Stolen Sister

LINDA HUBER

Stolen Sister

To my cousins, Martin, Ruth, Fiona and Lucy

Also by Linda Huber

The Paradise Trees
The Cold Cold Sea
The Attic Room
Chosen Child
Ward Zero
Baby Dear
Death Wish
The Runaway
Daria's Daughter
Pact of Silence
The Un-Family

www.lindahuber.net

Prologue

Twenty-two years ago

Saturday, 17th March

Smoke. She could smell smoke.

Paula rolled onto her side and grabbed the travel alarm. The figures on the clock face were dim in the faint moonlight shining through thin cotton curtains. Half past midnight. She sat up in bed, sniffing. Was it really smoke? Or just a woodland-after-rain smell? She'd lived in a city all her life; she wasn't used to country smells. She poked Joe beside her, but he snored on.

Paula thrust the duvet back and swung her legs to the floor. Two steps and she was at the window. Maybe a compost heap was smouldering in the hotel grounds? But all seemed quiet. From here in their room above the old coach house she couldn't even see the main building, just tall trees and the pathway up to the hotel. She stumbled to the door, brushing against the cot at the bottom of the bed, but Erin didn't stir.

As soon as she stepped onto the landing, Paula knew. A pungent, scorched-wood smell filled her nostrils and made her breath catch. That was definitely smoke. Heart thudding, she yelled at Joe to get up, then banged on Sylvie's door.

'Sylvie!'

No answer came. Paula rattled the handle, surprised when the door opened. 'Syl!'

The room was empty. Where had Sylvie gone at this time of night? They'd arrived at nine yesterday evening, and she and Joe had crashed out as soon as they'd unpacked and settled Erin down to sleep. Travelling with a six-day-old baby didn't leave you much energy for extras, and they wanted to be awake at tomorrow's reunion. Had Sylvie gone up to the bar by herself?

A crackling sound and a muffled bang beneath her had adrenaline surging through Paula's veins, turning her limbs to so much jelly. *Shit*, no, that was more than smoke – that was a fire, and it was *in the building*. Out, out, they had to get out of here. Her baby… Panting, she fled back to the bedroom, snapping the light switch down as she went, but no light came. The phone? Dead. She scrabbled on the table for the bulk of Joe's mobile, but it was switched off and she wasn't familiar enough with it to get it going quickly in the dark. No, no.

'Joe! Fire, we have to get out!' Shuddering sobs caught at the words as she shook Joe, then slapped his face until his eyes opened and he jerked upright.

'Shit!' He leapt up, then fell back on the bed, coughing.

Paula plucked the baby from the cot and wrapped her in a blanket. She grabbed Joe's hand and pulled. He shuffled after her, bending double in the hallway as they were met by a waft of acrid smoke bulging up the stairs. The landing glimmered in front of Paula's eyes as her heart thumped wildly in her throat. That didn't smell like wood smoke now – that was… rubber? Hell – what was in the underneath room of the coach house?

Joe thudded to his knees behind her, gasping hoarsely and clutching his throat. 'Need… my inhaler.'

'We don't have time. You'll be better when we're outside, come *on,* Joe!' She pulled at his arm, but he lowered his head, gasping for air.

The baby coughed too, and Paula pressed her mouth against her daughter's head, whimpering as more bangs came from below, sending a thicker cloud of grey up the stairwell.

She wheeled round, yanking Joe's arm. 'Quick! We can climb out the window.' But Joe wouldn't move from his place on the floor, and Paula lurched back into the bedroom. Her bowels felt loose with fear and her breath was coming in gasps that weren't all down to the fume-laden atmosphere she was breathing. She couldn't lift Joe or even drag him; he was a big man and her body was still weakened from giving birth. Where was his inhaler? Bloody asthma. She put the baby on the bed and rifled through Joe's jacket pockets, then a movement from outside caught her eye and she dropped the jacket to bang on the window.

It was Sylvie, teetering down the path in those ridiculous heels. So she *had* gone up to the bar. At that moment Sylvie saw her and stopped dead. Paula fought with the sash window, her arm muscles screaming in protest as it inched upwards and smoke-laden March air rushed into the room.

'Sylvie! Fire! Get help!'

The baby wailed and Paula grabbed her, holding her in the window where the air was cleaner.

Sylvie's hands flew to her mouth and her shoulders jerked up to her ears. Her eyes were round Os as she stared at the lower part of the building, then raced to stand beneath the bedroom window.

'Paula – throw me the baby! And then get out of there!'

Another explosion downstairs, and the floor beneath Paula's feet shook. She could feel the warmth now, and–

'*Paula*! Throw me Erin!'

Tears coursed down Paula's face as she wrapped the blanket right over Erin's head and leaned out. Thick, choking smoke puffed from the lower part of the building, enveloping Sylvie, now standing with outstretched arms. It was years since Paula had prayed, but she begged now for her baby's life and her own. *Please, please, this can't be happening.* She let go of the most precious thing on earth tonight and screamed as Erin fell like a stone into Sylvie's arms.

'I'll get help. Climb out!' Sylvie fled back towards the hotel, the baby clutched to her chest.

Paula tottered from the window as her child vanished in the darkness. Help was two hundred yards up the path; they had to fend for themselves now.

'Joe! We have to–'

The floor beneath her feet gave way as the air thundered around her and the coach house shattered into the night.

PART ONE

BRAVE NEW LIFE

Chapter One

Two days beforehand: Thursday, 15th March

The phone was ringing as Maisie let herself into the flat after her Thursday morning visit to the library. She dropped her bags in the hallway and hurried through to the living room, unbuttoning her coat as she went.

It was Paula. 'Hi, Maisie, I'm wondering if you can help us this weekend?'

Maisie blinked. She'd called her niece just last night, and there'd been no mention of help needed. 'What's the problem?' She shrugged out of the coat and lowered herself into the armchair to talk in comfort.

'It's Stella. You know, my friend who's looking after Vicky and Jamie this weekend while we're at the reunion?'

Maisie had met Stella, who lived two streets away from Paula and was a tower of strength, bless her. Jamie had severe cerebral palsy, but Stella was the most un-fazeable babysitter anyone could wish for. She'd taken four-year-old Vicky and almost three-year-old Jamie while Paula was in hospital having baby Erin. In fact, the children were still staying with Stella at night, though she brought them home to visit every day.

Paula went on. 'Her husband's been taken into hospital

with a burst appendix. Please say no if you don't want to, but–'

'Of course I'll take Vicky and Jamie,' said Maisie. 'I'm not decrepit yet, you know. It's just two nights, isn't it?'

'Mais, you're a star. Yes. We're driving to Carlisle tomorrow to meet up with Sylvie, then we'll all go on to the hotel in her car. The reunion's on Saturday and we'll be home on Sunday afternoon. I'd really like to go if you're sure you can cope, and we're taking Erin with us, of course.'

Privately, Maisie thought that taking a not even week-old baby to a party wasn't what she'd have considered doing, but what did an old maiden aunt know? And Paula deserved some fun – the poor girl was rushed off her feet most of the time.

'Oh, sweetheart. I only wish we all lived closer and I could help you more.' Maisie pulled a face. Her Edinburgh flat wasn't a million miles from Paula and Joe's home in Glasgow, but it wasn't near enough to make daily visits. Especially when you were pushing seventy and didn't have a car.

'You're a gem. We'll bring them over around eleven, then head south from yours.'

Maisie put the phone down. Well, that was her weekend planned. Vicky would be no problem, but poor Paula, there weren't many people she could ask to take care of her son. Maisie stood up and squared her shoulders. To work – she had a guest room to prepare.

Maisie's apprehension doubled the moment she opened the front door the next day. Vicky's cheeks were tear-stained, Jamie was whining and dribbling in his buggy, and Paula was pale but smiling determinedly. Maisie caught Joe's eye and he grimaced.

14

'Be good for Auntie Maisie, now. She'll need your help with Jamie.' Paula kissed Vicky, who shook her mother off, scowling.

'Jamie'll be fine,' said Maisie, taking Vicky's hand. 'I could do with some help making chocolate crispy cakes, though.'

'Ooh, yes!' Vicky ran off into the kitchen without looking back.

'Off you go. Don't worry about us.' Maisie kissed Paula and the sleeping baby in the young woman's arms, and patted Joe's arm. She waved as the car drove off into early spring sunshine, then strode towards the kitchen with the buggy. She would have to be super Great-Aunt Maisie for the next few days, that was all. She'd manage that, wouldn't she?

***

And manage she did – the first day. Vicky was happy making her crispy cakes and loved her lunchtime beans on toast, then Jamie slept in his buggy all through the afternoon outing to the park.

'Ice cream on the way home?' suggested Maisie, when Vicky was tired of the swings. 'I saw a van near the gates when we were coming in.

Vicky jumped up and down, but the van was gone when they arrived at the entrance, and the child's face crumpled.

'There's a café on the main road,' said Maisie. 'We'll go there. It's a bit chilly for ice cream outside, anyway.' She took Vicky's hand and pushed the buggy along the uneven pavement to the café. Once inside, she ordered banana splits for them both, crossing her fingers Jamie would stay asleep while they were eating.

He did, almost. Maisie was wiping her fingers on her serviette when the little boy jerked awake and began to whimper. Past experience told Maisie that screams were only moments away, and something akin to panic rose in her throat. What a fool she'd been, bringing him in here. Dear Lord, why had she thought she'd be capable of looking after these children, even for just two days?

Sweat breaking out on her forehead, she smiled brightly at Vicky, who was on the last third of her treat. 'Nearly done? I think Jamie would like to go home soon.'

'We're not going home. We're going back to yours.' Vicky pushed her plate away, her lips trembling.

Maisie rocked the buggy as well as she could, but the whimpers were changing to a high-pitched whine that would soon be screams. She signalled to the waitress, who was eying them with an apprehensive expression.

'Time to go, Vicky, sweetheart.' Maisie paid, then stood to help Vicky with her jacket.

The little girl burst into noisy tears. 'It's not fair! I didn't get to finish my banana split. I want Mummy!' She kicked the table leg.

Maisie pushed the buggy to the exit, shooting the waitress an apologetic glance. The woman had the door open before they reached it, and Maisie escaped thankfully.

'Maybe in summer we can go again, just the two of us,' she said to Vicky, who was scuffing her feet along the pavement. The little girl didn't reply.

By the time she'd settled the children into bed that night, Maisie felt as if she'd run to Cape Town and back. She was leafing through the TV magazine when the phone rang beside her chair.

'We've arrived, Mais. The hotel's great – a big country

house kind of place just beside Killington Lake. The three of us and Sylvie have rooms above the old coach house in the grounds, so it'll be nice and peaceful for Erin no matter what time the party goes on until. Are the kids okay?'

'Fast asleep,' said Maisie. She chatted for a few minutes, then put the phone down. This weekend would do Paula and Joe the world of good. She *could* do this for them. She'd organise reinforcements tomorrow. Helen next door would help, and Jane, her closest friend. Another day and a half looking after Vicky and Jamie was doable, surely.

Chapter Two

Saturday, 17th March

The blast reverberated in Sylvie's ears as she fled towards the hotel. A roar filled the air behind her, then sudden heat flashed across her back and she increased her pace, lungs bursting and heartbeat thudding in her ears. Smoke seeped into her chest, slowing her flight. Almost there… here was the fork in the path, right to the hotel and left to the car park. Sylvie turned and looked back. A ball of fire flickered where the coach house had been just moments ago, dust and smoke and heat wavering in orange-hued air and the crackle of flames replacing the boom of the explosion. Oh no, no. Sylvie's gut shifted and she gripped the baby to one shoulder as she vomited gin and tonic and peanuts onto the grass at the side of the path. Erin squawked, and Sylvie wiped her mouth with one hand and peered at the baby. They were both illuminated, horribly, by the fire. It wasn't good for Erin, being out in this. Voices shouted ahead and Sylvie made a swift decision. Her breath coming in pants, she ran along the path to the car park, thankful her handbag was still looped over her shoulder and more thankful the car keys were inside. The air was better here. She fumbled the key into the lock and opened the boot of her

Vauxhall. Paula had transferred her box of baby stuff when they'd continued the journey in Sylvie's car. Poor Paula, with Jamie the way he was, she'd never not need a supply of nappies, wipes and bottles in the boot wherever they went. Tears blinded Sylvie as horror hit home. If Paula had still been in the coach house when it exploded, she would never need anything again. The remains of that afternoon's bottle of milk were there, and Sylvie offered the baby a drink. Erin sucked a few times, then turned her head towards Sylvie and fell asleep. Sylvie stood motionless, her forehead touching Erin's. This poor scrap… but the little face was relaxed now, and she was breathing easily.

Sirens wailed, distant at first then swooping closer, and blue lights flashed towards the coach house. Sylvie hesitated. She should go and speak to someone – they wouldn't know she wasn't in there. And maybe, oh please, Paula. Joe… She wrapped the blanket more securely around the sleeping baby and strapped her into her infant car seat, thankfully still in the back, then inched a front window open and locked the car. She wouldn't be long.

Two fire engines and a police car were blocking the way back to the coach house. Sylvie looked around. Further up towards the hotel, a police officer was talking to a man she knew was the bar manager, and she trailed up to them.

'If you'll just wait inside, madam,' began the policeman, but the bar manager recognised Sylvie – hardly surprising considering he'd spent the last couple of hours chatting her up.

'Sylvie! You're okay? Jim, this is one of the guests in the coach house.'

The officer grabbed his radio. 'Are your friends out too?'

'They were still in there when I–' Sylvie bent over,

weeping into her hands as Paula's face at the window flashed before her eyes.

The officer gripped her elbow and supported her towards the hotel while he spoke into his radio, confirming two people had been inside the building. A crackling answer came. No one had been found yet. Sylvie rubbed her cheeks with gritty palms, sick with horror. The hotel was buzzing. There was a function on tonight and all the guests were running around gawking at the scene outside, yacking excitedly and oh, God, get her away from this. The officer took her into a small room off the hallway, sat her on a hard chair and shouted for water.

'Do you need a doctor?'

Sylvie wiped her face on her sleeve. 'No.'

He nodded, sitting down opposite as a bottle of water and a glass appeared. Sylvie took a sip. The water was cold, and carbonated more than she liked, but it was wet and felt good on her throat. She would be fine, but... did the baby need a doctor? She closed her eyes. No. Erin needed a mother.

'My friends...?' Her voice trailed off.

'If they were inside the coach house, I'm afraid they're gone. They weren't in the bar with you?'

'No. They went straight to bed when we arrived. I came up here for a while, then when I went down the path again Paula was banging on the window and I saw smoke on the ground floor...' The memory was appalling. Sylvie forced herself to continue. 'I was running back up the path to get help when the building exploded.'

The officer was writing in his notebook. 'And your friends – do you know anything about their next of kin?'

Sylvie sniffed. 'Joe has no one. He grew up in care. Paula has an aunt in Edinburgh. Maisie, um, Gibson, I think. She's looking after the kids. I don't know her address.' She sipped her water again, her teeth chattering against the glass.

The policeman looked grim. 'We'll find her. Are you going to stay here?'

It was the last thing Sylvie wanted. 'No. I'll drive home to Carlisle now.' And hopefully he wasn't going to breathalyse her. Those gins must be long out of her system.

He took her details, warning her they might need to speak to her again. Sylvie escaped as soon as she could. Home, home. She would deal with Erin herself – take her to Carlisle first and on to Edinburgh when they'd had some sleep. She switched the car seat into the front where she could keep an eye on the baby, and sank in behind the wheel.

The dashboard clock informed her it was ten past two as she started the engine, her throat burning with a mixture of smoke and tears. It was the worst night, the worst day.

***

By Saturday morning, Maisie wasn't so sure about coping. Jamie had wailed from 1am until four, and nothing Maisie did made the slightest difference. Vicky was awake for much of the time too, pouting and covering her ears in the bed beside Jamie's travel cot. Eventually, Maisie put the little girl into her own bed and lay down in Vicky's, rocking the cot and trying to rest. This was dreadful. How on earth would Paula cope with a new-born as well as her son?

At eight o'clock Maisie opened her eyes to sunshine splitting the skies, and a sore back from dozing on the too-soft mattress of the guest bed. Jamie was asleep, and she tiptoed from the room and made coffee, trying to ignore the horrible dragging feeling of not having had enough sleep.

Still in her dressing gown, she was hunched over her mug when the doorbell rang. Jamie wailed loudly and a thud from the bedroom told Maisie that Vicky was up now too. Cursing whoever was outside, she went to open the door.

Two tall police officers were standing on the step, their faces grave. Both held up identification, and the older one spoke.

'Miss Gibson? We need to speak to you. Can we come in?'

Speechless, Maisie stepped back, alarm bells shrilling through her head. Policemen at the door... dear Lord, had something happened to Paula and Joe? Sick dread rose in her throat as she led the men into the living room. Vicky followed and grabbed hold of Maisie's hand.

'Can the little girl wait in another room?' said the older officer.

Vicky pressed herself against Maisie's side, and Maisie stroked the tousled blonde curls.

'Why don't you watch TV in here, darling, while I talk to the policemen in the kitchen? Look, there are still some sweeties in the bowl.'

Hands shaking, she put on cartoons for Vicky, then led the way to the kitchen, closing the spare room door on Jamie's whimpers on the way.

The younger officer pulled out a chair for Maisie and her legs collapsed beneath her.

'I'm afraid it's bad news,' said the older man, leaning towards her. 'There was a fire at the hotel your family were staying in last night. They didn't survive. I'm very sorry.'

***

Maisie closed the front door after the police officers, then crept back to the kitchen and slumped into her chair. In the space of half an hour, everything had changed. Heart pounding, she gripped the mug of tea one of the men had made her. What was she going to do? Those poor children – Vicky singing along with her cartoons and Jamie whining away in the guest room. He wouldn't understand, but very soon now, Maisie would have to destroy Vicky's little world. And the baby... oh, Erin. Less than a week in this world, and gone already. Hot, choking sobs rose in Maisie's throat, and she forced them back. She had to stay calm, for Vicky.

The officers had explained that one woman survived the blaze. She wasn't in the coach house when it exploded and she'd talked to the police. The heat had been so intense that nothing was left to bury or cremate – just a huge, blackened hole in the ground. Maisie pushed her tea away and wiped her eyes. Where was the woman who'd escaped? Maisie had been too shocked to ask, but it must be Paula's friend, the one they'd joined up with on the way.

'Auntie Maisie!'

Oh, dear Lord, this was it. Maisie went into the living room and sank down on the sofa. Credits were rolling after the cartoons and Vicky was kneeling on the floor, much too close to the set and surrounded by sweetie wrappers, but what did it matter, today?

The little girl gave Maisie a rare beam. 'What did they want? Are we going to the park for ice cream soon?'

No time like the present. Maisie patted the sofa beside her and Vicky clambered up.

'Darling–' Her voice caught, and Maisie had to stop to gather her thoughts. She clasped her hands to stop them shaking, squeezing so tightly it hurt. 'Vicky, love, a very,

very bad thing has happened. That was why the police were here.'

Vicky's eyes were huge, and Maisie put an arm round the small shoulders and inched up close. 'There was a big… accident… at the place where Mummy and Daddy were staying, and they went to heaven. It was all very quick. I know it'll be hard for us, without them, but we'll manage, darling. Try not to worry.'

Vicky jerked back, her eyes widening. 'But they're coming home tomorrow. Mummy said so.'

'No, darling. They won't be back.' Maisie tried to cuddle Vicky, but the child pushed her away.

'They'll be home tomorrow. I know they will.' She ran through to Jamie and began to sing nursery rhymes.

Maisie slumped into the sofa. How did you make a four-year-old understand that Mummy and Daddy were gone for good? In Vicky's world, fairies inhabited the earth and Santa Claus was real. They would have to get help with this, counselling or a psychologist or something. Maisie massaged her head with both hands as a high-pitched wail joined in the song in the guest room. The first thing was to get Jamie up and fed, then she would ask Helen next door to take Vicky for an hour while she made some calls. She had said they would manage, and they would. She would do her crying later.

Jamie screamed the moment Maisie touched him, but Vicky was there to comfort her brother while Maisie dressed him. The little girl fed him a yoghurt while Maisie pulled on her clothes, choking back shivers as the enormity of the situation hit her again and again. She would have to go to Glasgow, pack up more things for the children. Who would see to the family's affairs there, the house and so on? Joe had no one, and she was Paula's only adult relative. It would all be down to her.

Helen next door was horrified and immediately offered to take Vicky to the park. She hugged Maisie on the way out and murmured, 'You've told her. Let it sink in for a while. She'll come back to you about it.'

Maisie hugged back, then waved from the window as the pair started up the street, Vicky skipping beside Helen, the picture of a happy child on her way to the ice cream van. As soon as they rounded the corner, Maisie dropped to her knees and burst into tears.

Fifteen minutes later, she crept back to the sofa to dry her eyes, the first hot pricks of anger stabbing through her chest. Why Paula? Why Vicky? The standard answer, 'Why not?' was just wrong. But cope, Maisie, cope.

A call to her GP surgery produced shocked promises of referrals to a counsellor for Vicky and the community nurse service for Jamie, and by that time Maisie had remembered Paula's friend's name – Sylvie Raynott. She would phone Sylvie, just to touch base after such a catastrophe. Maisie frowned – there couldn't be many Raynotts in Carlisle. Directory Inquiries might help.

Five minutes later she was writing down the number for S Raynott. Maisie hesitated, the phone still in her hand. Under the circumstances, Sylvie might still be asleep. She would wait a few more hours.

The nursing service called while she was trying to comfort a screaming Jamie. Maisie shut the kitchen door on the wails, then nearly burst into tears too when the woman on the phone promised help, assessment, day care – whatever it took to let Maisie organise her new life. Someone would be round on Monday – would Maisie manage until then? The call ended and Maisie had another cry. Being offered help when you so desperately needed it was… she didn't know what it was, and it didn't change the emptiness in her soul.

Nothing was good about the day, although Helen and Simon next door were gems with the children. Somehow, Maisie got through the hours and by eight that evening, the children were in bed – Vicky having made no further mention of her parents – and Maisie was alone, clutching the mug of hot chocolate Helen had made before she left. Now to try Sylvie's number.

Three, four, five times the phone rang. The poor girl could be staying with family, of course. Six, seven, eight… And then a voice.

'Hello?'

'Sylvie? I'm Maisie, Paula's aunt–'

A sound at Sylvie's end had sudden sweat breaking out all over Maisie's body. Her hands shook so violently she could barely hold the receiver. A funny little high-pitched cry with a wobble and hiccup at the end of the breath – *Erin*. She was alive.

***

Dawn had been seeping through the darkness when Sylvie pulled up outside her first-floor flat on the south side of Carlisle early that terrible morning. Traffic had been light, of course, but she hadn't trusted herself to drive fast, and twice she'd had to stop to gain control of the shakes that were shuddering through her body. How was she supposed to deal with this? Just thinking about Paula and Joe was unbearable, so she tried not to. But every time she stopped concentrating on here and now, Paula's scream as she dropped her daughter from the coach house window echoed through Sylvie's head.

The baby was asleep in the passenger seat, and Sylvie went for the box in the boot. The supplies it held were meagre, but they would give her the chance to settle Erin and then get some sleep before thinking about how best to get the baby to Maisie Gibson. The box held a couple of sachets of baby milk, the kind you got in hospitals as freebies when you had a baby. Not that Sylvie knew about that, but Paula had told her. And how ironic it was that she, who had wanted a child for so long, now had one, but would soon be handing her over to an old woman who would in no way want or be able to bring her up. Or would she?

Box under her arm and car seat in the other hand, Sylvie climbed the stairs to her flat. The baby was grizzling now, so the first priority was to feed her. Sylvie put the car seat on the kitchen table and turned to the box. The grizzling turned into a howl, which continued the whole time Sylvie was boiling the bottle to sterilise it and making the milk, but when the feed was cooling in a jug of iced water she lifted the baby and changed her, and the howls returned to grizzles.

'Here you go. Breakfast,' she said, her voice sounding odd in her ears. She wasn't one of those people who talked to herself, and in a way she *was* talking to herself. This tiny creature didn't understand the words, but she understood the bottle perfectly, latching onto the teat and sucking vigorously. Sylvie went through and sank into the living room sofa, weariness making every bone in her body ache. She closed her eyes, and Paula's face loomed.

Erin nodded off again when the bottle was empty, and Sylvie held the baby upright against her chest, rocking gently, feeling the comforting warmth of the little body and smelling the peculiarly baby smell of Erin's sweaty little head. The burp came and Sylvie wiped away the splodge of sick that came with it, then took the baby through to the bedroom. Sleep, she so needed to sleep. And she needed a baby bed. Sylvie looked around, then upended the drawer containing winter jumpers and turned it into a makeshift cot before crashing out on the bed.

Her sleep was haunted by darkness split by flames and horror, and it was after eleven when Sylvie wakened to the sound of the baby howling in the drawer. The memory of what had happened slammed into her head, and she moaned. She lifted Erin, but the howls didn't stop and Sylvie's nose told her why.

Changing the baby and inserting her into the one spare sleepsuit helped her focus on the present, and it gave her a plan of action, too. There were only two nappies and one sachet of milk powder left in the box – she would need to go shopping. Sylvie made a bottle for the baby and coffee for herself, and they breakfasted together while she made a list in her head. Baby milk, nappies, spare clothes for Erin – you could get all that in the supermarket.

Sylvie slumped at the thought of going out. This tiredness was laming; it was if her limbs had turned to so much metal. And she had to get hold of Maisie Gibson's phone number and let her know where Erin was, too. Then there was Dave – what would he think if he saw news reports about the fire? And the others who'd be arriving at the hotel around now, ready for twenty-four hours of nostalgia and indulgence, only to hear that two of their number were... Sylvie sat still, not daring to close her eyes. Paula's face would haunt her for the rest of her life.

The phone rang in the hallway, and she jerked out of her trance. She laid Erin on the armchair and boxed her in with cushions before hurrying to lift the receiver.

'*Syl*, thank Christ. I've just seen the news – what happened?'

Dave. They'd met a few weeks ago at the gym where Sylvie worked as receptionist, and several dates later she was beginning to think this might be what she'd been waiting for all her life.

'A fire. It was horrible, Dave, and Paula and Joe... they didn't make it and–' Her voice stuck.

'I'm coming over.'

'No!' Sylvie gripped the phone. If he arrived here now she would melt into a ball of helplessness and she couldn't afford that luxury, not with the baby to deal with and Maisie to find. 'I need to sleep, Dave. I'm fine, not a scratch. I'll call you later, okay?'

He took a bit of convincing but at last Sylvie could ring off. She stared at the phone in her hand. She hadn't told him about the baby. Erin gave a little bleat from the living room, and Sylvie went back to stroke the soft little face, then touched her head to the baby's. They were both here, and they so easily might not have been. Now she was the one who had to keep Erin comfortable until... later. And they still needed nappies and stuff.

***

She was draping newly washed baby outfits over the radiator when the phone rang again. Sylvie dived to lift it before it woke the baby. This would be Maisie, heck, she hadn't–

It was Jen, one of the school-friends she should have been celebrating the reunion with right now.

Sylvie listened to appalled exclamations and rang off as

soon as she could, loneliness surging. Other people would be able to turn to their family at a time like this, but she was the only child of older parents and her dad had dementia. Mum had either forgotten about the reunion or not seen the news, or she'd have been on the phone already. Sylvie pictured her mother's tired face. She couldn't dump all this on Mum until she was feeling more in control, and anyway, her parents were in Devon, too far away to pop by for a comforting chat. She could call a friend, of course, but the thought of explaining everything again and then the horror on Sue's or Janice's face... No.

Erin awoke, ready for a feed, and Sylvie did the needful, marvelling at the sheer amount of time looking after a baby used up. But what a good little soul this was, flexing long fingers and blowing bubbles. Everything felt better with Erin in her arms. Sylvie cuddled more comfortably into the sofa and reached for the remote.

The end of a film danced before her eyes before the news came on. Sylvie watched, uncaring as the usual politics came first, then she jerked upright as a picture of the North Bank Hotel spread over the screen, and oh no, there was the garden and no, no, the hole where the coach house had been, the hole she might have died in...

Moaning, she clicked the TV off and cuddled the baby close, her body quivering as the explosion rocked through her soul yet again. Erin's little face looking up at her stopped the scream before it erupted from Sylvie's throat and she sat there, panting, her face pressed to the baby's. It was okay, she was here and so was Erin. They were two survivors together. Sylvie kissed the downy head, slowly relaxing as her breathing returned to normal. Right. She wouldn't watch the news for a while. She wouldn't watch anything. She would look after the baby and recover from her ordeal, and then she would contact Maisie Gibson and take Erin home. Sometime.

They were cuddling on the sofa again that evening, Erin sweet-smelling and wearing a new outfit, when the phone rang. Sylvie boxed her in with cushions again, and went to the hallway to lift the receiver.

'Sylvie? I'm Maisie, Paula's aunt–'

The baby squawked in the background, and Sylvie heard a gasp in her ear.

'You've got Erin! Oh, thank the Lord! Nobody told me, I thought she was–'

Searing guilt and misery almost choked Sylvie. 'Hang on a moment, Maisie.' She put the phone down and went to gather up the baby, murmuring and shushing on the way back to the phone.

'I'm sorry, I was going to call you. To be honest, um, I'm not sure anyone knows Erin was with us at the hotel. I was so upset when it happened... then the police didn't mention her and neither did I.'

'It doesn't matter. I'll come and get her, I'll...' Maisie stopped, and Sylvie's mind raced.

No. *No.* The baby couldn't go home yet. They were helping each other, she and Erin.

'Not at all, I'll bring her. But you must have enough to do for the moment, with the other children and everything. I can keep Erin for a few days, a week or two, until you're organised. I've got some time off work, and I'm going...' Sylvie cast around for somewhere realistic to go to. 'To my aunt on the east coast tomorrow. She'll help with Erin. I'll give you a call when I'm back in Carlisle, shall I, and we'll get something sorted?'

Maisie sounded doubtful. 'Well… that would be a huge help. If you're sure?'

Sylvie breathed out. 'No problem at all. She's being so good, poor little mite.'

They exchanged a few more platitudes, then Maisie rang off and Sylvie went back to the sofa, leaving the phone off the hook. Visiting her aunt was a lie, of course, but for the moment Erin was better here, she was better for having Erin here, and Maisie would be better off not having a baby as well as two kids to deal with this week. Win-win-win.

Chapter Three

Wednesday, 21st March

Maisie's hand was shaking so much she couldn't fit the key into the lock. This was Paula and Joe's home, but they would never be back here, and neither would Vicky. Maisie's friend Jane had come to help today while Helen and Simon next door looked after the children in Edinburgh. And this wretched key…

'Let me.' Jane reached for the key, and in seconds the door was open and the fusty smell of unaired rooms greeted Maisie as she stepped inside.

For a brief moment she stood still. It was an ordinary semi on an ordinary street in Glasgow, and all around was evidence of ordinary family life, but it was a ghost house now.

Jane hugged her. 'Best if we just do the job, Maisie. What time's the van coming?'

Maisie stuck her chin in the air. 'Two o'clock. We should pick out things for the children, and I'll need all of Paula and Joe's paperwork, etcetera. The police advised me to get a lawyer to deal with it after the inquest, when we have death certificates.'

'Why don't I start packing clothes, then, and you can do

the more personal things?'

Jane went out to the car to fetch in the boxes and cases they'd brought, and Maisie opened the sideboard and pulled out a selection of folders, which she piled into a box. She would sort through them at home.

Paperwork boxed up, Maisie went through to the main bedroom, trying hard not to think too much. Why was this happening to her family? But death was no respecter of good people. Now their already tiny family was even more minute.

'Anything more?' Jane came in with a mug of tea in each hand and sat down on the bed.

Maisie wiped her eyes. 'Just Vicky's bedroom furniture, and Jamie's cot and things to get ready for the van. Did you pack their books?'

'Yes, and I put all the photo albums from the living room bookcase in too.'

'I'm really glad you're here, Jane.' Maisie sipped her tea. Please, please, she must manage to make a happy home for Vicky.

At one o'clock they ate their sandwiches, then Maisie went round emptying the bins. She had to keep her mind on the job in hand. Paula's friend Stella had a key and would deal with the fridge and freezer, then all they could do was wait until the formalities were completed and she could get on with selling the house, which might not be for a while, according to the police.

The van arrived, and the driver manhandled the few pieces of equipment and furniture and the many boxes into the back and drove off. Maisie locked the door with a steady hand. She would be back, but next time it wouldn't be so painful.

At home in Edinburgh, they managed to fit everything into Maisie's flat, and the driver took a vanful of spare-room furniture to the charity that would use it. Maisie and Jane arranged Vicky's things in the bedroom and filled the drawers of Jamie's changing table in the bathroom.

'Vicky'll like having all her own things here,' said Jane encouragingly, as she pulled on her jacket to go home.

Maisie wasn't so sure. A bedroom with all her clothes and toys from Glasgow would destroy any hope that Vicky had of going home – it was impossible to predict how the child would react. Plus, she was sharing with Jamie now. Maisie's legs were heavy as she trailed next door to fetch the children.

'Did you bring Jamie's toys too?' Vicky stood in her bedroom doorway, her little face expressionless.

'They're in the box under his cot. You can show me which are his favourites.'

Vicky ignored this. She went over to her dolls' house and stared inside, then emptied the furniture out and began to rearrange it. Maisie sat on the bed making the odd comment, but the child didn't reply until all the furniture was back in the house.

'They have a new home now.' She put the three dolls in, then turned to Maisie. 'What's for tea?'

Sick at heart, Maisie heated soup. It was awful, knowing she should he helping Vicky work through her grief, but not knowing how.

By the time the children were asleep that night, Maisie was more exhausted than she'd ever been. She poured herself a glass of sherry, too tired even to watch something mindless on television.

The box with Paula's photo albums was beside the bookcase. Maybe looking through these would help Vicky talk about her parents? She could ask the counsellor tomorrow. Maisie rifled through the box until she found the most recent album, and sat down with it.

Tears leapt into her eyes as she leafed through the pages. The album began last November, so there was Paula's birthday, then all the Christmas photos, and a family visit to the transport museum in Glasgow, where Paula was noticeably pregnant. The album ended two weeks ago with a couple of snaps of Jamie in his buggy.

Maisie blinked. No. *No.* That couldn't be the last photo. She scrabbled through the box, searching in vain for something more recent, then sat back, allowing the tears to flow for the first time that day. There were no photos of Erin here. Either they'd been somewhere in the house where she and Jane hadn't found them, or, more likely, they were still in Paula's camera. And cameras had been conspicuous by their absence today, which was entirely reasonable, considering the couple had been going to a reunion. So all the photos of Erin's first week in the world had been destroyed in the blast.

Fierce longing for her younger great-niece swept through Maisie. She lifted the phone, but Sylvie didn't answer. Of course, she was away. Maisie hesitated, then called Stella in Glasgow.

'Cameras? I'll go by tomorrow and have a look for you, but I imagine…'

'I know. It's just… I don't have any photos of Erin.'

Stella's voice was kind. 'I have a couple, Maisie. I'll get prints made for you straightaway.'

Comforted, Maisie rang off. She would manage this. She would.

***

Darkness was closing in, and with it came danger. Sylvie's

heart was thundering as she fought to escape, away, away, but her legs wouldn't move and heat, the heat was coming. She had to wake up and – boom! The world rocked, and Sylvie shot upright in bed, panting and covered in sweat. She struggled from the bed and scooped up the baby, sobbing as she clutched the small bundle to her throat. Baby, baby, please help… Four times since the explosion she'd gone to bed exhausted; four times the nightmare had descended and wrung her out.

Gradually, the world returned to everyday calm. Sylvie sat on the edge of the bed, still holding the sleeping child. Erin was the only one who could help. They had survived together and now they were helping each other but oh, it was hell on earth.

The clock on the bedside table came into focus as 4.59am became 5am. It wasn't worthwhile trying to sleep again – the baby would be looking for a feed any minute. Eyes closed, Sylvie kissed the small head cradled against her neck.

Erin bleated, then jerked awake and began to grizzle. Sylvie rocked her. Time to start the fifth day. Tomorrow, Erin would have lived as long without her parents as she had with them, and on Friday, longer. On Friday, Sylvie would be more Erin's mother than Paula was. Did babies this age remember back five days? She kissed the small head, and Erin's eyes closed again.

Sylvie laid the warm bundle back in the drawer and went to make a bottle. 'Thanks, kiddo,' she murmured. The thanks were well-deserved; Sylvie shuddered to think how bleak life would be with nothing to think about apart from the nightmares. The baby was keeping her sane. Sylvie was exhausted, but that was infinitely preferable to being alone.

Talking of alone, she should call her mother today. They

usually chatted once a week at least, and Mum still had no idea what was going on in Sylvie's life. Late afternoon was the best time – she had a whole day to get through first.

The new routine of feeds, baths and nappy changes swallowed the hours up, and at half past four Sylvie lifted the phone. She listened as the ring tone gave way to her mother's voice rattling off the number.

'Hi, Mum. How... how are things?'

Impossible to start with the information that two of her friends were dead and she was falling apart.

Her mother sounded as exhausted as Sylvie felt. 'Oh Sylvie, love, your dad's had a terrible week. I'm up every night with him now. We were at the doctor's yesterday, and he's going to put Dad on the urgent list for a place in a home. But I don't know...'

Sylvie forced her mind down to Devon. 'That sounds like the best thing, Mum. You need a break. Any idea how long it might take?'

'We should hear this week. I don't want him to go, Sylvie, but I can't do this any longer. Doctor Adams said some homes would take married couples, but I'm not ready for that yet.'

'No, of course not. What you want is Dad somewhere local, where you can visit easily. Mum, I'm a bit tied up this week, but I'll come down as soon as poss.'

'It's all right, love. I know you're busy. If you can come and help move him in, that would be a big help. I'll–'

The doorbell rang, and Sylvie frowned. Oh, for one of these cordless phones. She stretched forward as far as she could and managed to open the door, her mother's plans still in her ear.

It was Dave. He kissed his fingers and touched her cheek on his way into the living room. Sylvie concentrated on her call.

'–so Morton House would be the best place for him. I'll let you know as soon as we hear anything.'

Sylvie chatted for a few minutes, then rang off. No way could she burden Mum with what had happened to her and Erin. And shit, now she had to deal with Dave. Why couldn't people just leave her in peace?

He was on the sofa, leafing through yesterday's paper on the coffee table. He nodded towards the empty bottle of milk on the floor by the armchair. 'Been babysitting again?'

Sylvie sank into the armchair, her mind whirring. If she told him Erin was here twenty-four-seven, he'd be round all the time, 'helping'. And she needed space. He was the best bloke she'd ever met, and part of her was aching to tell him what was going on, but it was better to stay in a nice little cocoon with the baby until her head calmed down.

'I still am. She's asleep in the bedroom, so no singing, okay?'

He grinned. 'What a good neighbour you are.'

Sylvie made spaghetti for them both and opened a bottle of wine. Erin woke, and Dave sat jiggling her on his knee while Sylvie made coffee. It was good to have help… but no. If she told him more, she'd have to admit she was only just coping, and then she might not cope any more. Soon she would know when Erin was going to Edinburgh, maybe she could tell him then. He could drive them north.

Sylvie slumped into the armchair. Taking Erin to Maisie was the last thing she felt like doing.

Chapter Four

'I don't want to go to school! Jamie doesn't like it when I'm at school! You're mean!' Vicky stamped both feet on the kitchen floor.

Maisie pressed cold fingers to her cheeks. Don't cry, Maisie, you mustn't cry. This was Vicky's fourth day at school and they had the same conversation every morning. A week after losing her parents had seemed to Maisie a ridiculous time for the child to start a new school, but the counsellor suggested trying it. The Easter holidays were approaching, and a few days at school first might help settle Vicky into her new life. Maisie was sceptical, but she left Jamie with Helen next door and accompanied Vicky the first morning, surprised to see the little girl smiling as she joined in with the class, giving every indication of having a good time. The normality and the distraction had done Vicky good. But they still had the same discussion every morning.

'All children go to school, darling. And a lady's coming this morning to talk about finding a nice school for Jamie too, so we couldn't go to the park anyway. Get your schoolbag, now – Erica will be here in a minute.'

Erica lived further along the road and had kindly offered

to take Vicky to school every day along with her own little girl. Vicky flounced off to her room, and Maisie went back to dressing Jamie. He was all cheekbones today – had he lost weight since he'd been here? A carer now came every evening to help feed Jamie and put him to bed, but it wasn't nearly enough. Sick worry settled heavily in Maisie's chest. The social worker had been positive about finding a nursery place for Jamie, but then she hadn't met him yet. A child who could howl for an hour at a time might not be suitable for nursery.

Erica appeared and Vicky ran off without saying goodbye. Maisie clutched a hand to her chest, gripping her cardigan as if it would save her from drowning. It was all so heart-wrenchingly sad, and the guilt about not being able to provide what Paula's children needed was crippling. Vicky understood now that Mummy and Daddy were never coming home; she was confused and unhappy, and who could blame her? To complete the misery, they were all suffering from lack of sleep. Jamie slept badly no matter what Maisie did. The nightly screaming sessions might not be entirely her fault, but it felt like it. She hadn't even told anyone where Erin was. The last thing she needed was social services deciding she wasn't able to look after a baby, but poor Sylvie – she must be longing to get her life back.

By nine forty-five Maisie had the flat looking respectable, and Jamie clean and in his special seat. Maisie wiped a thread of dribble from the little boy's chin. Life would be so much easier if he could go to nursery for part of the day.

The social worker and a young occupational therapist arrived bang on time at ten o'clock, and Maisie was amused to see the surprised look on both women's faces when she opened the door. They'd probably expected someone half her age.

The social worker spoke. 'Miss Gibson – Maisie – I'm Yvonne and this is Jill. Shall we sit down and have a chat?'

Maisie led the way into the living room, where both women greeted Jamie very kindly. Maisie offered coffee, which was refused, and a cold drink, which was accepted, and they sat around the coffee table, Jamie blowing bubbles and babbling like a good child. Maisie's stomach began to churn. This imitation of a sweet, happy little boy was coming at the wrong time. Supposing they said an easy child like Jamie didn't qualify for help?

She needn't have worried. All the women were interested in was organising assistance. Maisie was promised a nursery place for Jamie every weekday, plus an additional carer to help get him up in the morning.

'That'll be short-term and then we'll review again,' said Jill, reaching out to touch Jamie's cheek. 'He's very thin – does he eat well?'

By the end of that conversation, Jamie had been promised a hospital appointment to be assessed for tube feeding.

'Thank you so much,' said Maisie, tears of gratitude burning in her eyes. 'Everyone's being so kind.'

Yvonne couldn't have looked more sympathetic. 'It must have been horrendous, losing your family like that. Do the children have no other relatives?'

Maisie explained their miniature family, her stomach cramping. This was where she should tell them about Erin. No, get Jamie sorted first. She would call Sylvie today and see how things were.

Jill was frowning. 'Maisie, I don't want to sound pessimistic, but Jamie's a handful, and that'll get worse as he gets older. It's heroic you're prepared to take him on, but how long you're able to care for him even with help, well, it might be limited.'

'I know,' said Maisie. 'But for Vicky's sake, I want to keep them together as long as possible. I'm fit, and as you see, he's tiny for his age.'

The women stood up. 'Let's make another date, two weeks today, to check how you're getting on,' said Yvonne. 'If you need anything in the meantime, give one of us a call.'

Maisie promised, but she knew it would take an extreme situation for her to make that call. If these women thought Jamie was too much for her, he would be removed and Vicky would be even more unhappy. If only Erin was home already – it would help Vicky to have her little sister here, but... Maisie's heart sank to her boots. Jamie didn't leave her enough energy to cope with a baby. She'd have to find the energy someday, though, wouldn't she? Or lose one of these children for good. What a mess this was.

That evening, Maisie waited until the children were in bed, then tapped Sylvie's number into the phone. The younger woman must be back at work now; she would probably be glad to have the baby off her hands. Apprehension wormed through Maisie. She should have told Yvonne and Jill about the baby.

She was about to give up when the phone was lifted. 'Sylvie, dear, how are you? And little Erin?'

Sylvie sounded very far away. 'We're fine, thanks. Erin's no trouble, takes her feeds beautifully and sleeps six hours through every night now.'

Lucky you, thought Maisie. 'Excellent. I'm calling about coming to collect her. Jamie will be starting nursery in a day or two, so I'll be able to manage the three of them. Paula would want them to be together, and it can't be easy for you, juggling work and a baby.'

There was a long pause and Maisie wondered if they'd been disconnected. 'Hello?'

'Yes, still here. Just thinking. Maisie, I'm fine with Erin. There's a crèche in the gym where I work so there's no problem there. You must need more time to get Vicky and Jamie settled. You have the hard part, let me help you with the easy bit. It's not as if we have the authorities breathing down our necks, and this is much the best arrangement for Erin. Until you're properly ready for her, of course.'

Maisie gripped the phone. Oh, how tempting that was. Another two weeks with Erin in Carlisle would get the school holidays behind them. And she still had a memorial of some kind to arrange, not to mention the Glasgow house sale. And Sylvie was Paula's friend...

'Are you sure? It would be a help, I must say.'

'Sure as sure. I'll give the baby a kiss for you, shall I? Oh, and there she is awake. Speak soon, Maisie.'

The call disconnected and Maisie leaned back in her chair. How helpful Sylvie was.

'Who were you talking to?' Vicky was standing in the doorway, teddy in hand.

Maisie got up. 'Can't you sleep? I'll tuck you back in, shall I? That was Sylvie, your mum's friend. She's looking after Erin for us.'

Vicky didn't answer, but she allowed Maisie to settle her back into bed, the duvet tucked right under her chin the way she liked it. Maisie sat on the bedside, stroking flyaway curls from the child's forehead and humming softly. When Vicky's breathing was slow and regular, Maisie rose to go.

Blue eyes shot open. 'Who's Erin?'

****

A smile tugged at Sylvie's lips as she laid Erin in the new cot in the corner of the bedroom. The baby shop in town was having a closing down sale, and it had been too good an opportunity to miss. The cot, an armful of bedding and a couple of new toys had made their way into the flat. It wasn't really extravagant, was it? Sylvie pondered the conversation with Maisie. More lies... but she could tell Maisie didn't really want Erin home yet, and this made it easy to say what Maisie wanted to hear. And it was all true – Erin was happy. She belonged here.

Sylvie leaned over the cot side, humming softly. It was wonderful, having a baby. Erin was thriving, nearly three weeks old and guzzling her bottle like a champ every time. Two or three times a week now Sylvie managed to sleep through with no nightmare, though the nights were still short, as the baby woke her around five every morning. But she could nap with Erin during the day, because in spite of what she'd told Maisie, she hadn't returned to work yet.

The problem was, she was supposed to start again after the Easter weekend. Sylvie pulled the blanket up under Erin's chin and tiptoed from the bedroom. No way was she going back to shift work on the gym reception, even if they did have a crèche. When she'd told the doctor about the terrible stress after watching her friend die in the fire, he'd been reluctant to give her even this much time off work, so it was unlikely he'd agree to another couple of weeks. Sylvie shrugged. She would take a few weeks' unpaid leave. There was enough in her bank account for that, then afterwards she would see. If only Maisie Gibson would leave them alone.

Thinking about Maisie reminded Sylvie about Joe and

Paula's car, and she went to the window and peered into the gathering darkness. The Fiesta was parked ten yards along the street, but she didn't have the keys. There would be spares somewhere, but it would probably be easier just to have a garage come and deal with it. Phil Brady from the flat upstairs drove round the corner in his VW and parked under the lamppost, and another idea jumped into Sylvie's head. She hurried to the door. Phil was always head-first under the bonnet of his car; if anyone could help, he could.

She met him on the landing and explained.

'No problem,' he said, his big brown eyes shining in sympathy. 'Shall we have a look in the morning, when it's light? I can get into it for you and we'll see if the spare keys are there. And if they're not, once you have the car's papers you can ask for advice at the Fiesta garage.'

Sylvie went back inside feeling that one thing at least was under control. Okay, this might be a good time to call Mum. Her father was due to move into a local care home in four weeks, which meant Mum was back in full coping mode, now she knew it wasn't forever. Sylvie had a long chat before hanging up. Her mother still had no idea about either the fire or Erin, but on the phone it was easy enough to keep all that secret.

The baby was still asleep. Sylvie poured a glass of Merlot and took it to the sofa. Heck, this time tomorrow she'd be with Dave. He was lovely, and if the whole horrendous fire and baby – not that the baby was in any way horrendous – situation hadn't happened, Sylvie knew she'd have been dancing on sunbeams right now. But Dave still thought Erin was a neighbour's child. It worked quite well, actually, as Sylvie and Carrie across the road really did exchange babysitting duties. Every time she left Erin was like a stab in the back, but she couldn't take her to the dentist with her, and it was best the doctor didn't know about her either. Sylvie had lied, telling Carrie she was looking after her sister's baby for the summer while poor Gemma was in hospital, and as Carrie was even newer on the street than Sylvie, there was no reason for the other woman to be suspicious. Not one person knew the truth about Erin, which meant Sylvie could never spend the night with Dave, but this only seemed to make him keener. Sylvie rubbed her face. If it was just her and Dave and Erin for ever and ever amen, how wonderful that would be.

The baby bleated in her sleep and a rush of longing washed over Sylvie. Could she persuade Maisie to sign Erin over?

This bubble burst as soon as the thought crossed her mind. Maisie was planning to keep the children together, that was clear. And the old woman was right about one thing: it *was* what Paula would have wanted. Sylvie bit down on her knuckles, tasting blood. She should have done more that night. If she'd yelled at Paula to jump... and what the hell had Joe been doing? It was all wrong, all wrong. Sylvie grabbed a cushion and huddled over it as the horror swooped up yet again. The pain was physical and it swept right through her every time Paula's face rose in her mind. And the scream was coming again...

Sylvie flung the cushion to the side and skittered through to the bedroom, where she plucked the baby from her crib. The only thing that helped was holding Erin, soaking up warmth and comfort. Clutching the sleeping child to her heart, Sylvie sank into the armchair she'd moved here from the living room and leaned back, her cheek against Erin's head. Breathe, Sylvie. Erin's here.

Slowly, the horror receded. Sylvie remained in the chair,

her breath still ragged. She looked around the room, with the crib and the changing table with the fish mobile hanging over it, and all the other baby bits and pieces. Being a mother was the only good thing tonight.

***

When she saw how quickly Phil managed to get into the Fiesta the next morning, Sylvie wondered why more cars weren't stolen – she was sitting in the front passenger seat within minutes.

Phil slid out the drawer under the driving seat. 'Look, here's the service book and the car's details. Doesn't look like the spare key's here, does it? But they'll help you at the garage.'

'Thanks, Phil.' Sylvie pulled a bundle of pamphlets and papers from the glove compartment and stuffed them into a plastic bag. 'I'll take everything personal out now. Do I just close the doors normally when I'm finished?'

'Yup. If you need to get into it again, just shout.'

Sylvie waved as he walked back to the flats, then clambered across to the driving seat. She wanted to cry, but no tears came. It was Paula and Joe's car, but still just a car. The baby was a more tangible reminder. For a moment Sylvie sat there, remembering how she and Joe had once been a thing, long before Paula, then she closed everything up again and went inside.

Putting the car's papers to the side, she rummaged through the plastic bag. Old maps, takeaway flyers and a notepad Paula had used for shopping lists were all designated to the bin, then Sylvie lifted a yellow booklet and stared, leafing through well-thumbed pages. The cover was torn, it was pretty shabby, but wow – this was her friend's antenatal clinic booklet. Paula's weight, girth, blood values and a multitude of other pregnancy information was here, including the results of two scans and details of the post-natal check-up. Why had it been in the car?

Sylvie leafed through again, wishing it was her name on the front and not Paula's, then grimaced. Paula would keep this in the car because then she wouldn't forget to take it to appointments with her. She was inventive like that, was Paula.

Later, when the baby was up and fed and looking gorgeous in a new pink outfit, Sylvie sat down for a cuddle and another look at the clinic booklet. Paula had put on twelve kilos over the course of the pregnancy, and her due date had been March 7th.

'You were late, miss.' Sylvie dropped a kiss on Erin's head.

In the back of the booklet she found a couple of pages with information about contacting the hospital and registering the baby after the birth. Sylvie frowned. Paula and Joe hadn't done that yet; they'd talked about it on the way down to Killington Lake. She scanned the page. Ah, no problem, you had six weeks to register a birth in England. Maybe this was something she could do? Because Erin was going to be here for a whole lot longer than six weeks, wasn't she?

Humming again, Sylvie rocked back and forth with the baby. Back and forth, back and forth, making everything better.

Chapter Five

Saturday, 31st March

'Auntie Maisie, can I have more toast?'

Vicky was perching at the kitchen table with chocolate spread on all ten fingers and a generous smear on her chin, too. A pinprick of warmth comforted its way through Maisie. Paula wouldn't have allowed the chocolate spread anywhere near the child, but it had put a smile on Vicky's face, and Maisie blessed it now.

And today was Saturday, which meant the morning carer came later. Jamie was still in bed, but he'd had his milk and was babbling away to himself. All in all, it was the best morning they'd had since the children arrived here.

''Course you can.' Maisie rose to put another slice into the toaster and waited, rubbing her back. Bending over Jamie when he woke in the night wasn't helping her old injury, but there was nothing to be done about that. The toast popped up as the doorbell shrilled, and Jamie screamed from the bedroom. Maisie hurried to let the carer in.

The postman had been, and two envelopes were lying on the hallway floor. Maisie took them into the kitchen to read while the carer dealt with Jamie. One had a Glasgow postmark, and Maisie slit it open eagerly. From Stella? It was. Maisie pulled out two photos: one of Paula, Joe and Erin, the other of Paula, Erin and Vicky. Maisie blinked furiously. How happy Paula looked. And surely Vicky would remember her sister when she saw this. Maisie glanced at the child solemnly working her way through the second piece of chocolate-covered toast. Maybe she should wait. Right now, Vicky was happy, and they still hadn't arranged when Erin would come home. Maisie turned back to the envelope and pulled out the note accompanying the snaps. *I couldn't find any cameras at the house, but here are two photos I took. If I come across any others I'll send them on. By the way, Chris and I are moving to Liverpool in June, but I hope you'll have everything settled with the house before then. Stella x.* Maisie hoped so too. She took the photos through to her bedroom and slid them between the pages of her father's old family bible until she had time to put them in the album.

By half past ten the children had gone to the park with Helen and Simon, and Maisie was baking scones for her book group meeting that afternoon. It was her turn to host and she'd decided to go ahead. She had to have some kind of life apart from the children, and six ladies for afternoon tea should be possible. She hadn't managed to read the book but that was a minor detail. She was sliding the scones into the oven when the phone rang, and she hurried through. A phone call during the morning used to mean a chat with a friend; now it had the potential to mean something had happened to one of the children.

'Hi, Maisie, it's me.'

Sylvie's voice on the other end did nothing for Maisie's peace of mind. They'd only spoken on Thursday. 'Sylvie! Is Erin all right?'

'She's fine, sorry, I didn't mean to scare you. It's Joe and

Paula's car. I was wondering what you'd like me to do with it?'

Maisie sat down on the hall chair, feeling foolish. The car had never crossed her mind, but now she remembered the arrangement to leave it at Sylvie's and travel on south in her larger vehicle. She thought swiftly.

'I suppose we should sell it. Or do you want to keep it?'

'No, I don't need two. If you agree, Maisie, I can arrange with the garage here to sell it for you?'

'That would be a big help. Would you do that?'

Sylvie assured her it would be no trouble at all, and Maisie warmed more and more to the younger woman.

'Get a good deal for the car, and you can keep the money, Sylvie dear. It'll be a small repayment for everything you're doing for Erin.'

'I couldn't possibly – I love having Erin here.'

'You must – I insist. It's so hard with Jamie. He's a terrible sleeper and if I had Erin here too I don't think I'd cope. You're giving me the chance to get things organised properly. It won't be much longer, I promise.'

Sylvie gushed some more about the baby before ringing off, and Maisie put the phone down with a smile on her face. She shouldn't have blurted out her woes like that, but Sylvie was such a gem, and now she could repay the debt, in a small way.

Maisie went back to her scones. They had risen perfectly.

***

Sylvie glanced at her watch and went to pack Erin's nappy bag. The tiny girl was spending the afternoon and evening with Carrie across the road while Sylvie and Dave went to a beer exhibition in town, followed by dinner. Sylvie didn't want to go, but it was the only way to keep Dave happy, and oh, if only they could be a family, the three of them. She was looking for a spare dummy when the doorbell rang, and to Sylvie's horror Dave's voice called through the letterbox.

'Anyone home?'

'Shit!' Sylvie hissed under her breath, seizing Erin and going through to the hallway.

To say Dave looked surprised would have been the understatement of the century. 'Hello! Have I got the day wrong?'

Sylvie tried to sound nonchalant. 'Nope. I, um, I'm watching her while her mum's having a nap. Tough night, apparently. You're early, I was just about to take her back.'

'I thought we could go for lunch first, so I came by on the off-chance you were home. Syl, are you sure your neighbour's not imposing on you? You seem to spend a lot of time playing childminder.'

Sylvie managed a smile. 'Not at all. You can hold her while I get ready, then I'll drop her off when we leave.' No way did she want Dave here alone while she delivered Erin to Carrie. He might go for a wander and notice all the baby things in the kitchen. She thrust the baby into Dave's arms, propelled him into the living room and dived into the bedroom.

After the vertical take-off, their day out was perfect in that Dave sampled lots of beer and enjoyed himself thoroughly. Sylvie missed Erin so much it was like a physical pain in her gut. It was getting more and more difficult to be away from her girl. Fortunately, the exhibition hall had a bank of payphones in the entrance, and a quick call to Carrie while Dave was in the loo put Sylvie's mind, somewhat, at rest.

'Let's go for a walk before we go to La Trattoria,' she suggested, as they left the exhibition. It was odd, this dating like a normal person. But mums with a baby and nightmares were normal people too, weren't they?

'Good idea.' He fanned his face with one hand. 'I'm glad I have a few hours to sober up before I have to drive home.' He exaggerated his wobble along the pavement and Sylvie laughed, linking arms as they walked.

'If you had a town flat like me, you wouldn't need to drive so much.'

'True. But maybe it'll be a nice long time before I'm driving home again,' he said, nuzzling her ear.

For a second, Sylvie froze. He was hinting he'd like to stay the night, and in different circumstances they'd have fallen into bed long before this, but... Tell him you have a baby, said the sensible part of her mind. I can't, said her inner fear. Telling Dave would change everything, and she didn't want the lovely fuzzy dream she and Erin were living in to end. Sylvie pouted inwardly. She *deserved* Erin, after all she'd gone through. Paula's face loomed again and Sylvie clenched one fist in her jacket pocket.

'Syl? If you'd rather wait, that's fine. I just thought–'

She managed a smile. 'Let's take it as it comes.'

Over dinner he was funny and romantic, and Sylvie realised he was working his way into her bed, but while part of her wanted this too, an eleven o'clock deadline at Carrie's meant a sleepover was going to be hard to organise without confiding in him. The moment they arrived back at hers he grabbed her for a long kiss, and her body melted into his.

The phone rang beside them and Sylvie lurched towards it.

'Why don't you get us something to drink?' she said over

her shoulder, and Dave went into the kitchen. Sylvie grabbed the receiver.

'Sylvie, good. I've been trying for half an hour. My Tina's a bit unsettled. Would you mind awfully–'

'I'm on my way.' Sylvie replaced the receiver and put her head into the kitchen. 'I'm going to bring Erin back here for the night. Carrie's still half-dead.' She ran out before he had a chance to reply.

She collected the baby and walked home, thinking furiously. Dave would almost certainly have been in the loo by now, and he'd seen the kitchen. If only she'd had time to tidy the place before he'd arrived this morning.

He was waiting with two glasses of red on the coffee table. Sylvie sat down beside him, Erin still in her arms.

'Does she often stay over? I noticed all the things in the kitchen.'

'She's here a lot, yes, but I don't mind, really. Look, she's asleep. I'll put her down. Don't worry about it, Dave.'

She laid Erin in her crib, then swept most of the baby items into the cupboard. She would let Dave stay; moving their relationship up a level would distract him nicely from the important things. Sylvie stroked her finger down Erin's soft cheek.

Chapter Six

Tuesday, 17th April

It was the same every morning. Maisie would get up, go to check the children and find Vicky in Jamie's cot, arms around her brother. The little girl was always in a deep sleep and Maisie worried about having to wake her. No one would get a good rest in with Jamie, who twitched and moaned all night. Maisie rubbed her face, trying to force the weariness away. She spent the first half of each night running back and forward to Jamie; if she got there quickly enough, Vicky on the other side of the room wouldn't waken. But at some point, Maisie would fall into a deep, exhausted sleep, and the next person to react to Jamie's cries was his sister.

On the surface, their lives were well organised. Carers were in and out to help with Jamie, and the little boy was collected by the school bus and taken to nursery each weekday morning. He had lunch there, so it was almost two o'clock before he was home each day. Vicky had been happy enough, doing things with Maisie in the holidays, and seemed to be coping well with her lessons, but... Maisie sighed. The little girl so rarely acted like the child she was. Jamie was the entire focus of her world – was Jamie happy, was he hungry, should she give him a drink? The ironic thing was, Vicky was much better than Maisie at comforting Jamie and getting nourishment into him, so it was always a relief when the child did these things, but dear Lord, she shouldn't be depending on a four-year-old.

Then there was Erin, still in Carlisle with Sylvie, who was never home now when Maisie called. The guilt about effectively abandoning Paula's baby was second only to the guilt about not telling the social workers about her. Maisie had a dream: her, Vicky and Erin all living together, with Jamie in a lovely home somewhere.

She closed the door after the departing carer and turned to find Vicky in the hallway, arms crossed and scowling.

'I wanted to give Jamie his breakfast. He likes it best when I do it.'

Maisie fixed a smile on her face. 'Jamie's going to school too. He'll be here when you get home.'

She gave the little girl a quick hug, hesitating. Vicky's remark that night had haunted Maisie ever since. *Who's Erin?* It seemed incredible that the child wouldn't remember her sister. But then, Paula and the baby were in hospital for two days, and even after their discharge, Vicky had spent the bulk of her time at Stella's. In a way, it was understandable that the change of routine and the horror of losing her parents had suppressed the child's memory of her sister. Vicky couldn't have said anything at her counselling sessions, either, or someone would have asked Maisie about it.

Now, she stroked bouncy curls from the cross little brow. The best thing was to get Erin safely back home, but dear Lord, she was seventy next week. Would she really be allowed to keep a baby?

'It would be fun if we had Erin here too, wouldn't it?' she said to Vicky, who stared, but gave no answer. 'You know –

our baby.'

'Jamie's my baby.'

The doorbell interrupted them, and Vicky grabbed her schoolbag and ran. Maisie went back to Jamie. The school bus would be here any minute, then when she had peace and quiet, she would try Sylvie's number again. And if there was still no answer, vowed Maisie, she would call every hour on the hour until Sylvie was home.

***

Maisie flicked through the TV magazine, the phone tucked between her ear and shoulder. Yet again, Sylvie wasn't going to answer. Apprehension wormed through Maisie. This was the third day of trying – not every hour, but mornings, lunchtimes and evenings. Surely Sylvie wouldn't have taken Erin away again without saying anything? Maisie began to tremble. It was too long since she'd spoken to the woman; it was shameful.

She was stretching the receiver back towards its base when she heard the click, and yanked it back to her ear. 'Sylvie! Thank goodness.'

'Oh... Maisie. I was going to phone you this week.' Sylvie's voice was distant.

'I'm so sorry, I should have fetched Erin back long ago. It's been hectic here but that's no excuse. I've imposed on you much too long. I'll come and collect her.' Maisie stopped to draw breath.

'Not at all – I love having her. That's why I was going to call you. I'm going to my aunt's again for a few days at the weekend and I'd really like to take her with me, if that's okay?'

Her conscience pricking, Maisie compromised. 'Of course. I'll come for her next week, though.'

'That'll be fine. I'll call you when we're back, shall I? And don't worry – she's an absolute joy.'

'Where does your–?'

But Sylvie was gone. Maisie replaced the receiver thoughtfully, then came to a decision. Next time Sylvie phoned, she would make a definite arrangement and collect Erin immediately. Vicky needed her sister. Something was telling Maisie loud and clear that she wouldn't be able to look after Jamie for much longer. Her back was playing up, and Jamie was looking less and less healthy. It took hours every day to get enough food into him, but the doctors weren't keen to start tube feeds. Maisie scowled at the phone. If these doctors had to feed Jamie, they'd change their minds in no time. But they didn't, and she was the one left to cope. Except she wasn't coping, was she?

Chapter Seven

Friday, 27th April

Sylvie was sitting on the floor, leaning back on the sofa, legs bent up with Erin lying on her thighs – it was their favourite face-to-face chatting position. At least, it was Sylvie's, and Erin seemed to enjoy it too. The little face was alert as Sylvie sang 'The Wheels on the Bus' time and again. Did Erin like it? There were no smiles yet, but lots of arm waving and mouth movements were going on.

It was so amazing, watching this little person grow – worth all the worry and expense. Funds had run out and Sylvie was back at work, putting Erin into the crèche and telling them the same story she'd told Carrie, that the baby was her sister's. Chatting to some of the mums made Sylvie realise how little she knew; all the talk about baby clinics and various brands of milk powder was like a different language. Erin looked as if she was thriving, but the guilt in Sylvie's soul was torture now. Maybe they should be going for jabs or something? She should find out about that.

New uncertainty flooded through her as she waved a rattle in front of Erin. Tiny fingers were stretching in the air – when did babies start to grab things? Heck, she really should get Erin checked. Since her return to work, together-time was doubly precious, but the outside world was still there, glowering in the background. Maisie was another huge source of irritation. If only the old woman would just disappear from their lives. Sylvie hadn't phoned back yet, and nine times out of ten she ignored the phone ringing, too.

'We'll stick together, you and me, won't we?' she said, and Erin looked at her seriously. 'Forever and ever and ever.'

Sylvie swung the baby in the air and kissed her on the way down again, nuzzling the soft cheek. Everything was better with Erin here. Paula's face didn't appear half as much when there was lots of baby stuff going on, and the nightmares came less frequently too. Sylvie stuck her chin in the air. She needed Erin as much as Erin needed her, and anyway, every baby needed a mum of her own. Juggling Dave and Erin was tricky but it had worked for the past... how long? Sylvie stared at the calendar and panic surged anew. Somewhere along the way, she had lost a week. Erin was over six weeks now. She should be smiling now surely, and she wasn't – what did that mean? And, oh *God*, she should be registered too.

Sylvie slid the baby into the new bouncy seat and scrabbled in the drawer for Paula's clinic booklet. Yes, six weeks. What the shit was she supposed to do now? Could she just... not do it? But that would mean the baby would have no birth certificate, and everyone needed one of those.

Sylvie stared at the booklet in her hand. The front page, where Paula's details were, was so shabby as to be almost indecipherable. An idea was hovering, a brilliant one, a fantastic one, the end to all her problems. If she could register Erin as her daughter, she would *be* a mum and Erin would *have* a mum. Box ticked for both of them. With a bit of care, she could change Paula's name on the booklet to hers. Her

Christian names were Laura Sylvia; it wasn't much of a leap from Paula to Laura, and she'd always been good at artwork. There was nothing she could do about Cairns and Raynott, though, except maybe lose that part. It had to be worth a try.

Bent over the kitchen table, pen and pencils to hand, Sylvie worked on the booklet and her plan. Thirty minutes later, the booklet was as good as she could get it. The front was even scruffier than before, after a smear of baby sick from a burp cloth and some work with a rubber. *Laura* looked as if it had always been that way, and the only legible letters on the surname were *a* and *n*, and the *l* was disguised as a *y* now. Sylvie had simply scored through Paula's address, making sure the street name was illegible, and added her own. The day and month of Paula's date of birth was lost under the sick smudge, and there was nothing else to show this wasn't Sylvie's antenatal booklet. It was worth a try.

A call to the registration office resulted in an emergency appointment that afternoon and Sylvie turned up well on time, feeling as if she was about to sit the most important exam of her life. If this went horribly wrong she could lose everything.

The registrar, a woman in her forties, lifted the clinic booklet by one corner.

'Sorry it's a mess,' said Sylvie, depositing Erin in the car seat onto a chair and sitting down beside her. 'She was sick on it while we were getting ready for the post-natal check-up.'

The registrar looked at the baby, her expression softening. 'She's a cutie. Okay, do you have any other documentation from the hospital where she was born?'

Sylvie had thought this through. 'She was born at home, here in Carlisle, though I stayed with friends in Glasgow for most of the pregnancy. They do, um, alternative birthing courses. We came back here for the birth.'

The registrar stared at Sylvie over the top of her glasses, then leafed through the documents Sylvie had provided – her own birth certificate, a utility bill and the rental contract for her flat – and started to fill out a form. 'And the father?'

'We weren't in a relationship. I don't want him on the certificate.'

The registrar went back to the booklet. 'And the baby's Christian name is still Erin?'

'Christine Erin,' said Sylvie, making a snap decision. 'Christine after my mum.'

Erin started making little 'ah' sounds and the registrar smiled at her. 'Have you got Grandma's name? You're a lovely girl, you are, yes.'

Erin stared solemnly at the woman, dribble escaping from her mouth.

Sylvie grabbed a cloth. 'You shouldn't dribble at people who pay you compliments, kiddo. They might not do it again.'

Erin turned her head to look straight into Sylvie's eyes, and a huge, definite smile spread across the little face. Sylvie burst into tears.

The registrar opened a drawer and thrust a box of tissues across the desk. 'She knows who her mummy is, doesn't she?'

'That was the first smile,' said Sylvie, sniffing into a tissue.

'And all for you.' The woman went back to scribbling on the form. 'I'll just make some photocopies and send this off. You'll get the full certificate in the post in a few days. If you need to make changes later, phone for an appointment.'

Sylvie left the office on cloud nine. She was Erin's mother. Now all she had to do was somehow get rid of Maisie Gibson.

***

Maisie awoke at quarter to six to a shriek from Vicky. She tumbled out of bed and hurried through, the smell hitting her as soon as she went into the children's room.

'Jamie was sick on me!' Vicky was standing in the cot, her face aghast, pink pyjamas streaked with yellow vomit.

Jamie was breathing rapidly, his eyes closed. Maisie lifted Vicky from the cot, her back twinging violently, and pulled the girl's arms free of her pyjama top. 'On you go and have a nice wash. I'll help Jamie.'

Vicky vanished into the bathroom and Maisie bent over Jamie. His brow was hot. No nursery today, then. Dismally, she began to remove the soiled bedding, and Jamie woke up and screamed. Maisie felt like screaming right back. She bundled the bedding and pyjamas into a pile on the floor and went to fetch a cloth to wipe Jamie down. A proper wash could wait until the carer arrived.

Vicky returned, fully dressed, and Maisie blessed the fact that the child was so independent.

'Can you stay with Jamie while I fetch him something to settle his tummy?' she said, trying to sound matter-of-fact. 'If he looks like being sick again, call me.'

Vicky took up position by Jamie's head, stroking his brow and singing softly. The call came as soon as Maisie entered the kitchen, and she arrived back in the bedroom to see vomit dripping from the cot onto Vicky's slippers. Dear Lord in heaven. Vicky was crying again and Jamie was howling. Maisie grabbed a towel and used it to wipe the sick up.

'I'll need to call the doctor,' she said to Vicky. 'We can't do this alone.'

'No! They'll take him to hospital – he doesn't want to go!' Sobbing loudly, Vicky pushed Maisie away.

Maisie closed her eyes for a moment, then opened them to see Jamie start one of his rare epileptic fits. She pulled him onto his side. 'I'm sorry, lovey. We need a doctor for Jamie.'

When the fit was over she phoned emergency services. Jamie being sick again interrupted the call, and Maisie was still holding his head when the ambulance drew up outside.

'Right, ladies, what do we have here?'

The paramedic was young and cheerful, and Vicky scowled at him.

'Jamie doesn't want to go to hospital,' she said, her voice trembling.

'Don't you worry, sweetheart. They'll fix him up and he'll be home before you know it.' The other paramedic was wrapping Jamie in a blanket.

Maisie called Yvonne, the social worker, who offered to meet Jamie at the hospital while Maisie dealt with Vicky. The little girl was distraught, and Maisie came to a decision: no school today.

'We'll pop you in a lovely bubble bath, then we'll go and see Jamie.'

'And bring him home?'

'We'll need to ask the doctor, won't we?' Was it wrong to hope Jamie would need several days in hospital? It would be so good to sleep all night again.

'It's a tummy bug,' said the doctor, later that morning. 'Nothing serious, but we'll hang on to him for a day or two – he's pretty dehydrated.'

'I want Jamie home and that's what he wants too,' said

Vicky, before Maisie could draw breath.

'I'll make sure he gets the very quickest medicine,' said the doctor. 'Miss Gibson – Maisie, is it? We'll do a full assessment while Jamie's here, then have a chat with you.'

Dread filled Maisie's soul. 'Of course,' she said, cuddling Vicky.

What were they supposed to 'chat' about? Would they even let Jamie come home? Despair brought tears to Maisie's eyes. With no Jamie, it would be so much easier to cope with Vicky, and Erin, too. But oh, poor Vicky.

**

Church bells outside and Dave snoring beside her woke Sylvie, and she opened her eyes to see Erin staring across from the crib. Sylvie pulled a face at the baby, revelling in the answering beam. They'd had lots of smiles since the first one – it was so cute. And having Dave here was brilliant too. Both her favourite people were within arm's reach, and how amazing was that?

Dave mumbled beside her and pulled her back across the bed, but Sylvie wriggled away.

'Shh – we have an audience.'

He opened his eyes and propped himself up on one elbow. 'Morning, Miss Erin. But Syl, for God's sake, I've stayed here three times this week and each time we've had to share the room with your friend's baby. She's taking advantage.'

Sylvie kissed his chin and slid out of bed. 'She's not. How many times has Erin disturbed us? She's a great sleeper.' No need to tell him he'd slept through the 5am feed each time. She lifted the baby and cuddled her.

Dave was still frowning. 'I know, and it's really kind

you're helping Carrie so much, but Syl, I don't think you should be. You're not right, you know.'

His eyes were fixed on hers, and a chill spiked through Sylvie. 'What do you mean?'

'I mean the baby hasn't woken me at night, but you have. Tossing in your sleep and moaning *help, help* and *go away*! You haven't been the same since the fire at the hotel. Maybe you should talk to someone about it? You shouldn't be looking after someone's child when you're not well yourself.'

Sylvie's gut cramped. What the hell had she said in her sleep?

'I'm absolutely fine, Dave,' she said, struggling to keep her voice steady. 'I'm allowed the odd nightmare after an experience like that, aren't I?'

'You are, but Carrie's still imposing.' He stomped off into the bathroom.

Sylvie went to make baby milk and coffee, her heart heavy. How was she to tell him that Erin was her baby, not Carrie's?

***

Maisie walked along the corridor to Jamie's ward, an odd mixture of apprehension and relief in her soul. She'd had a whole weekend's reprieve, but here they were, Monday already, and Jamie was being discharged tomorrow.

The ward was noisy and cheerful, and Maisie tried her best to feel cheerful too. She would tell Vicky tonight that Jamie was being discharged, and Vicky would be thrilled. It would be the best possible birthday present for her little great-niece. Maisie swallowed, love for Vicky swelling in her heart, all the greater because deep inside she knew it was hopeless – she was too old to be a mother to the child. The enormity of what had happened to her life hit Maisie like something physical, and she sank down into a chair in the corridor, fighting for control. It was too much. This was her life, the last part of her life – it was against the natural order of things that she should be mothering small children. It wasn't fair on any of them, least of all Vicky. Where was the justice here, and where was hope?

The nurses were busy. Maisie sat for a while then went into Jamie's room. He was up in a buggy today, looking more or less his normal self, apart from the new nasogastric feeding tube.

A staff nurse came over with a jug of pink liquid. 'The tube is a temporary measure,' she explained. 'If he doesn't get back to oral feeds, he'll need one that goes through his abdomen straight into his tummy. You can watch a feed today, then tomorrow you can do it under supervision before he goes home. It's very easy. The only tricky part is making sure he doesn't yank the tube out when he's waving his arms around.'

'What do I do if he does pull it out?'

'The district nurse can replace it.' The nurse went on to explain about what food to use, and Maisie left the ward half an hour later, her head reeling. From tomorrow, she'd be solely responsible for getting nourishment into Jamie. The carers with their Red Cross diplomas weren't nurses; they weren't allowed to do tube feeds. Ironically, she, Jamie's unqualified relative, was. And what would they do at nursery?

'Jamie's coming home!' Vicky's face was one big beam when she heard the news.

Maisie made a big effort to sound happy. 'Yes! This time

tomorrow, he'll be right here for you to play with.'

Vicky danced off to make sure Jamie's toys were ready, and Maisie shivered. It *would* be all right, because it had to be.

Chapter Eight

Wednesday, 2nd May

'Thanks, Carrie. I'll collect her before half ten.'

Sylvie handed over the baby in her car seat and hurried back to her flat. Dave would be here in twenty minutes, then they were going for a posh dinner before she drove south to her parents' tomorrow. She'd already made it clear he couldn't stay over – it would be very difficult to explain convincingly why Erin was there the night before a long trip.

She was waiting at the window when Dave's car came around the corner. Sylvie hurried down and settled into the passenger seat. It was easier leaving Erin tonight because it would be the last time.

Dave cupped her face. 'Hi, gorgeous! Ready for some serious protein?'

'Sure am.' Sylvie had to concentrate not to pull away. Doubt had been niggling for days. She'd so wanted to keep Dave, but things were only normal between them when Erin wasn't there, and Sylvie knew a choice was fast approaching. Bon Jovi was crooning 'Always' on the car radio and Dave joined in, grinning over at her in a pseudo-soppy way. Regret tugged at Sylvie's gut. This could have been 'their song'.

A few minutes later they were sitting at a corner table sharing a starter of garlic mushrooms, Dave squirming around on his chair and talking too fast about food. Was he going to plead to stay over in spite of her embargo?

The waiter removed the empty plates and poured more wine, and Sylvie sat back. 'You're jumpy tonight.'

He sipped his wine, then sat twirling the glass in front of him. 'Syl, I know it's early days, but I was wondering how you'd feel about looking for a place together? I want to move closer to work, and I think we'd be good together. How about it?'

It was the last thing she'd expected; they'd only known each other a couple of months. A vision of life in a lovely flat with Dave and Erin flashed through Sylvie's head... but no. No, no, no. That would never work, and anyway, it was *her* baby.

She reached out and tapped his hand. 'How about we talk when I'm back?' If she came back...

He nodded sheepishly. 'Okay. I didn't want to let you go away for God knows how long without saying anything.'

The waiter returned with sirloin for her and T-bone for Dave, and the subject was dropped, though he went on giving her long, sultry looks as they ate.

'The answer's no,' she said at last, laughing in spite of the thought that she might never see him again. 'You may not sleep over. I have a long drive tomorrow and anyway, you stayed last night.'

'I didn't get you to myself, though,' he said, then went on to tell her about the new DIY store planned for the area.

Sylvie's thoughts wandered. Another hour and she'd be home with her daughter. Tomorrow, she'd sort Maisie. And then, the rest of her life could start.

**

A shriek from Jamie at ten past one on his second night home dragged Maisie from a deep sleep, and she rushed through to see the little boy had pulled out his tube. Vicky was standing by the cot, sheer horror on her face.

'His nose is bleeding!'

'It's all right.' Maisie dabbed the small nostril as well as she could with Jamie thrashing around. 'It's where the Elastoplast was pulled off, see, it's stopped already. We'll get the nurse to come tomorrow and put the tube back in.'

She spent the next three hours running back and forward to Jamie, each time persuading Vicky back into bed. Eventually, Maisie lay down in her own bed with the little girl beside her agitating to go back to her brother, who was dozing and crying alternately. At six o'clock, the hundredth cry came, and Maisie dragged her weary body out of bed, careful not to disturb Vicky. And of course, Jamie had managed to loosen his nappy. Faeces were smeared over his pyjamas, bedding and hair. Maisie slumped down on Vicky's empty bed and buried her face in her hands. Help, she needed help. She stumbled to the phone.

The district nurse arrived at ten past seven to find the morning carer trying to wash a screaming Jamie, Vicky sleeping the sleep of the exhausted in Maisie's bed, and Maisie rinsing off sheets in the bath, her stomach heaving at the stench and horror of it all.

'Oh, Maisie, love, I can't let you go on like this.'

Sheer exhaustion made her snap. 'I can't go on any other way!'

And just an hour later, Yvonne arrived to take both children into foster care.

'It won't be forever, Maisie, but we have to get you back on your feet. You're exhausted. We'll assess your situation and work out what's best. You could get Vicky home quite quickly, but we'll need to think about Jamie and what's best for him.'

Vicky stormed through from the bedroom. '*No!* I won't leave Jamie! I hate you, Auntie Maisie.'

'She'll be fine,' mouthed Yvonne, as she bundled Vicky into her car beside Jamie, leaving Maisie in tears and Helen next door shocked and white, trying to comfort her.

Two hours' sleep made a big difference, and Maisie called Yvonne, ready to fight to have Vicky, at least, returned home.

'Sorry, Maisie, they're still being assessed. Yes, I know Vicky's no trouble, but we need to do things properly. As a special favour I'll ask the foster mother to call you for a reassuring chat, but it's best you don't see the children until we know what's happening. It won't take more than a day or two, and seeing you would upset Vicky all over again.'

Maisie knew this last point was true. An idea formed in her mind – she would go to Carlisle and fetch Erin while the children were in care. It might make a difference to Vicky if she knew her baby sister was home. Not that the child had given any indication of remembering Erin, but all little girls liked babies, didn't they?

Ava Cameron, the foster mother, called a few minutes later. 'They've settled in really well. You mustn't worry about them – have a good rest while you can. I'm sure you'll get Vicky home soon.'

It was exactly what Maisie wanted to hear. 'Thank you. I'm collecting the children's baby sister tomorrow. She's been staying with a family friend but I'm hoping to have her and Vicky back to live with me.' The moment the words were out, Maisie regretted them. Ava might tell the authorities about Erin. But then, they'd need to know sometime. She ended the call and dialled again. Now to try Sylvie.

The phone was lifted on the third ring. 'Maisie – I was going to call you today. I'm planning a holiday. Is it all right if I bring Erin to Edinburgh on Sunday?'

Not so difficult after all, was it? 'Yes, of course. I was going to suggest coming to collect her, but–'

'No need. I'm driving up to meet my friend, then we're flying from Glasgow on Monday. I'll call on Saturday and let you know what time we'll arrive, shall I? See you soon!'

Maisie was left listening to the buzz of a broken connection. Lovely. That would leave her plenty of time to visit her friend in Cramond tomorrow, have a walk on the beach and recharge her batteries. It sounded like the best idea in the world.

***

By two o'clock, Sylvie was hurtling down the motorway, the baby asleep in the car seat beside her. She hadn't left until after the lunchtime bottle, when there was a good chance Erin would sleep for a couple of hours. The turn-off for Manchester flashed past. They were making good time.

But oh, God. In three days' time Maisie would expect her to arrive in Edinburgh with Erin. Sylvie's stomach churned. She had seventy-two hours to find a way for her and Erin to disappear into their own world. Her job needed sorting too. The boss was getting increasingly stroppy about all the time off she was taking – sick leave, unpaid leave and now holidays. So maybe a new job was the answer, something she could do with a baby.

The journey took longer than she'd expected; the baby had a massive blow-out in her nappy near Birmingham, and a long screaming fit after Bath, and Sylvie's head was aching by the time they were driving through green Devon countryside.

The bungalow her parents had moved to from Glasgow ten years ago looked as idyllic as ever, a climbing rose waiting to bloom around the door and window boxes all over the place. Sylvie had never lived there but it still felt home-ish, with Mum and Dad. She would make a lovely home for her girl too, yes she would, she would.

Her mother hurried out as soon as the car stopped. 'Darling! Lovely to see you! But who's this?'

Christine Raynott's eyebrows were almost in the sky, and Sylvie beamed.

'Surprise! I'm adopting her, Mum. Meet little Christine.'

***

Two days later and still nothing was going right. Maisie had spent the time getting her flat ready for the return of Vicky and Erin, at least. The bed was kitted out with a new Disney duvet cover, and the cot was cleaned and disinfected and thank the Lord, now devoid of the vomit and poo aroma.

And then the phone call from Yvonne. 'Maisie, we're moving the children to another foster family. The Camerons couldn't cope with Jamie.'

Anger and bitterness exploded in Maisie. '*What?* I thought they were experienced foster parents?'

'They are, but... Jamie's difficult, you know that.'

'I want Vicky back here. Another change is the last thing she needs.'

Yvonne sounded doubtful. 'I know, and I'm sorry, but I don't think she'll agree to leave Jamie.'

'She's a five-year-old child, she–'

'Maisie, I *know*. Anyway, they've already been moved. As a special favour you can visit them, and we'll discuss this.'

The Noakes family lived on the other side of the city, and Maisie sat on the bus wishing she could drive. A young mother boarded, a baby on her hip, a folded buggy hooked over the same arm, her other hand guiding a small boy to a seat as the bus jerked along. Maisie winced. Not in a million years could she do that.

Sick certainty brought tears to her eyes. She was deluding herself – they would never give her the children back. In ten years, she'd be eighty and Vicky would be fifteen. How would an octogenarian cope with parenting a teenager? It wasn't going to happen, but she still had to fight for them, to show Vicky she cared.

May Noakes ushered her into a pleasant living room, where Yvonne and Vicky were already sitting on a squishy blue sofa. Vicky's eyes were as bleak as no child's should ever be, and Maisie's heart went out to the girl.

'Vicky, darling–'

The little girl ran across the room and clutched at Maisie's jumper. 'Jamie wants to come home to you, he'll be very, very good, he told me.'

Maisie hugged Vicky, feeling the tension in the small body. How could fate be so cruel to this poor child, and why was she so powerless to change things? And dear Lord, what would happen when Erin was home?

'I want you home too, darling, but–'

Yvonne spoke to Vicky. 'Auntie Maisie can't take Jamie

home, Vicky. He needs to be with people who're strong enough to lift him and carry him. Auntie May can do that now.'

'Can't I take Vicky home, at least?' The pleading tone in her own voice made Maisie cringe. This was what it had come to; she was begging for something that should be hers already.

'No! I won't leave Jamie! I hate you!' Vicky stormed from the room.

Home again, Maisie slumped into her chair, overwhelmed by the speed of the day's events, and dear Lord, what was happening with Sylvie? Shouldn't she have phoned by now to make handover arrangements? Of course the poor girl could have been calling in vain all afternoon. Maisie tried Sylvie's number, but there was no answer. She would try again in an hour or so.

Chapter Nine

Sunday, 6th May

At half past seven on Sunday morning, Maisie tried Sylvie's number again, but the phone rang on and on, and impatience swept through Maisie before she banged the receiver down. Sylvie would hardly have left home yet; Edinburgh was only a couple of hours from Carlisle. Was she going to arrive unannounced and leave the baby on the doorstep if Maisie wasn't home? It seemed a very casual way to go about reuniting the poor child with her family.

The phone remained stubbornly silent all morning and by lunchtime, fear had replaced Maisie's impatience. What would she do if no call came? Sylvie had said she was flying from Glasgow tomorrow. Maisie rinsed her coffee mug, and rubbed her face with the tea towel. Maybe she'd misunderstood; maybe Sylvie had meant she'd call shortly before she arrived.

Maisie didn't budge from the flat all day, but the afternoon went by with no word from Sylvie and by the evening, Maisie's fear had turned to anger. This was too bad of Sylvie. If the holiday had been cancelled for some reason, she should still have kept her word about the baby, or let Maisie know, at the very least. The best idea would be to take the train to Carlisle tomorrow and bring Erin home herself. Shutting out the *what if* voices in her head, Maisie phoned and booked her train seat.

***

'Look, Dad, you'll have a lovely view of the rose garden from here.' Sylvie perched on the bed in what would be her father's new room. Talk about Monday morning – Mum was nearly in tears and Dad's face was blank as usual.

Sylvie and her mother exchanged glances. He had no idea this would soon be his home – until his death, probably. They'd been bringing him to the care home for several hours a day since Sylvie's arrival, to ease him into the new life, but he showed no sign of recognising the place, even though most of his things were already spread around his bedroom.

'It's very comfortable, isn't it, dear?' said Christine, cuddling the sleeping baby in her arms. She sniffed loudly.

Sylvie swallowed. Mum was finding this hard, but she was head over heels in love with the baby, and that made things easier. There was always something to talk about, and babies were a more cheerful subject than care homes and dementia. And it was so restful. At long last Erin was accepted – loved, too – as Sylvie's daughter. This was how it should be, how it always would be now. All she had to do was concentrate on getting them away from the rest of the world, but oh, God, what was Maisie Gibson doing? How had the old woman reacted when no Erin arrived to grow up with her brother and sister? But Maisie wouldn't involve the police, would she? Sylvie shivered. She hadn't thought this through properly. Maisie was still a real danger, and Sylvie knew she couldn't live with the uncertainty. She came to a decision: if there was nothing about a missing baby on the news tonight, she would phone Maisie, make her understand that she was the only mother Erin would ever need.

A nurse came in with her father's meds. 'What a gorgeous baby! What's her name?'

'Christine,' said Sylvie's mother, pride oozing from every pore. 'After me.'

There was the usual interlude of baby compliments, then the nurse led her father out, and Sylvie and her mother looked at each other.

'Home,' said Sylvie, attempting cheerfulness. 'Then you can take E– Christine for a walk, if you like, while I get some stuff organised for work. Then we'll collect Dad again.' For the last time...

She didn't have a pram, but her mother had borrowed one from a friend who had one for visiting grandchildren. Sylvie stuck her chin in the air as they walked back to the car. This was going to work with Erin, because it had to. If she lost her baby now she would go mad. All she needed to do was silence Maisie Gibson.

When her mother and the pram had vanished around the corner, Sylvie sat looking at the phone. She could call Maisie... or she could just disappear from Maisie's life. If she and the baby relocated somewhere remote, she could start a new life. Dave's face swam before her eyes. Could she persuade him to come and live in Land's End, or the Shetland Isles? But no. The dream of father-mother-child was just that, a dream. Mother and child was reality, yes it was.

Sylvie opened the newspaper and turned to the situations vacant columns. Nothing, and nothing, and nothing. But she could keep looking. By the end of the week Dad would be settled and Mum would be settled without him, and she could go. Somewhere.

**

Monday morning sunshine was sniggering at Maisie everywhere she turned. Gripping her handbag, she stood outside Carlisle station and looked around for a taxi, trying to convince herself she was being silly, feeling so nervous.

The taxi meandered through the streets then stopped with a jerk at Sylvie's flat. Maisie grabbed the door handle. She was here, but where was Sylvie?

The middle-aged woman in the next flat to Sylvie's provided the answer. 'She's gone down south to help her parents. She wasn't sure when she'd be back – her dad's going into a home this week.'

Maisie grasped the faint hope with both hands. An emergency could explain why Sylvie had failed to contact her, and then something wrong with the phone lines, maybe? Perhaps a letter would be waiting on the doormat when she arrived back in Edinburgh. Maisie thanked the woman and turned away, her steps slowing as she thought of the call with Sylvie on Thursday. There had been no talk of visiting her parents then. And 'going into a home this week' sounded planned.

Cold, sick certainty burrowed into Maisie's heart. Care home, phone lines, nothing. Sylvie had run off with Paula's baby, that was what, and why hadn't she seen it coming? The increasing reluctance to phone, the excuses not to return Erin. It all made terrible sense now.

Maisie arrived at a bus stop and sat down on the grubby bench to think. The police would be able to find Sylvie, surely. But that might well mean Erin would land in a foster home too, separated from her siblings. It was impossible to know what to do for the best, impossible to guess what Paula would have wanted. A bus arrived and Maisie bought a ticket back to the station. She would go home and organise a visit to Vicky and Jamie, if possible, and think. The need to connect with at least two of Paula's children was pulling hard at her middle, and she could barely sit still while the train snaked north. Until she decided whether to call the police, there was nobody – not one person in the entire world – she could talk to about this. What a wretch Sylvie was.

Back home, Maisie dropped her case in the hallway and lifted the letter lying there. An official one, so not from Sylvie. She scanned the single sheet, then crumpled the letter in her hand. The children were to remain in foster care 'for the foreseeable future', but she would have 'generous visiting rights'. Maisie strode to the phone to call Yvonne Bradshaw and tell her she was going to contest this. Generous visiting rights would do nothing for any of them when Vicky was refusing to speak to her, and May Noakes was sounding more impatient every time Maisie called. A mean kind of satisfaction filled Maisie – the woman would be exhausted, looking after Jamie, and heaven knows, she knew how that felt. She listened as the phone rang out, then realised Yvonne would be home for the night now. Well – she'd call May and ask if she could visit the children tonight. Seeing them might help her decide what to do about Erin.

May was taken aback by the call; Maisie heard that loud and clear as soon as the other woman spoke.

'*Maisie?* Oh... I... didn't they tell you? They moved the children to another foster home this afternoon. They're in Glasgow.'

Chapter Ten

Tuesday, 8th May

The deed was done – her father was in the care home for keeps. And now Mum was in bits. Sylvie drove towards home, then changed her mind and turned into a rural pub on the way.

'Come on,' she said firmly. 'I'll buy you a stiff gin.'

'Oh, Sylvie, I don't know how I'd have managed without you,' said Christine, pulling out her compact and dabbing at her nose. 'Thank you, sweetheart.'

Warmth flooded through Sylvie. If only she could stay here, move in with Mum for a bit, find her feet and get a new job. But it wasn't safe. If the police were looking for her…

There had been nothing on the news last night, and nothing on the radio or in the paper this morning. Did that mean Maisie hadn't reported her? Sylvie bought a G&T and a soda and lime and they sat chatting about old days, Erin in Christine's arms.

'You will visit often, won't you? I'd love to watch her grow up.'

''Course,' said Sylvie lightly.

Home again, her mother settled down to feed the baby, and Sylvie pored over the situations vacant columns again. There were more today. One was for a receptionist in Bournemouth, another in Wales. And there was one in Scotland too, for a 'caretaker with desk duties' in a hostel in the Outer Hebrides. Sylvie stared. It was remote enough, though heaven knows what the job entailed. Might be worth finding out, though. She pulled the page from the paper and folded it up. Whatever she did, she should tell Dave. The tiny hope was still there – father-mother-child.

That night, while Christine was bathing the baby, Sylvie called him.

'Well, stranger,' he said, an edge to his voice, and Sylvie jerked in surprise.

'You didn't call either,' she said, then realised – she hadn't given him the number. And maybe that was a sign.

'Sorry. It's been hectic, getting Dad sorted. Hey – I'm going for another job, on the coast down here, or maybe up north in Scotland. Fancy looking for that place together up there?'

'You're kidding,' he said.

Sylvie remained silent.

'Oh. You're not kidding. Syl, no, I love my job. I have good prospects and anyway, I haven't been here long. Let's postpone coastal life, huh?'

'I can't,' she said. 'I mean, I don't want to. I'm serious about this, Dave.'

'And I'm serious about not doing it. In a few years, maybe, but not now.'

'I'm sorry. This isn't going to work. Thanks for everything, Dave, and take care.' Sylvie put the phone down and ran upstairs to her room. It was just the two of them now. A call to Maisie would show the poor old thing what would happen if anyone meddled with Erin, and it wouldn't even be a lie, would it? Which *proved* that she was doing the right thing. Mother knows best.

***

Yvonne couldn't have been more apologetic when Maisie eventually reached her on the phone on Tuesday morning, but that did nothing to quell the fury erupting in Maisie's soul.

'Maisie, I'm *sorry*. I tried your phone countless times yesterday. I even went twice to your home, but in the end we took them to Glasgow. May Noakes wasn't coping with Jamie, and you know–'

'I know all about Jamie. What I need to know, as a matter of urgency, is why you've removed these children so far from me, when I'm the only blood family they have?'

Lies, lies... Maisie bit her lip. She wasn't the children's only relative, was she?

'The new foster parents have years of experience caring for children with special needs. We know it will work with Amanda and Ted Grayson, and I'll take you to Glasgow to see them as soon as you like.'

Maisie sounded as nasty as she could. 'I want to go today. I'll be making a complaint about this, Yvonne. And if I'm not happy about the place, I'll be applying for a court order to bring Vicky at least back to Edinburgh.'

She had no idea if such a thing was possible, but she had to lash out somehow.

'I'll pick you up at one o'clock. You can spend as long as you like with them before we come back. This isn't the normal procedure, Maisie, but in this case–'

Maisie interrupted firmly. Was she supposed to sound

grateful? 'I'll be staying in Glasgow. I'm not letting you force me into abandoning those children.' She crashed the phone down and wilted into the sofa, hot, angry tears of frustration trickling down both cheeks. She had already abandoned Paula's baby.

The drive to Glasgow was frosty, in spite of the blazing sun. Maisie fixed her gaze to the left as hills and countryside alternated with towns and villages. Why was sunshine so hard to take when you were angry? And hurt. And feeling you were a stupid, stupid old woman. She should have told the authorities about Erin right at the start. Maisie closed her eyes, but she couldn't un-see what she'd done.

Glasgow wasn't the prettiest city. Despair engulfed Maisie as they drove along litter-strewn streets past shabby tenements, but soon they came to a leafier area, where red and beige sandstone houses were set back from quiet pavements. Yvonne parked in a broad driveway, and Maisie blinked up at a detached house with a generous garden. It was a pleasant place, made homelike by an assortment of toys left lying on the grass. Maisie forced stiff legs to the ground and hauled herself out of the car.

A tall, thirty-something brunette appeared in the driveway and shook Maisie's hand, rubbing her arm at the same time, grey eyes full of sympathy. 'Maisie? I'm Amanda. This is awful for you. The children are inside. Come through to the kitchen.'

Maisie suppressed a little surge of satisfaction when Vicky's foster mother led her inside after a mere nod to Yvonne. So Amanda thought this hadn't been managed well, too.

'I want Vicky back,' she managed, her voice breaking. 'But I can't cope with Jamie.'

'I know. Come through.'

Amanda led Maisie down a long hallway with bashed paintwork into an enormous and equally shabby kitchen. Maisie sank into a chair and gaped around her. It wasn't a posh place, but it was homely. Children's drawings were pinned and stuck all over the place, and the fridge held the largest collection of magnets Maisie had ever seen.

'Vicky doesn't know you're coming. Our student's with her in the playroom,' said Amanda, sitting down opposite while Yvonne hovered in the doorway. 'We can have a quick chat, then I'll take you to them.'

'Student?' Maisie sat clutching her handbag.

'The local college does a pre-nursing course and we always have a student from there to help with the children. As well as Vicky and Jamie we have a little girl with spina bifida, and a boy who'll be going home this week.'

'How many children do you take at one time?'

'Four, maximum. Ellen is long-term, though she goes home for a week or so every few months.'

Tears came into Maisie's eyes. She could see already this place was better for Jamie than the foster homes in Edinburgh, but oh, if the children stayed in Glasgow she'd end up being an occasional visitor in their lives.

'So they'd be permanent here? If I don't get Vicky back?'

'Yes. She's adamant about being with Jamie. Separation is a real fear, and I think for the moment it's best we reassure her this won't happen unless she wants it to.'

Maisie swallowed, nodding dumbly. Admit it, Maisie, this woman's right. I'm sorry, Paula.

Yvonne left, depositing Maisie's overnight bag by the table and promising to stay in touch, although the children would have a different social worker in Glasgow. Another stranger. Maisie felt whipped.

'Come and see the children, then I'll make tea,' said Amanda, getting to her feet. 'Ellen and Rob are at the park with my husband. You can meet them later.'

She led Maisie through a door into a back hallway, and from there into a toy-filled room with a large table where Vicky was colouring in, a dark-haired teenager beside her. Jamie was in his buggy, blowing bubbles and twitching in his usual way.

Maisie sank down and reached out to touch Vicky's arm. 'Vicky, darling. Are you all right?'

The little girl glanced up, and for one terrible moment it seemed to Maisie that all the hurt in the world was shining from the child's eyes.

'I'm sorry I wasn't there when they were moving you,' she said, but Vicky had returned to her drawing.

'Would you like Auntie Maisie to tell you what the plans are, Vicky?' Amanda nodded to the teenager, who left them to it.

'Uh-huh.' Vicky's gaze was still fixed on her drawing.

'You and Jamie are staying here with Auntie Amanda for now,' said Maisie, trying and failing to catch Vicky's eye. 'I'll be in a hotel very close by for a little while, and I'll visit every day to make sure you're settling in. Then sometime, you can come and see me in Edinburgh. You know you're in Glasgow now, don't you?'

This time Vicky did look up. 'I wanted to go back to Mummy and Daddy in Glasgow.'

'I know, sweetheart. They'll be watching you from heaven.'

Vicky ignored this. 'I don't want to go to Edinburgh. It's horrible there.'

Maisie sat in her B&B that evening, unanswerable questions filling her mind. Would she ever have a good relationship with Paula's daughter? With either of Paula's daughters? She had to find Sylvie – but what if she couldn't? And even if she did, she was unlikely to be given custody of a baby. If only she knew what Paula would have wished.

Four days later Maisie arrived home again, no clearer in her head, but reassured that Vicky was settling in well and building a good relationship with Amanda and Ted. There was nothing more she could do, except visit regularly. She was slumped in her armchair in the echoingly empty flat, ignoring the six o'clock news on television, when the phone rang beside her.

'Maisie, don't speak – I want to say something.'

Maisie jerked upright. Sylvie. She listened as the younger woman continued, her voice thin and breathless.

'I'm keeping Erin. You don't need to worry that she'll ever want for love, or care, or anything. She means the world to me, and I can give her a good home. We're going away somewhere you won't find us, but maybe someday–'

Maisie pressed her free fist to her chest as frustration threatened to choke her. 'I could go to the police, Sylvie.'

'I know. But if you did, would Erin have a good home with a mum who loves her? You know she'd be taken into care. I'm sorry, Maisie, but I have to do this. She's my girl.'

The phone went dead and Maisie sagged back in the chair, still clutching the receiver.

A mum who loves her. It was all any child could wish for.

Chapter Eleven

Late September

Sylvie drove south towards Stornoway, the sea swelling and grey on her left, the mainland invisible. The sky was wide here; everywhere you looked there was space. To the south of For and Harris lay the smaller islands of North and South Uist, with Skye, Rum, and Canna, and others too, to the east, and one day she wanted to visit them all. The Centre for Alternative Therapy on the northern tip of Lewis was their new home, and Erin was there right now, being looked after by Aileen, the secretary. Sylvie tossed her head back. Her baby was thriving in the peace here, and she was in the middle of it all, a mum.

It was a different life, being receptionist and general dogsbody at the centre, which held courses for alternative practitioners, patients and anyone else who was interested. Rather to Sylvie's surprise, business appeared to be booming. The hours were long, but it was more a way of life than a job because she could take the baby to work and attend to her in between tasks. And if she was busy, there was a multitude of others only too glad to change a nappy or mash a banana. The centre's philosophy seemed a little airy-fairy to Sylvie, but what the hell. She was happy here, and she was safe.

They were both safe.

At Stornoway, she pulled up by the Post Office and lifted her bag from the passenger seat, fingering the two envelopes inside, then opening one and leafing through the photos she was sending her mother. Erin in her buggy, Erin on the beach, Erin and Sylvie at home – Mum would love these. The planned fortnight in Devon was coming up next month and Mum was more excited with every phone call. Sylvie replaced the photos and stuck the flap down firmly.

The second envelope had Maisie's address on the front and a single photo inside: the one of Erin looking adorable in pink and beaming up at the camera. Sylvie fumbled for a tissue and blew her nose. The need to protect her baby had ridden roughshod over everything and everyone else. But Erin was her daughter, end of. She needed Erin to survive – imagine if she ever lost her… Sylvie shuddered, thrusting the thought away. From now on, her child was no longer Erin.

Inside, she stood in the queue for stamps, staring at the envelopes.

'Next.'

Sylvie stepped forward, sliding one envelope back into her bag. Another time, maybe. But not today.

She pushed the thicker envelope towards the woman behind the glass. 'First class, please.'

Chapter Twelve

Mid-December

Winter had come with a vengeance. Maisie could barely see Edinburgh castle, half-hidden as it was by flurries of snow as the bus trundled along Princes Street and on towards Haymarket. The scene was bleak, but the warm glow in Maisie's heart kept her warm. After months of indifference bordering on disrespect from her little niece, the tide had turned. This visit had been a good one. Vicky had shown Maisie the Christmas presents she'd made at school for Jamie, Amanda and Ted, and they had all gone to see the lights in George Square, Maisie's hand clutched in Vicky's small one.

'See? All she needed was time,' whispered Amanda, as Maisie's taxi arrived to take her to Queen Street station and the Edinburgh train.

Tears came into Maisie's eyes at the memory. Seven months was a long time when you were aching with love and sympathy and wracked with guilt, but oh, Vicky had kissed her goodbye. Up until today, she had kissed Vicky. Maisie hooked her handbag over her shoulder and gripped her overnight case, then stood to leave the bus. Her next visit was on Boxing Day. There would be presents to exchange and new toys to play with, so that should go well too. Two good visits must set a pattern; she hoped so, anyway.

If only she had a good pattern of visits with Erin, too. More guilt, even harder to bear. She had no idea where Paula's younger daughter was; Sylvie had disappeared with the child and Maisie didn't know how to start finding her without involving the authorities. If she did that, who knows what would happen, because Sylvie was right about one thing – Erin would be taken into care.

Hefting her case into the warmth of the flat, Maisie stepped over a pile of post in the hallway and dropped her bag by the coat stand. Post was little but cards at this time of year. She gathered them up and dumped them on the hall table to look through later.

It was considerably later when she lifted the pile – Helen next door had come through for the latest news on the children then stayed for a Christmas sherry, and Maisie had revelled in giving a positive report for a change. It was after ten when her neighbour left, and Maisie poured a cheeky half-glass and lifted the pile of cards.

The first she opened was a robin with a sprig of mistletoe in its beak. But the message had Maisie frozen to her chair, her heart thumping.

We are well and Erin is happy – as you see on the photo. Maisie seized the envelope and scrabbled for the photo she'd missed when pulling the card out. A chubby blonde baby in a pink suit beamed up at her, joy shining from her eyes. Oh dear Lord. Erin. Tears poured down Maisie's cheeks, and for a long moment she rocked in her chair, the photo pressed to her heart. At last she went back to the card.

This is what Paula would wish for; thank you for leaving me my girl. I won't be in touch again, but Erin will want for nothing.

Maisie dropped the card and returned to the photo of the baby. Nobody knew now what Paula would wish, but a happy, loved baby wouldn't be far wrong. And Vicky was happy too, at last, and Jamie was well-cared for, but dear Lord – was she really doing the right thing, letting Erin go?

Maisie turned the envelope and peered at the postmark, but it was smudged. London, wasn't it? The most impersonal city in the country.

Maisie read the card again, then ripped it in two, and four, then buried the scraps of Christmas in the pile of newspapers waiting for the church paper drive. She lifted the photo greedily; her third picture of Erin. Feasting her eyes on the child, Maisie finished her sherry, then took the photo to the bedroom, where she pulled out the old family bible. Paula and Vicky and new-born Erin were in there already. Maisie traced a finger down the baby on the new photo, then slid it into the bible. The past belonged in the past.

PART TWO

THE SEARCH

Chapter One

Twenty-two years later: Saturday, 28th October

What had she done? The memory crashed into Christine's mind, mocking her from all directions. She pulled the duvet over her head and rolled on her side, cringing into warm darkness as hot shame flushed through her. If anyone had seen them… Her stomach lurched, and she hugged both arms across her front and panted the nausea down. And oh no, her mother was coming up the stairs. If Mum came in here now…

And of course, she did. 'For heaven's sake, Chris, it smells like a rubbish tip in here. I hope you're pleased with yourself after last night. I've brought you some tea and toast, and you'd better have a couple of paracetamols too – I'm sure you need them.'

The clunk as a tray was deposited on the bedside table sent new daggers twisting into Christine's head, but her mother wasn't finished. The curtains swished open.

'I'll have eggs ready in half an hour, so make sure you're down to eat them. And you can phone Jess this morning and apologise, too. Her silver wedding party wasn't the right occasion to get blotto.'

The door banged shut. Christine curled into an even

tighter ball as tears pushed their way under her eyelids and ran across her nose. She'd been so bevvied and that was his fault; he'd filled her glass over and over, and she'd let him. Same as she'd giggled when he followed her into the ladies, and he'd giggled too. He'd been as drunk as she was. Horror and humiliation coursed through Christine as she remembered those few minutes in the narrow stall as they pulled at each other's clothes and– *no no no no no*. She'd had sex with her father's best friend.

Christine's gut shifted, and she wrestled the duvet aside, stumbling over last night's clothes as she made a dive for the bathroom, where she vomited bile into the toilet bowl. When the spasm passed she hung over the washbasin, then splashed cold water on her cheeks. The girl staring back from the mirror was pale, with mascara smudges under bleary eyes and dark blonde hair trailing limply over her shoulders.

'Christine? Are you all right?'

Frustration mixed with fierce longing made Christine close her eyes. Oh, to be six years old again and let Mum take care of her. But she was twenty-two and about to leave home to embark on the next phase of her life, which was not going to be welcome news to the woman on the other side of the bathroom door. Sylvie Adams had made mothering her only chick into an entire career.

Christine swallowed. 'I'm fine, Mum. About to have that tea. Give me five, huh?'

The stairs creaked as Sylvie retreated. Fingers shaking, Christine opened the bottle of make-up remover and cleaned her face before returning to her room to pull on leggings and a chunky sweater. It felt good, as if the sweater was hugging her, and God knows she needed the love today. She slumped on the bed, sipped the lukewarm tea and reached for the pills on the tray. Get a grip, Chris.

Her mother was ironing when she went downstairs, and her father was nowhere to be seen. Saturday was golf day.

Sylvie didn't look up. The concern she'd shown through the bathroom door had given way to her usual holier-than-thou expression when she disapproved of something her daughter had done. 'I'll make your eggs in a moment.'

'Mum, I can make my own breakfast. Big girl, remember?'

Christine slid a mug under the machine, then took her coffee to the table. The silver wedding party invitation stuck on the fridge with a daisy magnet made her stomach churn anew, and she sipped her coffee cautiously. She would never drink vodka again.

The iron glugged as Sylvie poured in more water, and Christine clutched her aching forehead. Heck, why was sex such a big deal? Two drunk people, and it wasn't as if she'd been a virgin. Okay, the memory now was appalling, but it had happened, and the consolation was that scumbag Drew must be feeling ten million times guiltier than she was. They'd both behaved badly, but he was the one who was married with teenage kids.

The warmth of the coffee mug in her hands was comforting. 'Sorry about last night. Drew gave me a shedload of vodka, and–'

'I don't remember you saying you'd prefer juice, Christine.'

'I know – I had too much. But getting drunk isn't a hangable offence, Mum.' Having sex with a man who played golf with her father might be, though.

Sylvie thumped the iron down and leaned towards Christine, tears shining in her eyes. 'I've never been so mortified. You could barely walk, and all that silly giggling–'

'For God's sake, Mum–' Christine broke off as her mother strode round the ironing board and poked her shoulder.

'Not one word more, miss. You were as drunk as a pig and I don't want to hear any of your nonsense. What would people think? Take that coffee to your room and stay out of my sight until you're back to normal.'

Christine stared, heat flushing through her. Not much empathy there, was there? Mum had the control freak thing down to a fine art, she really did. Had she never had too much to drink? Resentment seared through Christine. She wasn't a child now, to be moulded into Sylvie's version of an ideal daughter. But at least she could strike back.

Rising to her feet, she plucked a banana from the fruit bowl and stuck her chin in the air. 'With pleasure. Oh, and you'll be glad to know I'll be out of your sight more permanently soon. I've been offered a new job, starting January. In Glasgow.'

Sylvie's horrified expression was all Christine could have wished for, and a hysterical desire to laugh welled up in her head. According to her mother, Glasgow combined the worst aspects of a den of iniquity and a brimming pit full of poisonous snakes. But living with Mum and Dad, buried in the heart of the Aberdeenshire countryside, was doing her head in. It was time to fly the nest.

Chapter Two

Friday, 5th January

The taxi jerked to a halt in front of yet another set of road works. Crouching on the edge of her seat, Vicky bit back her frustration. It wasn't the driver's fault – orange-clad workmen seemed to be digging up every road in Edinburgh today. Would Maisie still be alive when she got there? The sweat of panic broke out, and Vicky pushed damp curls away from her face. An innocuous Friday had taken on a real nightmare hue, like one of those dreams where you're trying to go somewhere and it's terribly important you get there fast, but everything keeps going wrong, and you can't wake up, and oh, come *on*...

She hadn't trusted herself to drive all the way from Glasgow with her hands shaking like this, and the fifty-minute train journey had provided Vicky with time to allow the fact that she was going to lose her great-aunt sink into her brain. The call from the home had sounded so final: 'The doctor says she doesn't have long. She wants to see you before she goes – she has something important to tell you, she said.'

Vicky hugged her bag to her middle. This was going to be one of those days she would measure things by for the rest of her life. *It was just before/after Maisie died.* Hot tears stung Vicky's eyes. Suddenly and horribly, it struck her how alone she was in the world. She had two blood relatives, and one of them was going to die today. And how unfair it was that this should be happening now, when she and Ben had come home to Glasgow, finding yet-to-be-started jobs and a lovely new riverside flat. For the past five years Vicky had travelled up from Manchester every month to visit Maisie in her Edinburgh home for the elderly, and Jamie in his Glasgow home for the disabled. Now she was back for good she'd have so much more time for them both, but it was going to be too late for Maisie.

'Nearly there, love,' said the taxi driver, swinging round the obstruction at last, and Vicky fumbled her purse out. Train and taxi were very nearly as fast as coming by car, but how she wished she wasn't doing this alone. But Amanda, her third – and last – foster mother, hadn't been at home this morning and wasn't answering her mobile, either, and as Ben was still in Manchester this week there was no one Vicky could have asked to accompany her. Bleakly, she watched elegant Edinburgh streets pass by as the taxi rumbled along a row of grey stone houses, built in an era when rooms and windows were huge and ceilings were high. They took a right turn into Burnside Avenue and toped abruptly in front of Meadowside Home.

Colette Ferguson, the head nurse, ran out as soon as the taxi drew up, which did nothing to calm Vicky's nerves. Had the woman been watching for her? Was Maisie…?

'She's holding her own,' said Colette, taking Vicky's arm.

In other words, 'She's not dead yet'. Vicky winced, allowing Colette to lead her inside. As soon as you went through the front door you could tell this was a place where old, old people lived. Both ancient smells and institutional ones pervaded the hallway, lavender disinfectant and pee uppermost, and pity swelled in Vicky's throat. Poor Maisie. Living in a home was awkward no matter how you looked at it, moving from your own four walls where all your things were around you, to a tartan carpet you hadn't chosen on the floor, and meals you had no part in planning. And yet this was a good place.

'It was all quite sudden. She felt extra-tired yesterday, but she's been weak for months, as you know,' said Colette, lowering her voice and pausing on the dim first-floor landing. Maisie's room was on the left, and today the hiss of an oxygen tank was coming through the door. 'Then this morning her pulse was irregular, and her conscious level's up and down. The doctor will be in again soon. Maisie knows she doesn't have long, and that was why she wanted to see you so badly. I'll leave you to sit with her.' She pushed the bedroom door open and stood back.

Vicky crept across the room and sank into the chair by the bed, bending towards the slight figure lying there. Maisie was her mother's aunt, and well over ninety now. They'd had a fabulous party on the big day and Maisie had loved it. She'd never spoken before about something important that Vicky should know. But maybe it was simply the wish to have family with her when she died, and to say and hear 'I love you'. Fighting back tears, Vicky took the old woman's hand and squeezed gently. Maisie's head with its sparse grey hair moved, and she gave a deep sigh.

'Hello, here I am,' said Vicky, leaning forward to kiss the papery cheek. It was cool. 'Can I get you anything, Maisie love?'

Maisie blinked, then gripped Vicky's hand with surprising

strength, though her voice was little more than a whisper behind the oxygen mask. She pulled it away and started again.

'Vicky – I'm sorry. Sorry I let you go, back then. I wanted to keep you, but–'

'Hush,' said Vicky. 'I know. It's all right. It was for the best. You couldn't have taken care of me and Jamie both.'

Maisie closed her eyes and her chest heaved. Vicky's heart leapt. What should she do if Maisie stopped breathing?

The old woman's eyes opened again and gazed urgently into Vicky's. 'Vicky. There was a baby. You have a little sister. Erin. She was six days old when…' Her voice tailed off and her eyelids dropped.

Vicky could only sit and gape at her great-aunt. *No.* Was that even possible? Surely there couldn't have been a sister too when fate in the form of an explosion had robbed her and Jamie of their parents? She would remember, wouldn't she? Or someone would have told her. It had all been such a mess… She and Jamie were left with Maisie while Mum and Dad went to a party in England, but Vicky had no recollection of learning about their deaths. Losing your parents was every child's worst nightmare; she had blanked out a lot. But she'd been four years old – would she *really* have blanked out a baby sister?

'Hello, you must be Maisie's niece. I'm the GP. Alice Peterson.'

Vicky jerked back to here and now. The doctor was a middle-aged woman in a grey trouser suit, and she gave Maisie's shoulder a pat before shaking hands with Vicky.

'I'll have a quick look and then we'll have a chat.'

Maisie slept – or was she unconscious? – while the doctor examined her, then Vicky followed the other woman into the hallway.

'Her pulse is very irregular and her breathing is superficial. You know she's had problems with her heart for years. It's just her time – I'm sorry.'

The tiny hope she hadn't admitted to dissolved into nothing and Vicky nodded, pressing cold fingers to her cheeks. 'Thank you. Will she come round again? She told me something pretty way-out before she dozed off. I really need to ask her about it.'

'She may just slip away. She's in no pain, you can be sure of that.'

Vicky's breath caught. Maisie, Maisie, please wake up again. 'Has she been confused at all recently? I haven't seen her for a couple of weeks, but she was her usual self then.'

The doctor gave her a smile that was somehow sad and warm at the same time. 'No, she's still very with-it. She was raging about the government's latest proposals for NHS funding yesterday.'

'Okay, thanks.' That was Maisie, she cared about stuff. Vicky wiped her eyes and went back into the room. She sat by the bed listening to Maisie's breathing, and messaged Ben again. They'd been together for nearly four years, and Vicky knew she wanted him around forever. Like her, he'd grown up in Scotland then moved to Manchester, and when the chance to work in the IT department in the Queen Elizabeth Hospital in Glasgow came, he'd leapt at it, with Vicky's full approval. They'd moved flats on Tuesday, but Ben had gone back south to organise a few last things in his old job, intending to drive up again tomorrow. She'd called him as soon as she'd heard about Maisie that morning, and he was going to leave as soon as possible. The latest message she'd sent remained unanswered, which hopefully meant he was on the motorway now.

It was another hour before Maisie awoke. Vicky sat holding the cool hand, thinking wistful, disjointed thoughts about the past and about her own life. After her time in Manchester she felt she'd come home to her roots and what little family she had. Now this.

Maisie stirred, and Vicky brushed the wiry grey hair back from the old woman's forehead. 'Okay, lovey? You were asleep.'

Maisie's eyes were open, burning into Vicky's, and they were definitely sharp, she definitely wasn't confused. 'Vicky. Find Erin. Promise.'

'I'll try, but, Maisie love – I don't remember her. What happened back then?'

Swallowing the growing lump in her throat, Vicky pulled out a tissue. The answer was, a lot had happened back then and none of it had been fun. She could remember living at Maisie's. Jamie had cerebral palsy and was difficult to look after – even today he was as helpless as a new-born, with the mind of a three-year-old. All Maisie's friends had praised little Vicky for being 'a proper wee mother' to him. At not quite five years old it had been down to her to persuade Jamie to eat, to sleep, to allow Maisie to care for him without screaming the place down.

Vicky blew her nose and turned back to Maisie. But the pale blue eyes were blank and staring, and the bony chest under the pink flannel nightgown was motionless. Stunned, Vicky sat still. In half a second, in the middle of a conversation, Maisie had died.

It was depressing, and in a way shocking, to witness how efficiently the staff swung into their 'death' routine. Vicky was allowed to sit with Maisie for a while, then was ushered into a sitting room and brought tea she didn't want. Colette sat with her, talking about 'the long, healthy life' Maisie had enjoyed. All true, and no doubt kindly meant, but Vicky felt as if she had strayed into the wrong film at the cinema. After twenty minutes or so, her mobile rang, and Colette left her to take the call.

It was Ben. Vicky closed her eyes. Please be on the way, Ben, please. She tapped connect.

'Vicky – what's happening?'

Vicky felt her throat close. Her voice came out as a squeak. 'She's gone, Ben. I was sitting with her, and then she...'

'Oh hell, Vicks, I'm so sorry, love. I'm at Abington. I'll be with you in an hour.'

Vicky forced herself to speak. 'Drive safely. Love you.'

'Love you more.'

The connection broke and Vicky leaned back in her chair. He'd be here in an hour. It was the only good thing to happen today.

***

The drive back to Glasgow was silent for the most part, and Vicky was grateful that Ben hadn't demanded all the details the moment he arrived. There was nothing worse than talking about personal stuff in a public place. He'd simply hugged her tightly, then kept one arm around her until they got into the car. Now, travelling west along the M8 as speedily as traffic would allow, Vicky thought how truly awful it would have been to go home by herself on the train.

'Nearly home now. I'll make something to eat and we'll just relax. We'll start all the formalities tomorrow,' said Ben, as they passed Alexandra Park.

Vicky realised she had eaten nothing since breakfast. She should keep her strength up. There was still the funeral to arrange and Maisie's possessions to organise. And half their own possessions were still in boxes in the flat, and her new job started in ten days.

But the biggest question of all in her brave new world was: how was she to find out about the baby?

Ben dished up pasta with pesto and a green salad, and Vicky told him about Maisie's revelation.

He stared at her, chewing slowly. 'That's incredible. Wouldn't it be great if you had a sister? What are you going to do?'

Vicky put down her fork. 'Obviously I need to check it out, but I don't know where to start.'

Ben was frowning across the table. 'How on earth would you have been split up in the first place?'

'No idea. I suppose it's not impossible Mum and Dad asked someone else to look after a baby when they went to the hotel, but surely I'd have known about that? Maybe Maisie was delusional.'

'And wouldn't the authorities have placed you all together afterwards? I guess the first thing to do is find out if Erin exists.'

'I'll talk to Amanda, then I'll get onto social services and ask if they could look at their records for me. Maybe I can even find the social worker who dealt with us back then.'

Ben reached over and squeezed her hand. 'That sounds like a good place to start, and if Erin does exist I can have a scout round the Internet for you. Facebook, Instagram and so on? We might find her that way.'

'If she was fostered or adopted as a baby, she'd have a different name now. I wonder where I can find out how many kids my parents had?'

'The National Records Office? Have a look on their website.'

Vicky sighed. 'I think to begin with I'd like to talk to a person. Pity it's Friday. I'll phone social services early next week.'

They sat in silence for a few moments, Vicky thinking about her non-existent family. How good it would be to have a sister. But why would they have been separated so permanently like that, and above all, why had Maisie never told her about the baby?

Chapter Three

Monday, 8th January

Christine dived into the bathroom, fighting her stomach and losing. This was the pits. A week into her new job as an occupational therapist in one of the smaller Glasgow hospitals, and the suspicion was darker every day. It had prickled into her mind as she came down to the city at the end of December, driving the Mini her parents had given her for her twenty-first, your typical country girl arriving in the big, bad city. The first purchase Christine made in her new life was a pregnancy test, but she hadn't had the guts to use it. Yet. Today was the day.

Hands trembling, she pulled the slim, white tube from its packaging and did the needful. And waited. And waited, her heart racing so hard she felt dizzy. Yes or no? But she must be...

And there it was. PREGNANT.

Christine's stomach moved again, and she hung over the toilet bowl until the spasm passed. Why hadn't she gone for a morning-after pill? Talk about naïve. All she'd thought about that morning was the fact that she'd had the biggest hangover since time began, after vodka and sex with a man more than twice her age. And how had she managed to *not notice* the pregnancy all this time? She hadn't wanted to notice, that was it, and the nausea hadn't been troublesome at first. She'd even had a slight period since the wedding anniversary party, but her medical knowledge told her this could happen.

More retching. Her stomach muscles were aching. Panting and spitting, Christine leaned her forehead on the arm stretched across the toilet seat. The maths was easy – she hadn't had sex since, so she was about twelve weeks gone. And motherhood didn't sound like the best deal this minute.

The nausea receded and Christine sat back on her heels. At least she was deciding this well away from Mum. Sylvie had done her very best to dissuade Christine from taking the job, but Dad, bless him, had backed her up, and here she was. It should have been a lovely new life, sharing a flat at the top of Byres Road with Larissa, a friend from her old training hospital who was now a radiographer at the same hospital. They had the Glasgow West End on the doorstep, with work a short drive away. It was everything Christine had longed for since she qualified.

She stood up cautiously, then rinsed her face and went through to the kitchen, where Larissa was tying on running shoes. She always jogged to work when it was dry.

'Can you take my bag in the car, Chris?'

'Sure.' Christine filled the kettle. She had time for tea and toast before she left. It was all she'd keep down this morning. She glanced outside, where frost was sparkling on the windscreens of cars parked below. 'I don't know how you can stand running when it's as cold as this.'

'Nothing wrong with a January jog. See you later.' Larissa dumped her plastic bag with spare clothes by the flat door and departed. Christine sat nursing her tea, pondering the finality of no longer being alone in her body. She'd have to do something about it. But what?

By the time she arrived at work her stomach had settled, although the odd wave of nausea still washed through her. Christine changed into uniform. She was late – most of the other occupational therapists had already started. Luckily, she was on home visits this week, making sure that people who'd been discharged from hospital were coping with their various pieces of equipment. Today was the first time she'd gone out alone; last week, she'd accompanied a senior OT to learn the ropes.

She picked up her list from the rehabilitation unit reception and set off. As luck would have it, the first visit involved a baby – a young paraplegic woman with a two-week-old son. Christine admired little Justin, trying to ignore the aroma of baby sick that was invading the bathroom, where a special changing table had been set up over the bath.

'He's doing so well,' enthused Liz, the mother, demonstrating how the table swung out to allow her to slide underneath with her wheelchair. 'Having him has made my life a hundred per cent better.'

Christine's stomach jerked as realisation slammed home. She was *having a baby*. She watched as Liz snuggled her son into her neck. 'He's gorgeous. Is there anything you feel I could help with?'

'Not at the moment,' said Liz. 'The OT who set everything up for me said I could have a special buggy attachment for my wheelchair, but we agreed it could wait a few months. At the moment he's quite happy in a sling on my chest.'

'Yes, your buggy's on order,' said Christine, checking the file on her I. 'It–'

The baby farted loudly and a pungent smell filled the air. Christine stood still, breathing through her mouth and only just managing not to retch.

'You okay? Sorry about that.' Liz was staring, and Christine forced herself to reply.

'I'm sorry. My stomach's a bit, um… dodgy curry last night, I think.'

She escaped as soon as she could and took refuge in her car, sweat beading on her forehead. That had been way too close. And chances were she'd encounter a whole lot worse smells over the course of the week. A stop-off at a chemist provided her with a bottle of ginger ale and a packet of ginger sweets, plus the usual advice about seeing her doctor if things didn't improve. Somehow, Christine got through the rest of the morning. The sweets did seem to help. She arrived back at the hospital at lunchtime feeling better, and bought a sandwich from the Red Cross tea bar near outpatients, sitting at an empty table to eat. No way did she want to join the others in the rehab staff room – what would she do if she got queasy and somebody noticed?

Sliced cheese and cucumber on brown bread slid down without causing any major disruption in Christine's gut, and she relaxed cautiously in the plastic chair. Bad situation, Chris, but you do have choices. You can have the baby and keep it, have it and put it up for adoption, or get rid of it. A burning wave of misery flooded through her.

It was a decision she wasn't ready to make.

***

Vicky heaved the boxes containing Maisie's remaining possessions into the back of her Clio and banged the door shut. In the two days she'd spent in Edinburgh, she'd cleared the room in Meadowside Home, giving the furniture and most of the clothes to the Salvation Army, arranged the funeral according to Maisie's wishes and seen the solicitor about the will. Everything was left to her with the instruction to share with her siblings, which had caused the solicitor's eyebrows to shoot heavenwards. Vicky hadn't explained.

The M8 was quiet and she drove west on automatic pilot, planning. Today was Monday and the funeral was on Thursday. Thank goodness she wasn't due to start her job until the fifteenth. Between now and then, she aimed to find someone who had dealt with her family twenty-odd years ago, preferably a social worker. All she could hope was that Jamie was memorable enough to stick in someone's mind.

Glasgow city boundary flew past, and a smile played around Vicky's mouth as she immediately thought about Ben, working in his new job now. He'd been a rock since Friday. Losing Maisie was dreadful, but she wasn't doing this alone.

Here was their street, running parallel to the river just metres away. In spite of the still-unpacked boxes in the spare bedroom, their flat overlooking the Clyde was beginning to feel like home. It was in the middle section of a renovated block on the south bank of the river, and a passenger footbridge just opposite the building connected them to the city centre on the other side, so it couldn't have been more central. They had four generously proportioned rooms and a tiny balcony on the first floor. The mortgage was steep for Scotland but not for double-income no-kids couples like them, and the urban view down the river was terrific – and so was the flat. Light, modern and airy – exactly what she liked. They even had a couple of period features: cornicing in the living area and an original fireplace in the bedroom. Vicky manhandled the boxes of Maisie's things inside and went up in the lift.

The light on the landline phone was flashing as she went in, and Vicky tapped the display. Amanda had called an hour ago. Flopping down on the sofa, she pressed 'connect'.

'Vicky, honey – are you all right? I couldn't get you on your mobile.'

'I ran out of battery. Have you heard anything about my family?' She had spent Saturday with Amanda and Ted, basking in the comfort of being back in her old foster home. Amanda knew nothing about a possible sister, but had promised to try and find out.

'I've been phoning around on your behalf. I got in touch with the foster mother you came to us from, May Noakes, and between us we remembered the name of the social worker who dealt with you and Jamie in Edinburgh – Yvonne Bradshaw. As far as May is aware, there was no baby sister. I think it was more Jamie she remembered than you.'

Vicky made a wry face into the phone. 'I'll bet it was. The two of them had hysterics together every night we were there. You were much better with him. That's fantastic, Amanda, thanks.'

She hung up again after a brief chat. Bless Amanda. She had helped little Vicky through the grief and the muddles back then, managing brilliantly with Jamie until he moved to the home he was still in today.

Vicky scribbled Yvonne Bradshaw's name on an envelope and glanced at the clock on the microwave. Four forty-five. Not the best time of day to start looking for the woman and get some answers. She would do that tomorrow, and sort out Maisie's stuff now until Ben came home.

She opened the first box and immediately reached for a tissue. Knick-knacks were so pathetic, so unimportant, and yet heart-wrenching when someone you loved was gone. Maisie's precious Capodimonte rose, for instance. A rose in full bloom, delicate china petals blushing on a halo of green leaves. Lovely as it was in its way, Vicky wouldn't normally have given it house space, but now she would treasure it because Maisie had. Blinking, she rummaged through her great-aunt's possessions. A box of old books and ancient photo albums that Maisie had kept all this time so Vicky would too, a couple of pretty scarves she would wear, and the lovely green and blue paisley shawl Maisie had cherished. And Maisie's perfume, oh, how bittersweet – the smell of family. The photos Maisie had kept by her bed, the long-dead fiancé – another tragedy. No one died of appendicitis nowadays. These could go in the book box along with the photo albums, most of which were all similarly ancient. What had happened to the more recent snaps? Apart from a handful of pics of her and Jamie over the years, there were none. Vicky slid the photo of dead William into the box to deal with later, then noticed that one of the books in there was wrapped up in ancient and thin brown paper. She heaved it up and unwrapped it.

It was the family bible. Thinking back, Vicky remembered seeing it in Maisie's bedroom, way back, but she'd never examined it closely. Who had packed it into this box? Maisie, probably, years ago when she was moving into the home. Something was sticking out between two pages. Oh. Photos. Crouching on the floor beside the box, Vicky flicked through them, her mouth going dry. She'd never seen these. A blonde-haired baby, laughing up at the camera, full of the joy of life. Mum and Dad and a younger baby. And the last one – Mum and Vicky and the same baby, and it wasn't Jamie, because little Vicky had only been a toddler when Jamie was born and she was older in this photo.

Erin. It must be. She had found her sister. Was the older baby Erin too? And why had Maisie never shown her these? Hands shaking, Vicky stared at the last group. It was ages since she'd looked at photos of her parents, but she had their wedding album and a couple of others with snaps of her and Jamie. Why wasn't Erin included in that collection? The reason hit her like something physical, and Vicky sobbed. Her parents had died before they'd got round to sticking photos of their new baby into albums.

Vicky's brain buzzed. A baby meant a pregnancy… She stumbled through to the spare room, where the removal box with the albums was. Grabbing an old one, she flopped cross-legged on the floor and turned to the final few pages. There she was, a happy child. Her and Jamie and Mum and Dad and… not this one… nor this… but here. Mum and Jamie at the transport museum, and yes, Mum was pregnant. Vicky drank in the photo. She'd never noticed because she'd never known to look for it, but the baby bump was there. She sighed. Those were the years before the digital revolution, when people didn't take as many photos as they did now.

Vicky leafed through the albums, finding more snaps of her mother and unborn sister and oh, there had never been a bigger 'why?' in her life.

'She's tiny in this one,' said Ben, an hour or so later.

Vicky joined him at the window. 'She was only a few days old when my parents went to the party.'

Ben passed the photo back. 'Vicks – wouldn't they have taken such a young baby with them? Maybe she died too. Let's look up old newspaper reports, we might find the number of dead there.' He touched her shoulder. 'Sorry, sweetheart.'

Vicky shrugged. 'Maisie thought Erin was still alive, and she would know. And there's still the photo of the older baby to explain. But you know what I'd like to do? Pass by my old home on the way to the pub. The one I lived in with Mum and Dad. Seeing the place again might help me remember.'

Ben pulled out his car key. 'Good idea. I'll drive.'

They were going to Bridge of Weir, where Jim's Inn had the best pub food north of the border. Ben swung off the motorway at Hillington Industrial Estate, and a couple of minutes later they were driving through the streets Vicky would have seen every day as a young child. Hillington Road, with houses and flats and a school. Would she have gone there, if things had been different? Ben turned a corner before a garage and slowed down.

'Here we are – Muirhead Avenue.' He pulled into the side of the road.

'Let's get out and walk,' said Vicky. 'I'm pretty sure it was number fourteen. That's sort of stuck in my head.'

Hand in hand, they walked silently up the road. It was a quiet, attractive little street, the houses mostly semis with small front gardens and a larger space behind. Number fourteen was washed a pale yellow colour, with a rose bed along the front of the house.

Vicky stopped. 'I don't know. I thought I would remember the place, but I don't.' The disappointment was sharp.

Ben hugged her. 'You were four years old. Don't fret about it.'

He was right, thought Vicky, when they were sitting in the pub with salmon steaks in front of them. Her memories – or lack of them – were beyond her control. She needed to concentrate on what she *could* do – contact the National Records Office in Edinburgh and find out how many kids were registered to her parents, and look for Yvonne Bradshaw.

***

The following morning saw her sitting at the dining table, phone and laptop at the ready. After listening to the National Records Office canned music for way too long, and using the time to check her emails and the news, Vicky eventually found herself explaining the problem to a person.

The woman was obviously intrigued. 'Goodness, how fascinating. You can search and order certificates online, but – shall I have a quick look for you? We don't usually, but...'

'Please.' Vicky supplied the woman with the details she knew, and waited, listening to the keyboard clicking.

'Okay. Negative, I'm afraid. Two births are registered to your parents, Victoria Paula Cairns and James Joseph Cairns.'

Vicky's heart sank. 'Is there a death registered for Erin Cairns?'

More clicks. 'No. But there wouldn't be if she died in England. You'll need to contact the General Register Office there.'

'Thanks. I'll do that.' Vicky put the phone down and leaned back in her chair. This wasn't going to be the easy fix she'd hoped for. Maybe finding the social worker would be the better way to go. The Capodimonte rose was on the shelf beside her and Vicky touched the pink petals with one finger. She would keep her promise.

Chapter Four

Wednesday, 10th January

Christine stood in the Red Cross tea bar toilet, dabbing water on pale cheeks. Her new job was not going according to plan. She'd felt so awful all morning she'd had to go to the doctor, who promptly signed her off for the rest of the week. Her boss had been sympathetic, but then she had no idea that Christine wasn't suffering from an upset stomach that would be gone in a day or two. And what the hell she was going to do if this morning sickness didn't ease up pronto was more than Christine could work out right now.

'Are you all right, dear?'

The voice came from behind and Christine turned to see a middle-aged woman with a concerned expression hovering, waiting to get to the single basin.

'I'm fine. Just feeling a bit sick, that's all.' She moved to the side.

The woman washed her hands and pulled out her compact. 'No use pointing out you're in the right place. Or are you?'

Christine made a strangled noise halfway between a sob and a laugh. 'I'm in the worst possible place. Or my insides are, anyway.'

The woman stared at Christine's name badge. 'I've seen you up around where I live, haven't I? Court Place, near the top of Byres Road?'

'Could be. I live in Court Avenue.' Christine took a couple of shallow breaths. The anti-nausea meds were showing no sign of working. Please she mustn't be sick here, please.

The woman snapped her compact shut. 'I'm Kay D'Agostino. Why don't you let me get you a cuppa to settle your tummy? Or are you still working?'

'That's kind, and I'm finished now, but I should go home while I'm able to drive.' Christine saw the woman glance at her shaking hands, and stuffed them into her pockets.

To her dismay, Kay took her arm. 'I came by bus. Why don't I drive us both back in your car? Will your insurance cover that?'

At any other time that would have been funny, but today it only made Christine feel homesick. 'My mum has me and everyone else in the world insured to drive to the moon and back in my car. Thank you, that would be kind.'

She led the way to the staff car park where her Mini was, Kay clutching her elbow all the way. Fifteen minutes later they were pulling up in Court Avenue.

Christine managed a smile. The nausea was easing, so maybe the meds were beginning to work. Or maybe she was just relieved to be home. 'Thank you very much. I won't ask you in, if you don't mind.'

'Another time. You take care.' Kay handed over the car key and Christine trailed up the path to the front door of the flats.

***

The following morning, she drove north through cold and frosty Scottish countryside, anxiety and relief fighting to gain the upper hand in her mind. She would be home before dark, and while she wasn't looking forward to the approaching interview with her parents, it was good to be feeling more in control. The meds had kicked in and the nausea was all but gone, though to say she was tired was the understatement of the century. But now she'd decided what to do about the pregnancy, it was time to put her affairs in order, so to speak. Telling Mum and Dad was the first step.

The A90 swept round Stonehaven and continued northwards, closer to the east coast now. The grey North Sea on Christine's right was swelling. No sparkles today, just surging water under ominously dark clouds. Christine's stomach surged in sympathy. She looked away quickly and concentrated on the road for a while. Here was Aberdeen, the Granite City. Half an hour and she'd be home. They weren't expecting her.

The driveway was empty when she drove to the end of the village and pulled up outside her parents' house. Christine extracted her sports bag from the back and was rummaging in her handbag for her keys when the front door was yanked open.

'Chris! You didn't say– you look terrible, what on earth's wrong?'

Christine submitted to a fierce hug. Nothing new here, then. 'Gee, thanks, Mum. I've been a bit sick this week. Getting better now, but I'm off until Monday so I thought I'd come for some home cooking.' Nothing like buttering your mother up before breaking the news. Bad news? Probably. But it could wait until her father was here too. 'Where's your car?'

'Daddy took it. His is in for a service. Come in, let's get something calorific inside you. You're wasting away.'

'Mum, I've been gone less than two weeks. I can't be that much thinner.' Christine allowed Sylvie to lead her inside and feed her tea and a scone. Her mother fussed around with fresh butter and last year's homemade bramble jelly, which Christine couldn't face, but eventually, Sylvie sat down too.

'Tell me what's happening in Glasgow. How are you getting on sharing with Larissa? And your neighbours? And how's work going?'

One question at a time was fine, but a herd of them was suffocating. Mum wanted to keep her place right in the middle of her daughter's life, and she wanted to hear that everything was shiny-nice, too. Christine hesitated. She couldn't afford to antagonise Sylvie right at the start today.

'Larissa's lovely, she's been showing me around. We went to one of the cinemas in town on Saturday. Work's going...'

She was babbling. Christine took a sip of tea. Mum had missed her vocation; she should have been one of those cross-questioning lawyers. It was a relief to escape upstairs when her scone was finished.

Her bedroom had, of course, been tidied and dusted within an inch of its life. Christine sank down on the bed, one hand on her stomach, which wasn't quite as flat as it had been. Her breath caught as she imagined how she'd look by July. Was she doing the right thing? The decision had come in the night, after a dismal dream she barely remembered, but she knew this was the right way. She wanted her child to have the best possible life, and she wasn't in a position to give it that.

Her plan was to wait until after-dinner coffee before telling her parents about the pregnancy. Christine ran downstairs when her father arrived home from work, and was given another fierce hug – Dad's hugs were somehow more comforting than Mum's at the moment. Sylvie had set the dining room table with the best china and Christine was touched, though the chicken pie with creamy mushroom sauce was hard to get through. Christine shuddered inwardly. There was nothing worse than being fed your favourite meal when your hormones were going crazy and your stomach was in knots.

'You haven't eaten enough to keep a sparrow alive,' said Sylvie, her mouth drooping.

Christine managed a smile, then gathered up the plates. 'Still getting my appetite back. I'll make coffee, shall I? There's something I want to run by you.'

She set the machine to make espressos, then took the cups through and sat down, her heart pounding. Both her parents were looking at her with apprehensive expressions, and Christine fixed her eyes on the table top, fighting for courage. She had no idea how they would react.

She looked up. 'Mum, Dad – I'm pregnant. It wasn't planned, but I've put a lot of thought into what I should do, and… I'm going to have the baby and give it up for adoption.'

Silence echoed in the kitchen while she forced herself to look at her parents. One second, two, three.

Sylvie rose to her feet, her face flushed and aghast. 'No. Chris, no!' She burst into tears.

Christine gaped at her father, who was frowning into his cup. He reached out and pulled his wife back into her chair.

'It's Christine's decision, love. I assume you've thought it through, Chris?' His expression was an odd mixture of love and regret.

'Yes, of course. I… I'm sorry.' Christine reached a hand

out to her mother, then retracted it when Sylvie turned away. Christine's heart began to pound.

'The father doesn't know yet,' she said carefully. 'I wanted to tell you first.'

Sylvie rocked back and forth in her chair, her head in her hands. 'Think of all the medical stuff, the doctors and tests. Tell her she can't, Ron.'

Christine had never felt so helpless, or so bewildered. Did her mother want her to get rid of the baby? Her father was bending towards Sylvie, and to Christine's consternation, a single tear ran down his cheek.

'Sylvie, love, don't take on so. It'll be all right in the end, won't it, Chris?' He slid his chair closer to Sylvie's and put an arm around her, hugging her to his shoulder.

Christine felt as if she'd tumbled into a parallel universe. Somehow, this was now about Sylvie, and not about her and the pregnancy. She watched as her father stroked her mother's cheek.

Sylvie clasped both hands to her chest, her eyes wild. 'She'll have tests, Ron, and blood samples, and...' A strangled whisper died away.

'She has to know, Sylvie. This was always going to happen. You – we should have told her long ago.'

'Told me what?' Fear squirmed through Christine's gut. Was there some ghastly family illness she might pass on to the baby?

Sylvie motioned to Ron, and he reached across the table to grip Christine's hand. 'This'll be a shock, love. Your mum didn't know how to tell you, but... you were orphaned as a tiny baby, and Mum adopted you. I met the pair of you a year or so later, and here we all are today. We're still your parents, Chris.'

Whatever she'd expected, it wasn't this. Christine's heart leapt into her throat, and she slammed both hands on the table. The espresso cups rattled in their saucers. 'You're *kidding*! Shit – I had a right to know that.'

Sylvie moaned. 'You were *my* baby! I wanted us to be a family!'

Ron grabbed Christine's hand again, taking Sylvie's too and holding all their hands together above the table. 'Nothing has changed, love. We are a family. Aren't we, Chris?'

Christine glared. 'You tell me. Do I have any blood relations? Shit, if–'

Ron shook his head. 'There was no one left, was there, Sylvie? Your birth mother was a friend of your mum's, Chris.'

All Christine wanted to do was stamp out and never come back. But that would get her no answers, and who else could she ask? She glowered at Sylvie. 'You have a whole lot of explaining to do.'

'Give your mum time, love.'

'She's had twenty-two years.' The world had turned inside out.

Sylvie sat twisting her wedding ring, not looking at anyone. 'You were so tiny and perfect, and all alone. I couldn't have let you go to… strangers.' She raised her eyes to Christine's. 'Don't make decisions you might regret, Chris. Wait until the baby's here.'

Fury zipped through Christine. 'You have no right to tell me what to do. I'm going for a walk to get my head round this, and when I come back I want information about my birth family. Names, dates – everything. And then I'll make any decisions necessary.'

That night, Christine lay in bed thinking cold, sober

thoughts. She had seen press cuttings of the hotel in England where her birth parents had lost their lives, and she knew their names. Paula and Joseph Cairns. She'd been Erin; it was her second name now, but they'd never used it. Her parents had both been orphaned young and grown up in care, so there was no other family to take her as a baby, and no one left to search for now. Sylvie had been at school with Paula and they'd been friends since they were twelve. So in a way, she was as good as blood family, but the sense of betrayal was agonising. Christine had no recollection at all of a time when Mum and Dad hadn't been her... parents. They should have told her. End of.

Misery chilled through Christine as she lay grappling with another, equally uncomfortable thought. Here she was, condemning Sylvie and Ron, but wasn't she planning to do something very similar to her own child? She'd had no intention of telling Drew about the baby. But what if her son or daughter came back to her as an adult, wanting to know details of its birth family? Nowadays, that was more than likely. Would she lie to her child about its father?

That decision was still unmade when she went downstairs the next morning. Sylvie's mobile was lying on the hall table, and it felt like a sign. Christine slipped the phone into her pocket and took it into the loo, hoping Drew was among Sylvie's contacts. And he was. Christine keyed the number into her own mobile and replaced her mother's on the table.

Sylvie was tapping away at the computer in the study, but she came through when Christine put the kettle on. 'You sit down and I'll make you some toast. How are you feeling this morning? Will your tummy cope with an egg?'

Christine lifted her mug and sat at the table while Sylvie rootled in the fridge. Mum was trying to make peace, but...

No, that wasn't what she was doing at all, was it? Christine swallowed painfully. Mum was doing what she always did – ignoring the stuff she didn't want to see.

'I'm fine. The anti-nausea pills have made a difference.'

Her mother froze, fear all over her face. 'Oh, Chris, are you sure they're safe? That's how thalidomide started, you know. Anti-nausea pills. You mustn't take them.'

'Mum, this is the twenty-first century. The pills are harmless.'

'When do you have your next check-up?'

'Next week.'

'I'll come down to Glasgow for a bit, cook you some nice healthy meals.'

It wasn't even a question, and Christine choked back a sharp retort. Diplomacy might be best. 'Wait until the sickness is past, huh? The doctor said there's no need to worry.'

She started on her toast and heather honey, relieved when Sylvie went back to the PC.

'I have a couple of letters to draft for your dad. Why don't you walk through the village and get some nice healthy fresh air? You can get some farm eggs for me.'

Despair rose in Christine's throat, and she leapt to her feet, throwing diplomacy out of the window. 'Mum – *Sylvie*.' Her mother flinched. 'I'm sorry, we can't just go back to happy families as if nothing has happened. I can't believe you're ignoring what you've done to me. I'll go for the eggs and then I'm going back to Glasgow. I need time to think. I barely know who I am anymore.'

Glad to escape the kitchen and Sylvie's eyes, Christine set off down the lane. The wind was biting, freezing her cheeks in seconds and dusting the odd flurry of snow across the hill tops. Christine stuffed gloved hands into her pockets, grimacing at the bleakness surrounding her. Hopefully the weather would hold; she'd never driven on snow-covered roads, and Glasgow was a long way off.

She shivered. This new dilemma was as big as the 'what to do with the baby' one. How could they have kept it from her? This wasn't the 1940s; kids nowadays knew they were adopted. What had her mother – the word itself was a lie, today – been thinking?

Christine swallowed. Going back to Glasgow felt right. She needed time to digest her new identity, and she needed to be away from her mother's searching, frantic eyes and her father's keep-the-peace manoeuvres. A second decision formed in her mind. She wasn't going to inflict the same dilemma on her child in the future. She would tell scumbag Drew she was pregnant.

Christine smiled grimly. Telling him would allow her to torture him, just a little. Pulling out her mobile, Christine flipped it open, then stopped dead as a gust of wind chilled her icy cheeks. Did she really want to have a 'you're going to be a father again' conversation out here? It could wait until she was in Glasgow – which would give her time to plan the torture, too.

Chapter Five

Friday, 16th February

Vicky opened her flat door and breathed in the feeling of homecoming. Friday night, the weekend before her, and at long last all the boxes were unpacked. Ben was loving his new job, and she had settled into hers – secretary to a team of lawyers – well enough that she was no longer exhausted by five o'clock every day. It had been an intensive few weeks. She dropped her handbag on the sofa, glancing at the shelf where the Capodimonte rose was flanked by a framed photo of Maisie and the snap of Mum with Vicky and Erin. And she still hadn't found her sister. Truth to tell, she had almost given up hoping there was a sister alive to be found. Erin didn't feature in the birth or death records at the General Register Office in England, which seemed pretty definite proof, and Vicky hadn't been able to track down the social worker Yvonne Bradshaw, who'd be retired now, according to Amanda. For all Vicky had found out, Yvonne could be living it up in Spain or Thailand, or she could be dead. Paula and Joe's old school had a page on Facebook, and she'd posted to ask if anyone remembered them. Only three did, and Vicky had messaged them, but while two women knew about her and Jamie, they were unaware of a baby. The other only knew the couple were married. None of them had been in the same class or even the same year as her parents, though. Vicky searched through all the old news reports she could find online about the explosion, but a baby didn't feature in any of them. One woman had been booked into the coach house and survived the explosion, but the name meant nothing to Vicky. It might be worth trying to find her, but a social media search drew a blank, and anyway, surely the police back then would have known if a baby had survived and got her back to her family? It was hard to know where to go from here.

Vicky changed into jeans and a sweatshirt, then went through to the kitchen and put eggs on to boil. Ben would be home soon and she was making kedgeree – not a very glamorous meal, but it was a favourite of theirs.

'Now that work has calmed down, I'd like to try and find out about Erin,' said Vicky, when the kedgeree was finished and they were sipping second glasses of Sauvignon Blanc. 'Can you suggest anything IT-ish we could try?'

Ben pulled a face. 'Nothing more on Facebook?'

'Nope. It's so depressing. I'm beginning to wonder if Maisie *was* hallucinating before she died, if Erin never existed. That photo,' she waved towards the snap on the shelf, 'could be any baby.'

'Don't give up yet. Adoption records could be the way to go. We need to find Yvonne Bradshaw.'

'Oh, I'm not giving up. I promised Maisie. I thought I'd put an ad in the paper. There are loads of missing person posts in the online versions, and I can put one in a few physical papers too – in Glasgow and Edinburgh and a couple of the biggest cities in England.'

'Nice idea. And how about missing person sites online,

too?'

Vicky sighed. Somehow, she'd imagined that finding information about someone would be a whole lot easier. 'Good idea. Another thing I thought of is talking to the neighbours at my parents' old home. If any of them are still there from way back, they might know something.'

'That's tomorrow's outing sorted, then. Let's get your ad set up.'

Vicky went for her laptop, and between them they drafted a missing person post. *Searching for Erin Cairns, born in Glasgow–*

'Should I put a date of birth?' said Vicky, hesitating. 'Maisie said she'd been six days old, which would make her birthday around the tenth of March.'

Ben tilted his head to one side. 'No. If anyone calls saying they're Erin, you can check with the date of birth. Put: *now in her twenties.*'

Vicky made the addition, then glared at it, aghast. How awful. It was all she knew about her sister. *Possibly fostered or adopted as a baby*, she added, and sat back. 'I'll run this everywhere for a month. Some websites might keep it on for longer, too.'

'You're likely to get a shedload of weirdos responding. Better set up a junk email address for it,' said Ben, and Vicky nodded.

Half an hour's work later and the ad had been posted on five missing person sites and submitted to every Glasgow newspaper, three in Edinburgh and Inverness, and four of the big ones in England. Vicky sat back. She shouldn't hope too much, but oh, she was hoping for the world.

***

By mid-morning the following day they were back at Muirhead Avenue. Ben parked as close to number fourteen as he could, and Vicky pulled on her gloves. This was your typical cold and frosty morning, but at least it was dry. Together, they walked up the path at number fourteen and Vicky rang the bell, her stomach churning hopefully.

The door was opened by a man with a toddler in his arms, and Vicky launched into her question.

'We moved in two years ago and the people we bought the place from only had it for five years,' he said, shaking his head. 'Try Lynn Evans next door – she's been here forever.'

Vicky followed Ben down the path, depression settling on her shoulders as they strode through the wintry bareness of the front garden. She'd have run up and down here, picked daisies on the grass, enjoyed the summer sunshine. Yet the garden – in fact the entire street – felt foreign.

The woman who answered the door at number twelve was well into her sixties with dyed blonde hair piled roughly on top of her head in a style more often seen on a younger woman. Vicky began to explain who she was, but Lynn Evans interrupted her.

'Vicky! I remember you, of course I do. And your poor little brother. Such a tragedy, losing your parents and the baby like that. What brings you back now?'

Stunned, Vicky grabbed Ben's arm. Lynn remembered Erin – they weren't chasing a figment of Maisie's imagination. But oh, it was sounding more and more likely that her poor little sister had perished along with their parents.

The woman was leaning forward, eyes gleaming avidly, and Vicky swallowed. Spilling family secrets to a stranger didn't feel comfortable, but there was no sense in saying nothing, with the ad due to start on Monday.

'We're wondering now if my sister did die. There's been a suggestion she was adopted, but we've no idea where, and I'm trying to find someone who might know. Do you remember any friends my parents had?'

Lynn looked disappointed. 'There were a few people, but it was a long time ago and I can't say I knew them. Don't you remember any names?'

Vicky stared bleakly at the garden next door. 'I barely remember living here.'

'The street has changed a lot since then,' said Lynn. 'They widened the road a few years ago, and lopped about three yards off all the gardens. A lot of trees came down, too. If you like, I'll dig out some old photos and scan them to you.'

So maybe this hadn't been a waste of time after all, thought Vicky, writing down her email address for the woman. A photo might jolt a memory.

'The rate we're going, we'll have to contact every adoption society in the country,' she said to Ben on the way back to the car.

He clicked the key to unlock the doors. 'There'd be societies back then that don't exist any longer. Put your faith in the ad and cross your fingers we find Yvonne Bradshaw. Meanwhile, let's head down the coast and get some air in our lungs.'

***

Monday afternoon, and after a sunny weekend spent doing the Glasgow sights with Larissa and a group of others from the hospital, Christine was glad to be back at work for a rest. She was still taking meds to keep the nausea at bay, but the exhaustion had passed, thank God.

She had taken to going into the tea bar for a cuppa before setting off for home in the afternoon. Today, the first person she saw there was Kay. Christine took her tea and a digestive over to Kay's table. She hadn't seen the older woman since that day in January, and come to think of it, she didn't know why Kay had been here that day.

'Hi there. Can I join you?'

Kay's face broke into a smile. 'I've been wondering how you were!'

Christine sat down opposite. 'No complaints today.' If only. But no need to go into any of that with Kay. 'Were you visiting someone?'

Kay shook her head. 'I have a mild heart condition and it flared a bit in December. But it's fine now. I've just been signed off clinic for six months.'

'That's brilliant. Were you off work with it?'

'Only for a week. I'm the manager in the big charity shop in Argyle Street – you might have seen it from the bus on the way into town – so it's not too strenuous. I love it. I get to meet so many people.'

'I usually get the subway into town, but I'll look out for it.' Christine finished her biscuit and lifted her cup. 'Did you come by car? Or would you like a lift home?'

'A lift would be great.'

Kay chatted about this and that all the way home, and Christine found herself telling her neighbour about growing up in the Aberdeenshire countryside, and training in Aberdeen. Kay seemed genuinely interested, but she didn't bombard Christine with questions like Sylvie did. Christine found herself wishing communication with her mother was as effortless.

'Thank you very much,' said Kay, when they pulled up

in an empty space between their respective homes. 'Tell you what. There's a bakery on Byres Road – they do amazing cookies. Why don't I get a selection tomorrow, and you can come by after work and have your cuppa at mine?'

Christine smiled. 'Sounds good. Don't buy much for me, though. Little and often is my motto.'

Kay gave her arm a quick pat. 'Sounds like a cookie to me. See you around five? I'm number ten.'

Larissa wasn't home yet, and Christine sat down with her mobile. She had the usual messages from her mother, who'd taken to texting twice a day. Now was a good opportunity to make the call she'd been plucking up courage about for ages. She would phone Drew and tell him about the baby. He worked in Aberdeen and the odds were he'd be driving home in his posh car now. He'd have a hands-free, and hopefully for his sake, he didn't also have a car full of friends and colleagues. Anticipation mingled with schadenfreude as Christine pressed connect. How many times had she had this conversation in her head?

'Drew Miller.' The voice was clipped.

Christine's schadenfreude gave way to instant loathing. This man had seduced her and got her pregnant, and if she had anything at all to do with it, he'd be regretting it bitterly before the day was over.

'Hi, Drew, it's Christine. Just to let you know, I'm expecting our child.'

She heard a muffled exclamation – had he dropped the phone? – then car noises, followed by silence. It sounded as if he'd parked up. Then, 'For fuck's sake, Christine, what the shit do you mean?'

'It's not rocket science, Drew. I'm pregnant. It's yours. Which part don't you understand?'

'It can't be. You're lying.'

More silence, and Christine waited. It was small revenge, but still sweet.

'You can't prove it's mine.'

'Not right now I can't, but as soon as it's born that will be no problem at all.'

'You're not *having* it?'

The horror in his voice made her want to laugh. Poor Drew, all he'd wanted was a drunken fumble at a party. But she had the upper hand now. 'Of course. Come the summer, you'll have three kids. Good, huh?'

'Christine, I can't do this, and I'm sure you don't want a baby in your life. I don't care what it costs, but get rid of it. I'll pay. I do have some say in this, you know.'

It was a lovely mental image: Drew in his car, the sweat of sheer panic on his horrible slimy face. Christine pressed the phone to her ear and whispered, 'You have no say, Drew, but oh yes, you'll pay. I–'

'I'm telling you – get rid of it. I'm a lot more powerful than you are, miss.'

'You've already proved that, Drew. Seducing a woman half your age. Your child will be shocked when he or she is old enough to ask about Daddy.'

Christine rang off. That had gone rather well.

***

Kay's flat was the same vintage as her own, but with two extra rooms and a minimalistic, airy feeling that Christine liked. She settled down at the kitchen table the following day and accepted a cappuccino and a chocolate chip cookie. 'Have you been here long?'

'Twenty years. It's too big for me, but all the memories of my husband are here. I'll hang on to it in the meantime.'

'Oh. Is he…?'

'Cancer. He was only forty-six.'

Christine couldn't imagine what that must have been like. 'Life sucks sometimes.'

'You've said it. But there are good parts too. How's your life? I had the impression the first time we met that things aren't easy for you.'

Christine sat fiddling with her teaspoon, searching for words. But she'd have to tell other people eventually, and Kay was a good person to start with. 'You're right. I'm pregnant, and I…' Omitting the part about Drew, Christine explained what she had decided.

Kay listened, then came around the table and gave her a big hug. 'You're doing the right thing. You should always vote for life, because it's all we have. But, Christine – wait until the baby's here before you decide about adoption.'

Christine put her spoon down. 'That's what my folks said. But I can't possibly work and look after a baby and–' She stopped. Wasn't that what thousands of other women did? She tried again. 'It doesn't feel like the right time. But I'll have a hard think, I promise.'

'Good girl. And any time you need help, you know where I am.'

Christine walked home feeling as if she'd found a kind of mother substitute. Kay wasn't emotionally involved, of course, but her response was exactly what Christine had wanted from her mother. A hug to warm away the hurt and the loneliness. At least Dad had held her hand, though that hadn't warmed half as much as a hug would have. Christine let herself into her flat. Tonight's call would come through soon – Sylvie called every night now. Christine knew she wouldn't be able to put off the threatened visit much longer.

Right on cue, her phone rang. Christine dropped her bags on the kitchen table.

'Lovely news, darling. Daddy has business in Glasgow tomorrow, so I'm coming with him. We'll be there until the end of the week. I've found a hotel a few minutes from your flat – I'm so looking forward to investigating the city with you!'

Christine had to search for words. You'd think she and Sylvie were best mates instead of mother and daughter, and they weren't even that, were they? The sense of betrayal hit her again. 'I'll be at work during the day, remember.'

'You can give me your key, and I'll do all your washing and ironing, and have dinner ready when you get home. Do you have a freezer, darling? I could–'

'No freezer, Mum. I finish at four-thirty tomorrow. Why don't I come to your hotel and we can wait for Dad there?'

'I'm not sure what he'll be doing, but that's a good idea. We...'

Christine put the kettle on, her phone pressed to her ear as her mother chatted on about everything she planned to do at Christine's flat. No way, but they would worry about that tomorrow. And maybe, with several evenings in front of them, they'd be able to talk like adults about what had happened in their family. Christine sighed. She could hope, yes, but something was telling her it was a lost cause.

***

Two late afternoons and evenings spent with her parents had Christine's nerves in tatters. The biggest part of her still wanted to scream at them for not telling her about her birth family, but in a way it changed nothing. They hadn't been concealing hordes of aunties, uncles and cousins, and Sylvie was trying to make amends now. Christine was barely allowed to breathe without Sylvie inquiring about her well-being. It was ten times more claustrophobic than living at home.

After an hour in Sylvie's company the first evening, Larissa had upped and offed to her boyfriend's for the duration, and Christine couldn't blame her. If only she had a boyfriend to escape to. Roll on Sunday afternoon, when Mum and Dad were due to drive north again.

On Friday after work, Christine pulled up outside the Clarence Hotel, where Sylvie was waiting on the steps as usual, a plastic bag full of healthy groceries at her feet. Christine breathed in, summoning energy and patience, and waved. This was Mum's way of saying, 'I know I'm not doing the right thing here, but I don't know what else to do'. Sylvie had never asked about the baby's father, and she must suspect something, otherwise she would ask, wouldn't she?

'I heard the weather forecast at lunchtime,' Christine said, as Sylvie plonked down in the passenger seat. 'It should be fine for your drive up north. Have you anything planned for next week?'

Sylvie made a regretful sound in her throat. 'Jess and Drew are cooking us dinner when we get home on Sunday. I won't have the heart to enjoy it, though. I wish we were staying longer.'

Christine almost laughed at the mental picture of Drew having kittens, wondering if Mum and Dad knew what had happened. Revenge was very satisfying.

'You must come home for the weekend next week,' said

Sylvie, as they approached the flat. 'Then I can make sure you're not wasting away.'

'I think I might have a course, but I'll come soon, don't worry.' Mentally, Christine crossed her fingers. She only had to keep things sweet for another day or two. Things would settle down eventually with her parents. They had to.

Up in the kitchen, Sylvie started the dinner preparations while Christine set the table. As usual, it was one question after another. 'Have you made any other friends, darling? You've never mentioned the neighbours?'

Christine forced a smile. 'I've met a lovely woman who lives around the corner – Kay. She manages a big charity shop halfway along Argyle Street. The others in this building are students at Glasgow uni, they…'

And she was babbling again. Fortunately, her father arrived and they sat round the table eating her mother's signature dish of rump steak with peppercorn sauce, tagliatelle and green beans. Christine felt genuine nostalgia wash over her; they'd enjoyed this meal on birthdays and special occasions so many times in the past. How good it would be to turn the clock back ten years and stop time when she'd been a happy child.

After they'd eaten, Christine and her father cleared away while Sylvie leafed through the evening paper Ron had brought home.

'What a load of junk they print nowadays.' Sylvie was tutting every three seconds. 'This is seventy per cent adverts and thirty per cent celebrity gossip and sensationalism.'

Ron winked at Christine. 'I remember when I was a student, we had this rag…'

Christine listened to the story. Mum and Dad were good people and yes, she loved them. If only they hadn't lied to her; it would colour their relationship forever now. When the dishes were done she went back to the table, where Sylvie was gaping at the newspaper. Her face had gone red and blotchy.

Christine squinted at the upside-down page on the table. The paper was open at the personal ads columns, with the birth, marriage and death notices underneath. Had someone died?

Ron was still by the sink. 'Come on, then. Let's have the latest celebrity gossip.'

'There's just the usual trash. Please don't bring anything like this home again.' Sylvie stomped off to the bathroom, scrunching the newspaper up as she went.

Christine and her father met each other's eyes across the kitchen.

'She's feeling the separation on Sunday,' said Ron. 'She loves you, Chris. She gave up a lot to bring you up.'

Emotional blackmail, here they came. Christine flung the tea towel down on the table. 'Dad – she has to let me live my own life. Most especially she has to let me do what I feel is right about the baby.'

He patted her shoulder. 'I'll talk to her. Don't worry.'

Sylvie returned, and the evening played out with a series of holiday reminiscences, but when Christine went into the bathroom later, tiny shreds of newspaper were swimming in the loo.

***

Vicky clicked the TV off as *Pride and Prejudice* came to an end. It was a good film, just the thing for a Friday night home alone when your guy was out with his footie mates. She stretched, and was about to heave herself over to the kitchen to make some tea and toast before bed when an email pinged into her mobile. She tapped it open. *My daughter knows an Erin Cairns*. You can call me. A mobile number followed.

Vicky hesitated. They had arranged that Ben would follow up these claims, in case there was ever anything nasty. But this sounded innocuous enough, and Ben was probably pretty merry right now. She keyed the number in.

A woman's voice answered. 'Are you the person interested in finding Erin?'

Vicky's heart was hammering in her chest. Please, please, let this be it. 'Yes. She's my sister, and we were split up when Erin was a tiny baby. I've no idea where she is, or even if she's alive.'

'Oh. I'm sorry. The Erin I know was orphaned when she was fifteen months or so, then came to Scotland to stay with family. She lived in Surrey before that.'

Vicky swallowed. The disappointment was always crushing. 'It's not the same Erin, then. Thanks for contacting me, anyway.' She ended the call and leaned her head on the back of the sofa. One day. One day, the right call would come.

Chapter Six

Saturday, 24th February

Christine rinsed her breakfast coffee mug and sat down to pull on her boots, feeling the hardness of her still-small bump as she bent to pull up the zip. The baby was becoming real. She lifted her bag and pulled out the photo they'd given her at the twelve-week scan.

'Hi, little blob,' she whispered. 'I'm your mum.' Heck, now she was talking to a photo. She needed her life back. Well, when the baby was born – and adopted – she'd have that. Unexpected loneliness surged.

'What did you say?' Larissa trailed into the kitchen to put the kettle on. 'Is it safe to stay here today, or are your folks coming back for dinner?'

Christine stuffed the photo into her bag and stood up. 'You're okay today. We're having lunch in town, then Mum and I are doing the shops, and we're having dinner at their hotel tonight.'

She trudged through the Botanic Gardens to collect her parents. Last day and last chance. She'd failed miserably as far as getting her parents to talk frankly about what had happened in the past was concerned, but Mum had been right about one thing – after just a few days of home cooking,

Christine was feeling better. Or maybe it was the stage she was at; the second trimester was supposed to be the best bit of being pregnant. She should make the most of it.

***

Glasgow city centre on Saturday wasn't the quietest place to have lunch.

'Oh, darling. To think, this is the second-to-last meal we'll have together.' Sylvie crumpled her Willow Tea Room napkin on her plate.

'For heaven's sake, Mum. You'd think I was being guillotined at dawn. We'll have other days and other meals.' Christine had reverted to her usual sarcastic, humorous way of communicating with her mother, and actually, when had that started? She thought back. When she was about fifteen and fighting for independence, that was when. Humour didn't hurt, and hurting Sylvie was taboo.

Her father had been looking surreptitiously at his watch for the past quarter of an hour – he wasn't really an Eggs Royale in a tea room kind of guy. And Mum was revved up about something; her cheeks were pink and her fingers were pulling at the napkin on her lap.

'Ladies, you have an afternoon about town with a credit card in front of you,' said Ron, signalling to the waitress. 'So I'll leave you to it, if you don't mind, and see you back at the hotel.'

Outside, Christine almost jumped when Sylvie took her elbow in a cosy squeeze and marched her up Buchanan Street. They didn't normally take arms. What was going on in Sylvie's head? Regret about tomorrow's separation? Or was it about showing Christine how very 'family' they were? Christine opened her mouth to comment, then closed it again. Just get through the day, Chris. Keep the peace. She didn't have the energy to deal with Mum right now. They wandered through various shops and Christine submitted to being bought two pairs of maternity trousers and three tops.

'I'm so glad we're sorted, darling. I do want to make it up to you a little.'

Christine almost choked. Mum really was a hopeless case; you'd think they'd had a spat about how late she was allowed to stay out. How could five items of clothing make up for twenty-two years of lies?

They arrived back at Argyle Street and Sylvie gave Christine a hug, her eyes sparkling.

'I'm going to get you a little surprise, darling. Why don't we meet for coffee in half an hour?'

Thirty minutes to gather her thoughts. Good. Christine pointed to the building opposite. 'Let's meet at Jill's – remember, the coffee place on the top floor over there?'

Sylvie agreed, smiling brightly, and hurried off. Christine spent a peaceful thirty minutes browsing in the St. Enoch Centre, then crossed the street and took the lift up to Jill's Coffees. Thankfully, she grabbed the one free table and ordered a cup of Earl Grey.

Fifteen minutes later, there still no sign of Sylvie. Christine watched the stream of shoppers on the street below, feeling more anxious by the minute. Had Mum mistaken the café? But they'd been here before... She tried her mother's phone, but it went to voicemail. Christine tapped her fingers on the table. It wasn't like Sylvie to be late.

***

Saturday brunch with Amanda and the family rocked. Vicky drove across the city, feeling well-loved and pleasantly full. It had just turned two o'clock, so Ben should be back from his lads' lunch soon. She wanted to talk more about the non-success of the plan to find Erin, then tonight they were going clubbing – the first time in ages.

Vicky glanced out as the Clyde appeared at the roadside, meandering through the city on its way to the coast. Sunshine and blue water, and she loved living here – how could she have spent so long away?

Ben was hurrying over the footbridge as she parked outside the flat. He ran across the road and kissed her.

'You smell of beer.' Vicky hugged him anyway.

'I smell of two beers. You can make me a coffee in our fabulous flat.'

Vicky unlocked the flat and they went through to the living area, which was open-plan to the kitchen. She went to make coffee, gazing out across the river while the machine heated. The glass wall and roof of the St. Enoch Centre on the opposite bank were shining in the late February sunshine, and Ben was right – this was a brilliant place to live.

'Okay,' she said, when they were sitting at the table with steaming mugs in front of them. 'Progress on finding Erin is so far… negative. No proof she survived. Nothing new from Facebook et al. Plenty of responses to the ads in papers, but nothing useful. I'm wondering about rewording the text to say she may have a different name now.'

'Wouldn't people work that out for themselves? Change it on the sites where you can do it for free first and see what response you get.'

Vicky made a note on the pad she used to keep track of her campaigns, an odd thought sliding into her mind. 'I wonder if Erin knows her name was Erin? If she doesn't–'

The doorbell interrupted her, and Vicky pushed her chair back and went to answer it. Who on earth was this?

An envelope was lying on the floor under the letter flap. Vicky lifted it and opened the door. No one. How weird.

She wandered back to the living room, opening the envelope on the way. A single sheet was inside, with three words printed in large black letters: *Stop persecuting us*.

***

Sylvie was twenty minutes late now. Christine decided to have one more go calling her mother, then try her father if Sylvie was still incommunicado. She lifted her phone. Rats – no signal.

She grabbed the passing waitress. 'I'll have another Earl Grey, please – I'm just going out to the terrace to make a call.'

The roof terrace was tiny and full of smokers, but her phone beeped reassuringly as soon as she stepped outside. Christine was about to connect to Sylvie's number when she spotted a figure hurrying across the footbridge far below. Hell on earth, that was Mum. What had she been doing on the other side of the Clyde? There were no shops there – or were there? Christine went back inside and started on the second cup of tea.

Two minutes later Sylvie rushed in and plumped down in the opposite chair, her face red.

'So sorry, darling. I was delayed at the jeweller's, then they couldn't do what I wanted straightaway anyway. I'll have to take this home with me and give it to you properly when it's been engraved.' She slid an elegantly gift-wrapped box across the table. 'From Daddy and me, for our beautiful girl. It's to make up a little more for keeping you in the dark too long. It was because I loved feeling you were my own baby girl, but it was wrong, I know. And, Chris, I don't want you to feel bad about what's happened to you, darling – it'll all work out for the best, you'll see.'

Christine stared, then lifted the box. She couldn't imagine how getting pregnant after a drunken fumble with Drew would ever work out for the best, but the love in Sylvie's eyes was unmistakable.

'Aw, thanks, Mum. You shouldn't have.' A lump came into Christine's throat. Sylvie wanted them to be close. If only Christine could be content with what her mother was offering. She waved to the waitress to bring Sylvie a coffee, then pulled the gift wrap away to reveal a dark-pink jeweller's box. She opened it.

It was a golden guardian angel on a thin gold chain. Christine blinked. Whatever she'd expected, it wasn't this. They weren't Catholic, and her mother had never been superstitious. 'It's lovely, Mum. But... why an angel?'

Sylvie reached out and touched the angel. 'Because fate was looking out for you when you were a baby. You've brought us so much joy, Christine. I'll have all our names – yours, mine and Daddy's – engraved on the back. We *are* a family, darling.'

Christine was almost embarrassed. It was a sweet gesture, though the angel would have been more appropriate when she was about five.

She smiled across the table. 'Thanks, Mum. I'll treasure it.'

Her mother chattered on about family doings all the way back to the West End, where Christine pleaded for an hour to herself to change for dinner. Sylvie returned to the hotel, and Christine went home for a shower. She was washing her hair when she heard her phone's shrill ringtone on the window ledge, on and on, stopping only to start again a moment later. By the time she emerged, hair dripping and a towel clutched around her, the procedure had been repeated three times. Someone was keen to get hold of her. She grabbed the phone. Drew. No way. She didn't need any aggro tonight when she was achieving peace, of a kind, with her parents.

'You're popular,' said Larissa, when Christine went through to the kitchen. 'Who was it?

To Christine's horror, tears of frustration at the whole mess welled up, and two escaped. She grabbed a tissue and blotted as well as she could. There wasn't time to redo her make up.

'Chris? What's up?'

Christine took a deep breath. She'd told Kay about the baby; she should tell Larissa too. 'Do you have time for a chat later? Or tomorrow?' She blotted more tears.

'You're scaring me now. Are you okay?'

'No. I discovered – at least Dad told me – I was adopted as a baby. It was a shock, and there's a shedload more, but right now I have to go to the last supper. Or that's what it feels like, anyway.'

Larissa gave her shoulder a little rub. 'I'll be all ears when you get home, and Chris – I'll help as much as I can. You know that.'

She hugged Christine, then pulled back, staring at Christine's middle, her breath catching. '*Chris*? Are you…?'

Christine nodded, touched Larissa's arm, then lifted her handbag. 'Later.'

Chapter Seven

Sunday, 25th February

Sunday morning housework was giving her too much time to worry about the anonymous note. Vicky switched off the vacuum cleaner and pulled it back to the hallway cupboard, indecision niggling away in her head. Ben was convinced the note was connected to the search for Erin, but Vicky wasn't sure. Her job as a legal secretary meant she was privy to all kinds of sensitive information. And why would anyone connected to the search for Erin tell her to stop persecuting them?

'I still think we should go to the police,' said Ben.

He was making lunch, and Vicky leaned on the work surface and watched as he chivvied mushrooms around in the frying pan. Clients wouldn't appreciate the police sniffing around, and neither would her boss. 'No. I want to speak to them about it at work first.'

Ben added beaten eggs to the pan. 'I suppose. As long as you still feel okay here?'

Vicky considered this. A mysterious, mildly threatening note – it wasn't a comfortable feeling, but that would be what the sender intended. She was tougher than that.

'No problem. That's smelling pretty good, Jamie Oliver.'

'Oh, I make a mean mushroom omelette. Grab the bottle. Lunch is served.'

Vicky poured two cold glasses as he busied around dishing up. Swallowing her first mouthful, she waved her fork at him. 'To continue where we were so rudely interrupted yesterday – Erin. Amanda's managed to find the names of the first set of foster parents Jamie and I were sent to, bless her. Ava and Ian Cameron. We were only there a day or two, apparently.'

Ben reached out and brushed her cheek with his finger. 'You were a poor wee thing back then.'

Vicky shrugged. 'I was a mad wee thing, anyway. Poor Maisie – and poor Amanda, when we eventually landed at hers – but she made everything better for me, Ben. A lot of kids get a worse deal in life.'

'Do you have details for the Camerons?'

'A phone number. They've moved around a lot and they've stopped fostering. That would be why they were so hard to find.'

After lunch, Ben cleared away while Vicky sat down with her phone. For a few seconds, she stared at the display. She didn't feel good about speaking to the Camerons, and really, what would they tell her? They couldn't be expected to remember details about the families of children they'd fostered so briefly such a long time ago. She was ticking a box that didn't need ticking because she didn't know what else to do.

And maybe that was because there wasn't anything more to be done. Vicky slumped back on the sofa. It was nearly the end of February. She'd faffed around for all this time, searching for a sister who didn't even have a birth certificate, and that was most likely because the poor baby had died before she was ever registered as being alive. Apart from

Maisie, everyone was convinced Erin had been blown to bits along with her parents. Vicky pictured the scene: Paula and Joe, asleep in a strange bed, their baby in a cot beside them, then – boom! Pulverised. She burst into tears.

'Hey, hey. Come here. Leave it for now.' Ben was beside her, rocking her in his arms, and Vicky leaned against him, soaking up warmth and comfort.

'Inside, I think she's gone, Ben. I'm looking for her because I promised Maisie. I would so love her to be alive, but she can't be.'

For a long moment they sat holding each other, saying nothing. Then Vicky scrabbled for the tissue in her jeans. It was time to concentrate on the living. She had Ben, who was the best thing in her life. And she had–

'Get your jacket,' she said, standing up and pulling Ben to his feet too. 'We're going to visit Jamie.' She needed something feel-good for the rest of the day.

Jamie's home was deep in rolling countryside to the north of the city. A mile or two before Strathblane, Vicky turned left into a narrow lane that wound through a copse and emerged at a long, two-storey, grey stone building. The car park was almost full, and she pulled up in the second-to-last visitors' space and switched off the engine, glancing at Ben. He didn't often come here with her, but she appreciated the company today.

'Nice,' he said, getting out and admiring the view to the north. The predominant colour was green.

'It looks its best in the sunshine, doesn't it? We can ask if Jamie can come for a walk in his wheelchair.'

Vicky led the way inside and up to the second floor, where the young adults were. Jamie's unit consisted of ten residents, all around the same age. Vicky rang the bell, then pushed the door open and went in, Ben behind her.

Jamie was in the day room and gave a shriek of joy when he saw her, bouncing in his wheelchair and straining against the straps holding him upright. Vicky put her arms around him, hugging the thin body, feeling the tightness of the spastic muscles. He was laughing and dribbling, eyes shining, and a lump came into Vicky's throat. Her Jamie. The screams and unrest of his growing years were long gone, or maybe the meds were better now – it didn't matter. Jamie was happy. She hugged him again. 'Look, Jay-Jay – Ben's here.'

'Hi there, mate,' said Ben, pulling chairs from a nearby table and sitting opposite Jamie.

Vicky sat down too, still gripping Jamie's hand, her heart melting when she saw how warmly Ben was looking at the boy. 'Okay, Jamie – we've got doughnuts, sunshine, and Ben to push you. How about a walk in the garden?'

Two hours later, she was driving back towards Glasgow, peace in her soul and new determination to continue in her head.

Ben shifted in the passenger seat. 'Vicks. I've been thinking. You're right – logically speaking, Erin couldn't have survived the blast back then. And if she'd been left with a friend of Paula's, we'd have found her by now. Maybe it's time to stop searching.'

Vicky was silent for a few moments, then pulled up at a red light and shook her head at him. 'I've been thinking too. I want to give it another couple of weeks, for as long as the ads are running. If I leave any stones unturned, I'll regret it later.'

'I don't want you to get hurt. And that letter…'

'I won't get more hurt than I am already, Ben, and there's still the first foster parents to call, and Yvonne Bradshaw to find. I could go more public on social media – put another post on my parents' school Facebook page, saying I'm looking for Erin, get people to share it. Someone could see it who didn't see the first post.'

Home again, she went back to the number for the Camerons. *Big girl pants, Vicky. You can do this.*

A man's voice answered. 'Ah… Vicky, yes. Lovely to hear from you.'

Vicky explained. Even in her ears, the story was beginning to sound unrealistic. And as she'd feared, the call was for nothing.

'Sorry, love, I'm afraid I don't remember your wee sister, and Ava's not at home this weekend. I'll get her to call you back, shall I?'

Vicky agreed and hung up, unsure if Ian Cameron had remembered her and Jamie or not. Well, she had tried. Now for Facebook.

Chapter Eight

Monday, 5th March

Going to Kay's for tea – coffee turned her into a hyper lunatic now – had become a weekday ritual. Larissa was rarely home before half six, and Christine liked to talk after a day's work. Not that she had much energy to talk, these days. Working full-time was killing her, even though she had strictly non-lifting cases now. The exhaustion was back tenfold, bringing the nausea with it, and oh, for a nice office job where she could sit on her bum all day and get fat in comfort.

Kay answered the doorbell, her face creasing in concern, and Christine winced inwardly. She must look as bad as she felt.

'In with you. You need a cuppa.' Kay helped her off with her jacket and rubbed her back on the way through to the kitchen, which made Christine feel even more decrepit.

She sank down on a wooden chair and leaned her elbows on the table. 'You've said it. My stomach's been murder all day. If I wasn't feeling sick I was collapsing on the nearest chair or running to the loo. Sorry. TMI.' She accepted a mug of milkless Earl Grey and sipped.

Kay passed her a plain biscuit. 'Eat. If I know you, you

haven't had a thing all day. Chris, why don't you cut down your hours? More time to rest would do you the world of good.'

'I know. But I don't want to give up work too soon – it would make a difference to my pay, and I want to save. I've been wondering... about keeping the baby.'

It was an idea that had formed slowly, and in a really macabre way it was Sylvie who'd helped her make it. Mum had taken her on as a tiny baby – there was no reason in the world this baby wouldn't fit in with Christine's life just as well as she had with Sylvie's back then. Who was she to give up on her child? Another thing was, this baby was the only other person on the planet she shared genes with. And somehow, that was more important now than it had been a few months ago. She'd be keeping the baby for selfish reasons, but she could still love it, couldn't she?

Kay reached across to squeeze Christine's hand, her brown eyes warm.

'It's a big decision, Chris, but if you decide to go ahead, I'll be here for you.'

Christine smiled, then frowned into her mug. If she kept the baby they would need more than Kay here for them. But then, Larissa was around too, and Suze and the others from work, and she'd make new baby-mum friends at the clinic or whatever.

'Thanks, Kay. We'd need help, but it's not set in stone, yet.'

Or was it? Christine stared into the middle distance as she realised what she'd just said. Somehow, over the past few days, she and her baby had turned into *we*.

***

The following day she felt no better. Christine finished her hand-surgery patients, dragged her feet into the deserted staff room and lowered her backside into the nearest chair. This was dire. Eleven o'clock. She'd spent two hours sitting on her backside; exactly what she'd longed for yesterday, yet she couldn't be more exhausted. Kay was right. Working full time was doing her no good at all. She was five months pregnant, and this was still supposed to be the best time. How would she cope in another two months when she'd be the size of two elephants and moving around would be ten times more difficult? Christine stroked a hand across her bump, then froze, her breath catching as something – oh my God, the baby – surged against her hand. The first movement, and oh, how bittersweet it was.

Christine wiped tears from her cheeks with her fingers and went to put the kettle on. This afternoon was her twenty-week check-up and scan, and she was planning to ask the doctor about reducing her hours. Damn the decrease in pay. She poured water into a mug and added a tea bag, grimacing. Larissa was coming to the scan with her. It was a guilty feeling, because she could have asked her mother – Mum would have been on the first train south if she'd mentioned the word 'scan'. Christine touched the guardian angel around her neck, now suitably inscribed. No. Mum was too clingy, too desperate to make things good between them. It was hard work keeping her at a comfortable distance, but Christine had no intention of letting her mother take over. Larissa was a safer scan companion, and possibly birth partner? Antenatal classes started in a few weeks. Christine sipped her tea. It was something to think about.

***

The doctor glanced through Christine's test results, then peered at her over the top of his glasses. 'Your blood pressure's on the low side, and you're a touch anaemic, too. Don't worry, it's nothing we can't fix. You can go for your scan now, then we'll decide what to do.'

Christine and Larissa went two doors along the corridor to the scan room, where Christine lay on a narrow trolley while the sonographer, whose name was Alice, squirted cold gel on her bump.

'Ready? We might see what sex the baby is – do you want to know?'

Christine had thought about this. It seemed silly not to know, if Alice did. 'Yes. I want to know everything. You will check the size of the baby, won't you?' After all this sickness, she hadn't put on as much weight as she was supposed to.

Alice wagged her finger at Christine, and grinned at Larissa. 'Hospital staff are always the worst patients, aren't they? Okay, here we go.'

Grey fizz on the screen cleared, and Christine gasped. There was her baby – the head in profile, a little nose, two hands floating in front of the surprisingly round tummy, stick legs pulled up.

Alice moved the probe across Christine's bump, pressing firmly. 'Good heartbeat. The head looks fine, and so does the spinal column. Let's take some measurements.' She clicked around the screen. 'Perfect proportions. Well done.'

Christine swallowed. The sight of her baby kicking on the screen had unleashed a tidal wave of emotion, and she hadn't expected to feel this way. Protective. Weepy. Bitter that her child hadn't had a better start in life. She put a hand on her gelled-up bump and felt the answering surge in her womb. *Baby, I will do the right thing for you.* The thought arrived in Christine's head as distinctly as if she'd spoken aloud. She still didn't know what the right thing was, but she would do it.

'What's that near the top?' asked Larissa, leaning forward from her place on the other side of Christine.

'The placenta.' Alice shifted the probe, pressing harder. 'Sorry, Christine, the jury's out about the he or she bit. Do you want to give the baby a poke and see if it'll move into a better position?'

Christine breathed out. 'No, leave it.' It was enough for now that the baby had turned into a person. Knowing its sex wouldn't make the looming decision any easier.

Alice switched the machine off. 'Okay. Pics for the album coming up. And everything's fine, no worries.' She wiped Christine's stomach with a paper towel.

Back in the consulting room, the doctor wrote a prescription. 'Iron pills. You should feel less tired in a couple of weeks. How about I sign you off work for a fortnight? You look as if you need a solid week's sleep.'

Christine tucked the prescription into her bag. 'That sounds amazing. I'll finish this week, though – we have case meetings on Friday afternoon, so I can do my handovers there.'

'As you like.' The doctor scribbled on a pad and handed the sick note over. 'Come back and see me if you feel you're not ready to return to work in two weeks. Call the clinic and we'll fit you in the same day – staff perk.'

Larissa skipped beside Christine on the way back to the car. 'That went well, didn't it? I'm so glad you let me be a part of it, Chris. And we can talk any time you want.'

Christine nodded. Larissa would be a real help, if she kept the baby. Well, she had a few more months to decide, even with a mushed-up brain like hers. A few months more with her baby – or a lifetime more?

***

By Wednesday afternoon, Christine was wishing she'd taken the time off straightaway. After a disturbed sleep – the baby had spent the night doing gymnastics – she had no energy for work, and walked around with tears of self-pity brimming in her eyes. This was her child, but it was also Drew's. Suppose it took after its father? And while she liked kids, left to herself she wouldn't have considered having one for another five years at least. So maybe adoption *was* the best way to go.

At the end of the day, Christine bade her colleagues goodbye and trudged towards the bus stop, huddled under her umbrella. She hadn't trusted her ability to drive in this morning's exhausted state, and as her work was based in the rehab unit now, she didn't need her car to make calls. She walked up the road to her flat with water dripping from the bottom of her jacket, still feeling weepy. How pathetic she was. Or was this one of the famous mood swings you got when you were pregnant?

Her phone rang while she was heating soup for dinner. And of course, it was Drew. Christine rubbed her face. Today was getting better and better, but she should get the call over with, because he'd keep on trying. He always did. He knew now that aborting the baby was no longer an option, and was pressing as hard as he could for adoption.

'I don't have time for this, Drew.'

'Have you contacted anyone about the adoption? I'd like to get it organised. And I'll pay for a nice clinic for the birth.'

Was that the bait? 'I'm not at that stage, Drew. It's way too soon to worry about adoptions and nice clinics. Leave me alone.'

She disconnected, dismayed when he rang back straightaway. Christine rejected the call, and to her relief her mobile remained silent. Firmness appeared to be the way to go with Drew; she should remember that. She was still congratulating herself when his text pinged in. *Stop being childish. Am coming to Glasgow at the weekend. Will visit you. We need to talk.* Christine hurled her phone into her bag, then stood breathing quickly as panic surged. He could easily find out where she lived. A casual call to her parents, a question about how Christine was enjoying city life… Mum and Dad would think nothing of telling him all about the flat. *Shit.*

She was spooning up soup when her phone rang again. Christine grabbed it from the sofa. If this was Larissa to say she was staying over at her boyfriend's, she would howl. She needed some company tonight.

Oh. It was Mum. Pushing her bowl to the side, Christine took the call.

A hopeful and upbeat voice trilled in her ear. 'Hi, darling – how are you?'

Christine gripped the phone. Truth was out of the question – her mother would do a vertical take-off on a mercy dash to Glasgow if she knew half of what was going on in Christine's head.

'A bit tired. It was a long day. But otherwise fine. And you and Dad?' Hell. Since when had they started making polite inquiries about one another's health?

'All good here, but it feels like such a long time since we saw you, darling, and Daddy had a lovely idea. Why don't you and I go away for a little break, when your maternity leave starts? We'd have time to have a good chat about things. Or if you could take a day or two off sooner, we could make it a long weekend very soon?'

A mixed bag of emotions spilled open in Christine's head. A few days with her mother at her heels twenty-four-seven – she would go nuts. On the other hand… Fierce longing for the old days when she was a schoolgirl with a fussy mum and a humorous dad swept over Christine. The hormones were at work again.

'That's an idea,' she said cautiously. 'I do have some time off due. We could go this coming weekend, if you like?'

Sylvie's shriek of delight pierced right through Christine's headache.

But a couple of days away with her mother might get their relationship properly back on track. And not only that, it would allow her to avoid Drew.

***

Ava Cameron hadn't called back, and Vicky decided the woman remembered nothing and wasn't keen to re-establish contact. And as Yvonne Bradshaw the ex-social worker remained as unfindable as Erin, it looked as if the search would end that week when the ads stopped. Social media had brought her nothing new, apart from three more Facebook friends who'd known Paula and Joe but thought the baby had died in the explosion.

She was unloading the dishwasher on Wednesday evening when her mobile buzzed on the work surface. The number was a strange one, and Vicky's heart began to race. However unlikely it was she'd find out anything more about her sister, the hope was always there, quiet in the background, then swelling and piercing her heart at every message or response, only to be dashed again. She pressed connect.

'Vicky? Hi, honey, it's Ava Cameron. That clunk of a husband of mine told me two minutes ago about your call a week or two back. He said you were worried about your sister, but I guess he got that wrong? Is your brother…?'

Vicky abandoned the dishwasher and sat down at the table. This was going to be another dead-end conversation, and she didn't want to have it. 'Jamie's fine, in a lovely home.' Haltingly, she explained about Maisie's conviction that Erin was still alive. 'Thing is, I can't find any proof that Erin survived the explosion.'

Ava sounded puzzled. 'But that's very odd – there must be proof. I distinctly remember your aunt talking about the baby. A friend of your mother's was looking after her, wasn't she? I'm sure that's right. It must have been the second day you were with us, and we'd had a dreadful time with Jamie all night, and I remember I couldn't phone your aunt because she'd told us she was going to visit the baby somewhere in England, and of course in those days older people like her didn't often have mobiles.'

Ice-cold shivers were running down Vicky's spine, and she sat frozen to the spot. This was it. It wasn't proof positive, but it was as good as. 'You're sure? It was definitely my baby sister she was going to visit?'

'Yes. She said she was hoping to get you and the baby together at home, with Jamie somewhere else. Vicky, what happened? We didn't have you more than a few days and I'm so sorry about that – we didn't do well by you.'

Vicky concentrated on answering the question. She gave Ava a brief account of the search for Erin.

The older woman was audibly shaken. 'Oh no, honey – how awful. But I can't think what else you could do.'

'I've been looking for Yvonne Bradshaw, too.'

'She died a few years ago. Would there be records of some kind at the social work department?'

'I've gone into that as much as possible. There's nothing. Erin seems to have slipped through the net, somehow.'

'You need to find your mother's friend in England.'

'I don't suppose you remember Maisie mentioning her name?' As she spoke, Vicky realised what more she could do. She'd been asking people if they remembered Erin – she should ask about this woman too. She could be the woman who'd survived the explosion or she could be another friend, and some of those women on Facebook might help with that if she asked them different questions. Renewed energy flooded through Vicky. Erin, I'll find you…

Ava's sigh blew down the phone. 'No. I'll have a think, but…'

Vicky chatted for a few more minutes, then ended the call and thumped her fist on the table and yelled for Ben. Somewhere out there in the big, wide world, was her sister. It was time to open a bottle.

Chapter Nine

Thursday, 8th March

Vicky pushed the flat door shut and carried on through to the living area. Half past eight and she was home alone, as Ben was at the gym. She slung her handbag in the direction of the sofa and went to peer in the fridge. Time for food – she needed to mop up that Pinot Grigio. Thursday was the traditional staff pub night, when everyone in the office went to the wine bar across the road after work. Tonight, there had been nine of them. It was a great feeling, being part of a team who played together as well as doing the work.

A cheese sandwich was quickly made, and Vicky settled down on the sofa with the laptop. The knowledge that Erin had survived and was out there somewhere had given the search a new focus; she'd been thinking about it all day. This might be a good time to do a round of social media.

Scrolling through #missingperson on Twitter, Vicky pulled a face. A lot of these tweets had been sent by police departments, many in the States, and come to think of it, they had no guarantee Erin was still in the UK. Without a photo, tweets were unlikely to help, but she put out a new one anyway. Another thought struck Vicky as she scrolled.

The police – it might be an idea to speak to them now. Did they help with searches for people who didn't seem to be officially alive? Erin *was* alive; at least there were excellent grounds to think she was. But oh, what possible reason could Maisie have had to keep her a secret? Vicky's post-pub good mood vanished abruptly as the worst thought ever entered her head. She fumbled in her bag for her phone, beginning to feel sick. Please pick up, Ben…

'Ben. Do you think – could it be that something happened? An accident? If something fatal happened to Erin and it was Maisie's fault, that could explain why she didn't tell anyone.'

He was in the juice bar; she could hear the gurgling of the drinks machine in the background. 'Eh? I guess an accident's possible, but it doesn't explain the lack of a death certificate, or a birth certificate, for that matter.'

'But if she was never registered as alive or dead – oh, Ben – all Maisie would have to do is hide the–'

'Stop, stop, no. That's all wrong. It was Maisie who said, "Find Erin", so she thought she was still alive.'

The sweat of cool relief broke out on Vicky's brow. 'Oh, thank heavens, you're right. I'm getting muddled. Bloody wine bar. Maisie didn't know what happened to Erin, so something – or someone – else caused her to disappear. I'll get onto looking for the woman who was with Mum and Dad when they went to the hotel. Facebook, here I come. Thanks, Ben.'

'You should extend the ads too, now we know Erin's alive.'

Vicky disconnected, and pouted at her laptop. In less than half an hour, her feeling of home and peace had been replaced by lonely emptiness. The task ahead seemed too enormous to succeed. Maybe she'd never find Erin; this could turn into a lifetime search. Who read ads in online papers, and who bought physical ones nowadays? Nevertheless, she began to repost the ads they had set up, switching on the TV for company while she worked. A news channel blared into the room. Vicky pressed the remote to turn the sound down and glanced at the screen, where a banner was running along the bottom of the picture. '7-year-old girl missing in Edinburgh. Last seen 4.45pm in Bankside shopping centre. Police are...'

Oh no. Not this as well. It was bad enough for her, not knowing what happened to her sister, but how very much worse it must be for that little girl's parents. They'd be sitting at home right now, agonising about what had happened to their child, nightmare visions of perverts searing through their heads. The world was a cruel and violent place.

Vicky swallowed painfully and wiped hot tears away. Oh Erin, Erin, please be alive, please let me find you. Somehow, knowing her sister had survived made it even more tragic they'd been separated and heck, this was the wine talking. Or rather, crying. No way should she go on Facebook tonight.

***

Sprawled on the sofa, Christine accepted the plate of spaghetti bolognese and balanced it on her bump – she could do that now. She blew a kiss at Larissa. 'Flatmate of the year, that's you. I should have made the grub; I've hardly moved since this morning and you've done a full day's work.'

Larissa plumped down beside her and reached for the parmesan on the coffee table. 'You're allowed to blob when you're pregnant. I'm glad to be home – listen to that weather. It's pissing down outside.' She switched on the TV and *EastEnders* filled the room.

Christine twirled her fork. It was restful, an evening in front of the box with Larissa. Not that she needed to rest – the weather had kept her indoors all day, though Kay had come round in the afternoon with Danish pastries.

EastEnders rolled to a close and Larissa switched channels to get the news. 'Did you see the reports about the kid who's gone missing in Edinburgh? Must be awful for the parents.' She shivered, then reached for the evening paper she'd brought home from work.

Christine thought about the missing child. She'd heard a report on the radio earlier and the mother had been distraught. It was heart-wrenching to listen to. She passed her hand over her bump. If she gave up her baby, he or she would be missing from her life for all time. Even if they did make contact years later, it wouldn't be as mother and child. Was that really what she wanted?

'Chris? Have a look here.' Larissa passed over the paper, open at the small ads page. 'I was checking to see if there were any new car ads that might interest Jason, and this caught my eye.' She pointed halfway down the middle column.

Christine read it, a buzzing noise starting in her ears. *Searching for Erin Cairns, born in Glasgow, now in her twenties. Possibly fostered or adopted as a baby.* There was an email address, but no phone number.

'Your birth parents' name was Cairns, wasn't it?

Christine's heart was thundering away. Holy *shit*. What was this? The age was right. The name was right. And the place. But… who would be looking for her? According to Sylvie, Christine was the sole survivor of her birth family.

She said this to Larissa, who gaped.

'Dunno. A godmother? Or a family friend?'

Christine shrugged. 'But why now? It doesn't make

sense. If there'd been anybody like that, they'd have kept in touch right from the start. It can't be me they're looking for.'

Larissa looked doubtful. 'Erin Cairns isn't a common name. Why don't you email for more info? You might get a number to call.'

Christine laid the paper down on the coffee table. 'I could, but… I think I'd like to talk to Mum again before I contact a stranger. We'll have plenty of time for family chat when we're away at the weekend.'

Larissa tore the ad from the page and handed it to Christine. 'Sounds like a plan. Hang on to this, anyway.' She gathered the empty plates and took them through to the kitchen.

Christine folded the ad and slid it into her handbag, then lifted her phone. They hadn't finalised arrangements for tomorrow yet, and maybe a quick question now would put her mind at rest. Christine grinned as the ringtone started. Mum would have a heart attack; she wasn't used to being the receiver of calls from her – adopted – daughter.

Sure enough, Sylvie sounded as if she'd won the lottery. 'Darling, how lovely! Are you ready for our girls' weekend?'

Not really, thought Christine, then shook herself. This break was the ideal opportunity to get things sorted with her mother.

'I sure am. So what's the plan?'

'We'll meet in Edinburgh, and I'll fill you in then. Part of it's a surprise. Eleven o'clock at the meeting place in Waverley Station?'

'Lovely. Mum, can I ask you something? My birth family – you said there was no one left, didn't you?'

A heartbeat of silence, then to Christine's dismay, her mother spat down the phone. 'Oh, for heaven's *sake*, Chris, can't you just leave it? I've said I'm sorry. There was no one left, all right? I thought I was doing the right thing. All I've ever wanted is to be a good mother and help my child grow. I'm sorry if it wasn't enough for you.'

Yikes. Mum could do emotional blackmail every bit as well as Dad. Christine made a huge effort and managed to sound calm. 'Of course it was enough. But anyone would be curious about their birth family in the circs, don't you see? We'll talk more at the weekend, huh?'

Sylvie swallowed loudly. 'All right. Sorry, darling. All I want is to be the best mum I can possibly be.'

Christine disconnected and blinked at her phone. 'The best mum' wouldn't be ignoring the fact that her expected grandchild had a father, would she? And she wouldn't have hidden the facts about Christine's parentage, either. Heavy resentment thudded into Christine's gut. Maybe she *should* send a quick email to whoever had posted that ad. It wouldn't do any harm, and she'd use her junk address.

She sat staring at her email account for a full five minutes, deciding what to say. *I think I might know Erin Cairns. Can I have some more information? Chris.*

Send. There. Now it was up to whoever would read the email. Christine got up to help Larissa in the kitchen, not knowing if she wanted a reply or not.

***

Vicky clicked the TV off and rose from the sofa, circling her shoulders to ease the cramped muscles. She'd fallen asleep over the news – that had been the wine. A cup of tea sounded like a good idea. She would take it with her and have a bath; the warmth would help her relax. Her phone buzzed as she was waiting for the kettle to boil, and she pulled it from the

171

pocket of her sweatshirt. It was an email on her junk account. Idly, she tapped it open.

I think I might know Erin Cairns. Oh God, oh please. Vicky almost dropped her phone. Shaking all over, she stumbled back to the sofa, where her legs gave way. *I think I might know Erin Cairns*. It was more tentative than any other message they'd had, but somehow that made it all the more believable. There'd been several of the *Erin Cairns lives in Blackpool* variety, and Ben always checked these out, but each time the Erin in question had been either a false positive, like the one Vicky had answered, or non-existent. Vicky's fingers hovered over her phone, but her fingers were trembling too much to tap a response on the small screen. She took her laptop to the dining table, then called Ben while the machine was booting up.

'Another Erin message. It sounds genuine – I'm going to send my phone number.'

'Be careful, love. Get more details first. Ask for a date of birth.'

Vicky clicked into her email. 'This Chris is asking for details too. I suppose you're right. Hang on.'

She put her phone on the table, and tapped on the laptop. *What's your Erin's date of birth?* The answering email came, and swam in front of Vicky's eyes.

The eleventh of March. She didn't know Erin's exact date of birth, but if she'd been six days old when Mum and Dad went to the hotel, it could well have been the eleventh. And the year was right. Hell on earth. She grabbed the phone again.

'Ben – this could be it. I'm giving them my phone number.'

'Okay. Let me know what happens.'

Vicky disconnected, then emailed her mobile number,

staring at her phone on the table until it rang a few minutes later.

'Chris? I'm Vicky Cairns, and I'm looking for my sister Erin. She was separated from my brother and me as a baby, when our parents died. I only learned recently she exists.'

There was a long silence on the other end of the phone, but Vicky could hear unsteady breathing. Then a very young-sounding voice spoke. 'What were your parents' Christian names?'

'Paula and Joseph.'

'But that was my–' The connection broke.

Vicky stared at her mobile, then saved the number and put the phone down on the table as if it were made of wafer-thin porcelain. *But that was my...* Chris had said *my...* Vicky's head sank down on the table. Had she just spoken to her sister?

Her phone rang again, but it was Ben. She grabbed it. 'Keep off the line. I'll email you.'

Please, Chris, call back. But the phone remained silent as Vicky's fingers clicked over the keyboard.

Give her time, was Ben's response. *You could send a short email, but be careful – you still don't know for sure who she is.*

Vicky wiped her eyes. An email was an excellent idea. She tapped out a paragraph about her parents and Maisie and Jamie, then sent it off to Chris and sat back. She would wait now; if this was Erin, the poor girl would need time to think. And so did she.

Tea. Vicky went back to the kettle and clicked it on again, clutching her mug to her chest while she waited. People talked about grief, and fear, and anger, but she knew now what the most painful feeling of all was. Hope.

Chapter Ten

Christine spent the first half of the night rolling from one side of the bed to the other, unable to sleep. She'd always slept on her front, but the baby was too large for that now, and sleeping on her side felt unfamiliar and wrong. And the thoughts reeling around in her head made sleep even more elusive. She'd known she was Erin Cairns, daughter of Paula and Joseph Cairns. But… *sister to Vicky and Jamie*. That was surreal. Unexpected and it hurt like hell, because if it was true – and it couldn't all be coincidence, could it? – Sylvie had lied far more than she'd admitted. *Why?* Anger pulsed through Christine. She would have to speak to her mother, so it was very fortunate they were going on this long weekend together. Mum wasn't big on sharing info, but Christine would be able to pick her moment. And if Sylvie had lied about the 'no remaining family', well, there might not be a way back from that. The alarm pulled her from a troubled doze at half past seven on Friday morning, and Christine forced heavy legs over the edge of the bed. She had a train to catch and a plan to make – how best to approach the subject with Sylvie – so she'd better get going.

Larissa had left for work and the flat was silent as she

padded around getting ready, but the questions buzzing through her head made up for the stillness. A cup of tea soothed the still troublesome early-morning nausea – those books that assured you morning sickness got better after the first three months had no idea – and Christine was about to set off for the station when her mobile rang. Her heart rate soared. She wasn't ready for a call from Vicky Cairns. But it was Drew. Christine hesitated, then tapped to connect. This was as good a time as any to speak to him.

'I'm in Glasgow now,' he said abruptly. 'I'll come and see you after my meetings. What–'

'You won't, you know. Mum and I are away on a short break.' Mean and very sweet satisfaction filled Christine's mind as she heard his sharp intake of breath.

'You did that deliberately.'

'As a matter of fact, it was Mum's suggestion. Not that it's any of your business.' She could almost hear him panicking at the thought of her and Sylvie collaborating on how to do him for child support.

'I'll give you money, Christine, for expenses – everything. A lot of money. In return, I want nothing more to do with this.'

'With your child? Nice. Tell you what, Drew, you can put your blood money in an envelope and give it to Dad for me. And I'm not sure the courts would agree about you paying your way out of this, but we'll worry about that later. Please don't contact me again.'

Christine clicked her phone off and exited the flat, grinning at Drew's reaction. He was discombobulated, no mistake about it. The subway took her to Buchanan Street and she walked along to Queen Street Station, appreciating the sun on her face in spite of feeling her life was spiralling out of control. Christine bought her ticket and a latte, and stood on the station concourse waiting for the platform announcement.

The feeling of triumph over Drew didn't last long, and for the zillionth time Christine mulled over her relationship with Sylvie. Before all this, she'd have said they had an okay one, if a touch clingy on Mum's part. But, *sister to Vicky and Jamie... C*oncealing that was unforgivable, and *why?* Christine sipped her coffee and came to a decision. She would talk to Sylvie about it today, then she'd call Vicky back.

Sylvie was waiting at Waverley, a large-sized smile on her face. She kissed Christine, tapping her backpack. 'Someone's travelling light! Never mind, we can buy you anything you haven't brought.'

'I've brought plenty for the weekend,' said Christine, surprised. 'You didn't say I'd need anything fancy. We're staying in Edinburgh, aren't we?'

Christine took her arm and led her towards the other side of the station. 'That's the surprise. We're having our break just south of the border as usual. Come on, the car's along at the shopping centre.'

Christine stopped dead. 'As usual' was a bit of an overstatement. The family had spent several holidays in Yorkshire, in the north of England, but the last had been when Christine was about ten. 'Are you sure you want to drive all that way for just for a couple of days?'

Sylvie stepped onto the escalator up towards Princes Street. 'The forecast for this area's dire; we might as well get some sunshine. It'll be fun, you'll see.'

Christine shrugged. Yorkshire wasn't the other side of the moon, but this would mean she couldn't escape back to

Glasgow so easily if negotiations with Sylvie broke down. A large part of her wanted to scream at Sylvie right there in the middle of Waverley Station, ask what the hell she thought she'd been doing, but...

It was a tiny, but penetrating whisper. What if Sylvie'd had a reason, a good one, to conceal Vicky and Jamie? Or, even worse, suppose 'Vicky Cairns' was some kind of criminal, some chancer trying it on? Christine shivered. Surely it was too much of a coincidence; Vicky must be for real. They needed to talk about this like adults, her and Sylvie, and a spring break in sunny Yorkshire did sound nice. Hopefully she wouldn't regret that thought.

The first part of the journey was non-eventful, with Sylvie chatting about holidays and hotels for most of the time. They had lunch in Carlisle, after which Christine pretended to fall asleep, to gain some thinking time. She had to work out how to formulate a few questions that would elicit answers from Mum without pissing her off. Sylvie was planning to 'find a holiday flat or B&B in the first place that grabs us', so Christine had the rest of the journey to work something out.

The problem was, her broken night meant she really did fall asleep. Christine awoke to find they were in the middle of God knows where.

'Sleepyhead! A nap was just what you needed, darling. There's a little town coming up soon and I think it might make a good base for us.'

Christine rubbed her eyes. Sleeping in a travelling car had done nothing for the feel-good factor; it felt like the baby was bungee jumping around in her stomach and the nausea was chasing it. The sooner they arrived anywhere, the happier Christine would be. 'Where? Have we been there before?'

'Kendal. We passed through it a few times years ago, but

I'm sure you won't remember. There was a lovely farmers' market on Saturdays.'

Christine looked out to see rolling green countryside dotted with patches of woodland. This was the kind of area people wanted to retire to on *Escape to the Country*, but she'd never seen the attraction of living miles away from anywhere.

Kendal was a quaint little place, with whitewashed and stone buildings, some old and traditional, others modern. Sylvie pulled up near the tourist information on a hilly, cobbled street. 'I'll pop in here and see what they've got. Why don't you go and order us coffee and cake in that café? I'll join you in a few minutes.'

Christine got out and stretched stiff legs. It was a loo she needed right now, not a coffee, but presumably that would be available too. She crossed over and went into the café, which did have a loo, and ordered cappuccino for Sylvie and Earl Grey for her stomach, and a fruit muffin each.

Sylvie appeared wearing a pleased expression and jingling a set of keys. 'We have a lovely holiday flat near the river. Two bedrooms and all the etceteras, on the first floor. And there's a garden at the back we can use too.'

Christine checked Google Maps on her phone. Kendal was in Cumbria, not Yorkshire, and it wasn't far to Lake Windermere. And they made mint cake here too, which couldn't be a bad thing. She smiled at Sylvie. 'Sounds good. We'll need a supermarket.'

'There's a Tesco round the corner. We'll eat out a lot, of course. Oh, darling, isn't this fun?'

Christine sat back as the waitress came over with Sylvie's coffee. Fun? Well, yes. Sort of. At the moment. She had a feeling it might not stay that way.

***

Vicky pulled on a cardie and took her apple out to the balcony. She'd spent the last couple of hours drafting letters for work. Now she'd been in the team for two months, she was allowed up to two days per week when she could work from home instead of sitting at her desk in the city centre office. It was brilliant, being so flexible. She could work in the evenings and at weekends, and take time off during the day to visit Jamie or do the shops.

Dark clouds were scudding overhead, and the city was grey in sympathy. Even the river looked murky. Somehow, it fitted with her mood today. What would she do if Chris didn't get back in touch? The uncertainty was hard to take, rather like the feeling you have the day before an important exam. Vicky finished her apple and checked to see if anything had come from Chris, but there was nothing. Disappointment stung through her, then Vicky stuck her chin in the air. If she heard nothing today, she would send the girl a quick text or another email. And now to get on with some work.

She was finishing her last document when her phone buzzed. Oh. Jamie's home. Vicky tapped connect with a horrible sense of déjà vu. This was how it had started with Maisie, too. Please, Jamie, be okay.

'Vicky, Jamie was coughing all night, so we got the doctor in, and he's sending him for an X-ray. I don't know if you want to go along too?'

Vicky felt relieved. They'd been here before – Jamie was prone to chest infections. A course of antibiotics usually zapped them off. 'Poor poppet. I'll meet him at the hospital. Who's taking him?

'Mark. They're leaving now.'

'I'm on my way.' Vicky called Ben on her way downstairs and was given the news that he wasn't feeling great either and would probably come home after lunch. Vicky filled him in about Jamie. There must be some virus doing the rounds.

The hospital Jamie was heading for wasn't the huge one Ben worked at. Vicky drove along the M8 over the river, then turned into Great Western Road, where there were several smaller hospitals and clinics. Jamie's home usually sent their residents to one of these, and Vicky was glad. A smaller, more personal place was better for Jamie, and it was nearer, too. Ten more minutes and she'd be there, traffic permitting. Saturday could be iffy in this part of the city. Fortunately it wasn't today, and she turned into the hospital grounds and drove to A&E, glad to see the home minibus in the car park there.

The X-ray department was on the ground floor, and Vicky hurried along the corridor. She heard Jamie before she saw him. Loud wails were echoing through the building, interspersed by bouts of a hacking cough that sounded painful. Heck.

Jamie and Mark were waiting to go in, and Vicky hugged Jamie in his wheelchair.

'Hey, Jay-Jay, it's okay. We'll get you fixed up. Hi, Mark.'

The young nurse had worked in Jamie's unit for two years, and Jamie liked him. Vicky saw how her brother's eyes swept over her and back to Mark before the next wail came.

They were called through, and Vicky comforted Jamie while the technician and Mark placed him on the table, then she and Mark were sent out while the X-ray was taken. A doctor arrived with the result a few minutes later.

'Chest infection, as I'm sure you thought, and it's a bad

one, so we'll keep him in for a day or two.'

Vicky accompanied Jamie and Mark up to the ward, where Mark handed him over and said goodbye. Jamie was put into a hospital gown and settled into his bed in the corner of a six-bed bay, and Vicky's heart thudded downwards when she saw the uncomprehending misery on Jamie's face. She sat with him for a while and persuaded him to sip the juice the nurse brought, then left him asleep, his thin face pale against the pillow. Depression settled over Vicky as she walked back to the exit. What kind of life did Jamie have, helpless and disabled, with no family to love him except her and Amanda and Ted? He didn't understand where he was; he wouldn't know these strangers were trying to help him. She should call Amanda and let her know – she'd want to visit. Upset, Vicky walked across to the Red Cross tea bar and bought a large coffee and an egg mayo sandwich, then sat down to have lunch and call Amanda.

A short discussion about Jamie's quality of life did nothing to make her feel better, and she ended the call almost in tears. Why did stuff like this happen? Jamie's cerebral palsy was due to oxygen deprivation during his birth, how cruel was that? It would almost be better if–

'Chris? What are you do– Oh, sorry, I thought you were someone else.'

The voice had come from behind, but then the young woman in a white overall walked round Vicky and stood by the table, staring. Vicky's brain surged into action. This girl had mistaken her for… *Chris?*

The woman's name badge introduced her as Larissa Spence, radiographer. For a charged second neither of them spoke. Vicky's brain was whirring and she could hear a pulse beating in her ears.

'I'm Vicky Cairns,' she said at last.

Larissa slid into the seat opposite Vicky, staring back with an incredulous frown. 'You're very like Chris,' she said slowly. 'She's my flatmate. She told me about emailing with a Vicky Cairns – was that you?'

Vicky nodded. All she wanted was to grab Larissa and not let go until the girl had taken her to Chris who was probably, maybe, Erin, but she should take this slowly. Larissa looked as bewildered as she felt. Briefly, Vicky explained about the search for her sister.

Larissa's eyes were full of sympathy, and caution. 'Chris is feeling pretty emotional about it, but I know she wants to get in touch when she's back. She knew nothing about you, so it's all been a bit of a shock.'

'Back? Where is she?' Disappointment pinned Vicky to her chair.

'She's away for a couple of days with her mother.'

Vicky felt whipped. Erin's mother was dead. 'Can you tell me her – her mother's name?'

Larissa shrugged. 'Sylvie Adams.'

Vicky's brain whirred furiously. The woman who'd survived the explosion was Sylvie. So the odds were Erin had been taken by her mother's friend.

She stared at Larissa. 'I don't want to upset Chris. You know her – what do you think I should do?'

Larissa got up. 'I don't want to talk about her while she's not here. It would be best if you do nothing. I'll let her know you're definitely her sister. There's a real family resemblance – you have the same hair, though yours is a couple of inches longer, same features, same body shape, except she's pregnant. I'm sure she'll call you soon.'

A smile, and Larissa left the tea bar. Shell-shocked,

Vicky concentrated on just breathing for the moment. This was confirmation, surely – Chris was Erin. And *pregnant*? And did Chris work at the hospital too? That would fit with Larissa's reaction on seeing what looked like her absent flatmate here in the tea bar.

Vicky wandered across the car park and drove home in a daze. Ben was sprawled on the sofa looking sorry for himself, and Vicky told him about Larissa before making him tea and bundling him off to bed. She poured herself a small glass of Merlot. It was only two o'clock, but what the hell. Amanda was visiting Jamie tonight, so there was no reason not to stay in and celebrate.

Vicky sat in the armchair, sipping and thinking sad, sweet thoughts about her parents and brother and sister. And Maisie, who'd been such a love to her and Jamie, and she hadn't appreciated it. Vicky lifted the Capodimonte rose from the shelf and held it against her cheek.

'I think I've found her, Mais. I think I've found Erin.'

Chapter Eleven

Sunday, 11th March

'Rainy Sunday morning, darling, but I popped out for croissants and fresh orange juice. Come and have breakfast. Coffee's ready – and happy, happy birthday! We'll find you a little present today, shall we?'

Sylvie was beaming beside the old-fashioned filter machine, and Christine went for a hug then took her place at the table, pushing still-damp wisps of hair behind her ears.

'Thanks, Mum. You must have been up early.' She accepted coffee, juice, and a croissant, warm from the oven, unease adding to the nausea, but nowadays the nausea would lessen if she ate something. The unease might not. Sylvie was behaving like one of those mums on TV commercials, all sunshine and perfect and 'look what you can do with XX pre-rolled pastry'. Christine pulled out a smile for her mother, then bit into the croissant to save having to say more.

Her plan to thrash things out with Sylvie was going nowhere. The opportunities for an intimate chat were there, but every time Christine began, her mother slid the conversation round to something innocuous. They'd spent Friday evening settling into the flat, and all day yesterday exploring the area, visiting nearby Sizergh Castle before driving to Lake Windermere. The scenery was lovely in the early spring sunshine, fields and woodland waking up after the winter and sheep dotting the meadows, but Christine's increasing frustration meant she couldn't enjoy it. At one point they'd passed an old church by the roadside, ancient grey stone and a tall, square tower that looked as if it might have had bells, once upon a time. It was surrounded by an ancient graveyard, and Christine had suggested a quick stop. Wandering round, trying to decipher worn inscriptions on equally worn and often slanting gravestones, she'd said outright, 'Mum, I wish you'd tell me more about my birth family.'

Sylvie linked arms, pulling her back to the car. 'Later, darling. This holiday's about you and me and the baby. Let's leave the past alone for now.'

Christine had swallowed her objection and hadn't dared raise the subject again. There was something odd and brittle about her mother now, and the last thing she wanted was to fall out with Sylvie so far from home. Conversation for the remainder of Saturday had been superficial, and today was heading in the same direction already.

'So what's the rainy morning plan?' Christine slid out her phone as surreptitiously as she could. Ten o'clock. Shit. A whole day rattling round a small flat with Sylvie would drive her bananas.

'Let's go to the big supermarket on the edge of town and buy something nice for your birthday lunch. We can cook here, then go somewhere in the afternoon. The rain should have cleared by noon, according to the weatherman.'

It was as good a plan as any. Christine pulled up a map on her phone. 'Okay. We could try Killington Lake, maybe?'

Sylvie dropped the knife she was holding. 'There isn't

much to see there. Let's make for the coast, get some sea air in your lungs. It'll do the baby good.'

Christine sighed. They were back to doing the baby good. This break had been a mistake; she wasn't going to get any info out of Mum. It would have been better to ask about her birth family when Dad was there too. Tears blurred Christine's sight. If only she'd had that idea before they'd left. She tapped on her contacts list, then on Vicky's name. Was she looking at her sister's phone number? Christine ran a hand over her bump, feeling the answering kick and swallowing her impatience. A phone call to Vicky would bring clarity, but on holiday with Mum wasn't a good time to have a complicated conversation with a stranger, sister or not, and a text seemed too little, in the circumstances. She'd call first thing she was home. No matter what happened with Mum and the baby, she wanted to have contact with her birth family. Vicky would have photos, too; she could compare them with the ones Sylvie had shown her. Christine's breath caught. Her mother. Paula. Vicky's mother. Impossible for all this to be coincidence.

'For goodness sake put that phone away, Chris. All those rays can't be good for the baby. Come along and get ready.'

There was a new hardness in Sylvie's tone that had Christine thrusting her phone into her handbag and jumping up to clear the breakfast things. Yikes. Mum sounded like something in a horror film now, the kind where you began to wonder if this person was going to last until the end without going gaga and killing everyone. This was getting thoroughly spooky – she would phone Dad as soon as she could.

She had the opportunity a few minutes later when Sylvie vanished into the loo with her make-up bag, but what did you know, her father's phone was switched off. He'd be on the golf course, making the most of his freedom. Christine thought for a moment, then called Larissa.

'Chris! I–'

'Larissa, sorry, I don't have much time. We're in Kendal, and Mum's gone a bit off. I'm worried, but Dad's not picking up calls.'

'What do you mean, *off?*'

Christine described what had happened, glad to share the problem. 'I don't know when I'll get an opportunity to call Dad – could you let him know? He could call Mum and talk to her, and see what he thinks. I'd text him, but he's not big on opening them.'

'Sure, what's the number?'

Christine rattled it off, thankful that she knew it by heart. Two seconds after she ended the call, Sylvie appeared from the bathroom. Christine dropped her phone into her bag, but Sylvie had seen it.

'No phones today, darling. Why don't you leave it here? Let's go.'

Christine hesitated, then put her phone demonstratively on the kitchen table and treated Sylvie to her best smile. She wouldn't be able to answer it anyway, with Mum like this. A little grovelling could go a long way.

***

Sylvie's good mood reasserted itself in the supermarket, where the baby section had her beaming. 'Such lovely things, darling. It's going to be so good, having a little one in the family again.' She lifted a yellow sleepsuit and placed it in the trolley, along with a tiny pair of socks and a packet of bibs.

Christine stared, frustration rising by the minute. 'Mum. Don't buy things for the baby, please. I'm not even sure yet if—'

Sylvie cut in. '*I'm* sure, Christine. If you don't want this baby, I do. In fact, it would be better if you stayed in Glasgow, and left the baby at home with me. Yes.'

The brittleness was back, and Sylvie's voice was higher than usual. Cold fear slid down Christine's back. By the sound of things, her mother was having some kind of breakdown. The best thing would be to get her back to the flat, then try Dad again. Larissa couldn't have got contacted yet, or he'd have called Mum.

She jollied Sylvie along to the check-out, collecting salmon steaks, sugar snap peas and baby potatoes on the way. The drive back was amicable, after a brief disagreement when Christine wanted to drive and Sylvie wouldn't let her. Christine backed down quickly and, once safely in the flat, allowed Sylvie to chivvy her into starting the steak preparation.

'Are we driving back tomorrow?' Christine tried hard to sound upbeat. She should have some kind of timetable to tell her father.

Sylvie's answer brought the fear right back to centre stage.

'It would be better to stay here a few days longer, don't you think? Lovely fresh air for the baby. And you want to stay, don't you, Chris?'

Christine forced a smile. That had almost sounded like a threat. Fierce longing for her father swept through Christine. This couldn't be happening. Maybe it wasn't, of course, maybe she was the one going mad. The paranoia of mid-pregnancy, or something. She squinted at Sylvie, who was putting water on for the potatoes. Keep it happy, Christine. Or was she Erin?

'That sounds perfect. I'll just pop to the loo.' She grabbed her bag and almost ran from the kitchen. It really did feel like escaping. Come on, Chris. You can do this.

She was in the tiny hallway before she realised her mobile was still on the kitchen table and not in her bag. Oh God. Well, next time. Pregnant women were allowed to go to the loo every five minutes, weren't they?

The brief moment of optimism died as soon as she went back to the kitchen.

'Darling, I'm so sorry! Your phone rang a moment ago. It was Larissa, but I'm afraid I dropped it into the potato water.'

***

Vicky parked as close to Jamie's ward as she could get, worry grumbling in her middle. He'd had a restless night and was still asleep when she'd called at nine that morning. The antibiotics should be starting to work now, but of course the strange place, not to mention the strange people, would be disorientating to poor Jamie. She hurried up to the ward, unsurprised to find him in a single room – the other patients would need their rest as much as Jamie did.

She sat with him for two hours, then left when a nurse arrived with a ham sandwich and a yoghurt.

'He didn't think much of the Irish stew and plums and custard at lunchtime,' said the girl. 'So we called his home to ask what he liked. Banana yoghurt, Jamie!'

Vicky left them to it and wandered back downstairs. She passed a sign for the Radiography Department and hesitated.

Would Larissa be here today? Unlikely on Sunday, but it wouldn't hurt to go and look, and maybe she'd been in touch with Chris. It was odd, meeting her sister's flatmate before she'd met Chris – Erin.

She wandered along and hung around for a few minutes. The Radiography Department wasn't busy, but a few members of staff were there and... yes! There was Larissa, talking to a patient on a trolley. The younger woman spotted her and came over, not looking particularly pleased.

Vicky spoke quickly. 'I'm here visiting my brother – he's in Grampian Ward upstairs – and I just wondered if you were around.'

Larissa's frown lifted and a grin appeared. 'Of course – Jamie Cairns. He kept a few people busy last night, apparently.'

Relieved, Vicky smiled back. 'I bet. He has that talent when he's not well. I... I don't suppose you know when Chris'll be back, yet?'

Larissa stood still for a moment. 'Fancy a drink?' she said at last, then led the way to a machine along the corridor.

They let out cans of cola and stood sipping. Larissa was frowning again, and Vicky began to feel uneasy. Was anything wrong? Had Chris decided she didn't want to take things further?

'I'm not sure what to do, actually,' said Larissa at last. 'Chris called me this morning. She's worried about her mum, but her dad wasn't answering his phone. I said I'd get in touch with him for her, but he's still not picking up and now I can't get through to Chris, either. It isn't like her not to text back quite quickly, even if she can't return a call for some reason.'

'What's wrong with her...' For the life of her, Vicky

couldn't say 'mother'.

Larissa didn't seem to notice. 'She's very... nervous and upset. Chris is her whole world, so she took it hard when Chris left home. I'm sorry, I shouldn't be telling you this. I'm sure it'll all be okay, but...' She blinked miserably at Vicky.

Vicky put a hand on her arm. 'I shouldn't have asked you. Did you call his mobile?'

'Yes. I don't have a landline number – hey, that's an idea. They might be in the phone book. I'll check when I'm home. Thanks, Vicky. Chris should be home tomorrow and I'm sure she'll get in touch with you soon.' Larissa's pager went and she tossed her half-empty can into the nearby bin. 'Duty calls. Do you want me to text you to let you know I got hold of Ron and everything's okay?'

Vicky scribbled her number on a scrap of paper and went back to her car. The thought of Chris being away with someone who was definitely involved in her disappearance as a baby and was now 'nervous and upset' didn't sit well in her middle. It was time to intensify the Facebook search. Someone would have known Sylvie Adams back then.

At home, Ben was feeling better and was drilling holes in the bathroom wall for the new shelves. Vicky made them both a coffee and sat down at the table with her phone. Facebook. She pulled up the school group. Surely one of those Facebook friends who remembered Paula and Joe would remember Sylvie Adams – no, she'd been Raynott back then, hadn't she?

I'm Paula and Joe Cairns' daughter and I'm looking for Sylvie Adams/Raynott who was at the hotel near Kendal the year of the explosion, she typed. *I think she lived in England then. Does anyone know her?*

She posted the message and sat back. This might be a long wait; chances were the ex-pupils didn't open their Facebook every five minutes on Sunday afternoons. A text from Amanda pinged into her phone. She was on her way to see Jamie. Good. Vicky started a search for Sylvie Adams instead of Raynott on Facebook and found five: three were definitely not the right person and the others were too anonymous to tell.

The message icon at the top of her screen flashed. Golly, was this an answer already? Fingers unsteady, Vicky opened the message.

I was in Sylvie's class, though I lost touch with her a long time ago. It was from an Anna Henderson. Vicky punched the air. Bingo. Anna might know who was still in contact with Sylvie.

Could you call me sometime, please? Don't want convo details on FB. Vicky added her mobile number and sat back. If Anna had been at the hotel… Vicky got up and wandered over to the photo albums, still on the coffee table. Little Erin, and Jamie, and – heck. Going all soppy would get her exactly nowhere.

She was leafing through the albums when her mobile rang. Vicky lifted it and saw a strange number. Anna?

'Vicky, good to speak to you but I'll have to be quick – we have visitors. I remember your poor mum and dad, such an awful thing. What's the problem?'

Vicky explained briefly, hearing Anna's intake of breath.

'My God. I'm not sure I can help, though. Your mum and I weren't in the same clique at school and I wasn't at that reunion – we were abroad at the time. But I know someone who was there and knew Sylvie much better. Deirdre Sutton. She moved to the States years ago, though. How about I get try to get hold of her for you?'

'That would be great, thanks. You can give her my number.'

'Will do.' The connection broke.

Ben was still busy in the bathroom, and for a moment Vicky felt deflated. Things were moving forward, yes, but talk about baby steps and interminable waiting. Well, she would do more work stuff. She might be glad of the freed-up time later.

***

It was the afternoon from hell. Christine didn't dare say much about her ruined phone. For one thing, Sylvie offered immediately to replace it with a better one when they had the chance, and for another, there was something about her mother's eyes and voice that was scaring Christine. All she wanted was to go home.

They ate their salmon steaks for lunch, and Sylvie talked about the baby. Then they drove to Grange-over-Sands, and apart from a brief interlude when they bought Christine a new bathrobe for her birthday, Sylvie talked about the baby. Then they drove back to the flat, and it was baby talk all the way. The crazy thing was, in between, when Sylvie was talking to the woman in the café they stopped at for afternoon tea, or the assistants in the shops they wandered round, or the guy at the garage where they filled the tank, she sounded quite normal. The vague notion Christine had about asking someone for help came to nothing, because no one would have believed her. Why hadn't her father called to wish her a happy birthday? But then, maybe he'd tried Sylvie's phone if he hadn't got through to hers, and Sylvie hadn't told her.

Anything was possible today.

The best thing would be either to get hold of Sylvie's phone or get to a pay phone and call Dad. Thinking about his no-nonsense approach to life was comforting. He would be able to help, and Larissa should have called him already. Christine kept her eyes open, but pay phones were thin on the ground everywhere now, and seemingly non-existent in this corner of England. And Sylvie's phone was in her pocket. Christine considered simply asking for it to call her father, but if she came across as over-keen, Mum might be even more careful about not letting her have it. The best way was to watch, and take the first chance she had.

'Now, we've had a long day. I'm going to make you some hot chocolate, then it's off to bed with you,' said Sylvie, at nine o'clock that evening.

Christine had never felt so powerless. Her mother was treating her like a ten-year-old. She drank the mug of chocolate, kissed the proffered cheek and went to her room. Happy birthday, Christine.

Chapter Twelve

Monday, 12th March

Vicky spent half the night tossing and turning. There had been no reassuring text from Larissa yesterday, and nothing more from Anna or her friend Deirdre Sutton, either. It was agony, *feeling* so involved with Erin/Chris without actually *being* involved. Chris and Ron and Sylvie probably didn't even want Vicky to be involved in what seemed like a messy family crisis. Their family crisis, not hers. The nagging feeling that Erin was gone, and Chris was her sister in no way but blood, was hard to ignore, especially at 3am.

The alarm on Ben's phone woke her at quarter to seven as usual, and Vicky pushed the duvet aside. No way would she sleep again, with all of this crashing around in her head.

She sat on the edge of the bed. 'Feeling better today?'

Ben was already pulling work clothes from the wardrobe. 'I guess. Are you going in too, or is this a home day?'

'Haven't decided yet. I'll call the hospital at eight, see how Jamie is and take it from there.'

Ben vanished into the shower, and Vicky dragged her feet through to the kitchen. Seldom had a strong coffee been so necessary; talk about Monday morning. They were sitting in front of toast and cornflakes when a message vibrated into her phone on the worktop. Vicky grabbed it with shaking fingers. Was this Larissa? It was.

Sorry forgot to txt u last night. Ron's going to Kendal today for Chris + Syl so all OK. Speak soon. Larissa

Vicky gaped at the text. Kendal. The hotel where her parents had died was very close to Kendal. Why would Sylvie take Chris there? She connected to Larissa's number, her thumb sliding on the screen.

'Larissa, sorry, but why did they go to Kendal? Does Ron know what happened there?'

Larissa sounded bemused. 'I guess because of the scenery? Ron didn't say anything when I told him. I don't think he knew where it was at first. Why?'

'It's near Killington Lake, the place my parents were killed. It just seems odd, them going there.'

'Oh my God. I'm sure Chris has no idea about that. What are you going to do?'

As soon as she heard the question, Vicky knew what. 'I'll go there. Can you get Ron to call me ASAP?' She broke the connection and leapt up.

Ben was staring. 'Go where? Kendal?'

'Sylvie's taken Chris there. Ben, I have to find her – suppose she doesn't know that's where…'

She ran through to the bedroom for her handbag. Sylvie was unlikely to harm Chris; she seemed to have been a devoted mother to the girl, but… Tears burned in Vicky's eyes. The thought of Erin possibly being taken to the place their parents had died, and not being with her, was too much.

Ben followed her. 'I'll come too. I can pull a sickie. We'll find them, Vicks, if they're still there.'

If. Vicky hugged him tightly. 'I've never been there. To

the place they died. I should have gone long ago.'

Ben pulled up Google Maps. 'You'll be there in just over two hours from now. Come on – I'm driving.'

***

Christine opened her eyes to silence in the flat. She thrust the duvet to the side and reached for her phone before remembering it was dead, then grabbed her clothes and headed for the shower, swinging into the kitchen en route to get the time from the microwave. Bloody hell – it was after ten. She'd slept right round the clock; no wonder her head felt like concrete. And where was her mother?

Sylvie's bedroom door was cracked open, and Christine peeked in. The bed was made, the room deserted, and there was no Sylvie in the bathroom, either. Maybe she'd gone for fresh bread. Christine showered quickly and dressed, feeling better when she had her clothes on. Feeling vulnerable in your pyjamas was the pits.

In the kitchen, she started the coffee machine. The nausea was absent this morning, and a caffeine injection would help clear this wooziness from her head. Last night's chocolate mugs were still in the sink, and Christine started to rinse one, then stared. This one looked like an unwashed hot chocolate mug, but the other – the pink one she'd used – had a thick residue on the bottom. Christine poked it with a teaspoon, sick horror rising inside her. *No.* Had Mum put something in there to make her sleep? She massaged her bump, but the baby wasn't moving much. And she'd slept… like the dead. Panic rising, Christine filled a glass with water and drank it down, then grabbed her jacket. She would go somewhere and call Dad – she needed help fast. Clutching her stomach

– please, baby, give me a nice big kick – she ran to the flat door.

It was locked. Christine rattled the handle, then burst into tears and kicked the door. It had an elderly mortice lock, the kind you needed a key to open, and she didn't have one. Stupid, stupid. Why had she let Sylvie keep the keys? She was an adult; she should have a key of her own. What was she supposed to do now?

Drink your coffee and wait was all that came to mind. Christine sank down at the tiny kitchen table and sipped glumly, but at least the baby was kicking now. Ten minutes later, her mother's key in the door was a relief as well as a huge annoyance.

'You locked me in! What if the place had gone up in flames while you were out?'

Sylvie gawped at her, then dropped her plastic bags on the kitchen table. 'Goodness, darling, no need for this grumpiness! I was buying bread for your breakfast.'

The expression on Sylvie's face reminded Christine of an old film she'd watched recently, and she bit back a sharp response. Her mother really did look like one of the Stepford wives – a happy, plastic face and a bright tone to her voice. She should keep Sylvie sweet now, and wait for the chance to call her father.

Christine took the brown loaf from the bag and dredged up a smile. 'This smells good! So what's the plan today?'

'It's chilly out – let's zoom down to Morecambe and do some shopping. It's a big place; they're bound to have some nice baby shops.'

They were back to the baby. Christine kept up her end of the conversation by asking about the equipment Sylvie had used twenty-odd years ago, and comparing it to modern baby accessories. Sylvie was beaming over her coffee cup, but it still wasn't her usual smile, and renewed fear stabbed into Christine's gut. Somehow, the mother she'd known all her life was gone. But at least Sylvie was being nice to her…

Taking her courage in both hands, Christine pushed her plate back. 'That was yummy. We could look for a new phone for me in Morecambe, too. I don't mind paying for it. I was going to get a new one this spring, anyway.'

'Oh, that can wait until you're back in Glasgow. I'm sure they'll have a better selection there.'

Christine opened her mouth to object, then closed it again. Keep her sweet, Chris. She could make cow eyes later in Morecambe; surely they'd swing past a mobile place during their crawl round the baby shops? Eventually, Sylvie left the kitchen to look for the weather forecast on TV, and Christine seized her chance. Her mother's handbag was on the work surface – quick, get her mobile… yes! And the second door key while she was at it. Christine slid back into her chair, the mobile tucked in her jeans. Hopefully it wouldn't ring.

'The forecast's pretty poor, I'm afraid. Let's have a lovely blob here this morning, shall we, and do Morecambe after lunch?' Sylvie was back in the doorway.

A flash of sheer inspiration struck Christine, and she yawned demonstratively. 'That sounds wonderful. I'd love to put my feet up. Oh, do you know what would be lovely? Some baby mags. I saw some in the newsagent across the road the other day. You could be an absolute love and get a couple?'

Sylvie rose to the bait. 'Of course I will. You take our baby through for a rest on the sofa, and I'll clear off here and pop across the road.'

Christine was dancing with impatience by the time her

mother was ready. She didn't dare take the mobile out to make sure it was on silent, and sat with her feet on the coffee table, talking to Sylvie in the kitchen until at long last her mother lifted her bag and exited the flat.

Christine waited until the footsteps going down the stairs were inaudible, then whipped the phone out. Contacts, contacts. Open, scroll down to Ron, connect... And of course, he didn't answer. He wasn't big on mobiles at the best of times. Christine tried the landline at home with the same result. *Shit.* What could she do now? The police? No, that was a last resort. What the hell was Larissa's number? Hot tears of frustration welled in Christine's eyes. She couldn't remember.

***

'You are approaching your destination. Your destination is on the left.'

Vicky sat up straight and peered out as Ben turned into the car park beside the bus station. Ron had called on the way down and they'd arranged to meet here. She texted him. *We've arrived. Grey Nissan near the ticket machine.* She and Ben got out and stretched. Ron wasn't far behind them, but there wasn't much they could do until he arrived, as they had no idea if he knew where Chris and Sylvie were staying. Ben spotted a nearby café and went to get coffees while Vicky used the time to call Amanda, who gave her the news that Jamie was driving everyone at the hospital bonkers with his exuberance and would be discharged tomorrow. Good.

'The woman in the shop said the old town centre's just behind this street,' said Ben, handing over a cardboard beaker and a muffin. 'It seems to be really nice, and there's a tourist info place there too.'

They leaned on the boot and sipped and ate, and just ten minutes later a black Porsche drove past. The driver was a middle-aged man in a grey suit. He stared at them, then parked in a space three along and strode back, his face a curious mixture of bewilderment and regret.

'No need to ask if you're Vicky. I'm Ron Adams.' He shook hands with them both, then spread his arms out. 'I've no idea where my wife and Chris are. We'd better start calling round the hotels. Sylvie called while I was on the motorway, but when I tried to call back she didn't pick up.'

Ben fetched his iPad from the car. 'I'll pull up a list.'

Vicky nodded. 'They may have booked rooms at the tourist information office – we could go there and ask. Do you have a photo of your wife, Ron?'

He pulled a family snap from his wallet. 'Excellent idea. If anyone remembers them they'll see I'm on the photo too, and you and Chris are so alike you have to be family.'

Vicky stared at the photo, her head reeling. Chris was a younger version of herself, and how weird it was to see her sister – Erin – like this. Ben took her hand and squeezed, and she swallowed the tears.

They walked in silence up towards the tourist information, hope and fear hammering in Vicky's chest.

***

'Have you got my phone?' Sylvie burst into the flat and almost flung a selection of magazines at Christine, her eyes blazing.

Oops. Time for some tact. Heart racing, Christine put on her best bright smile and handed over Sylvie's phone, which she had switched off as soon as she heard her mother's feet on the stairs. 'You left it on the sofa.' Christine's heart was thudding so hard she could feel the pulse at her throat. God help her if Mum didn't buy that.

Fortunately, she did. Sylvie glared at her mobile, then dropped it into her handbag and curled up beside Christine. 'Let's have a look through those magazines.' She opened one at an article on sterilising equipment, the non-Sylvie smile back on her face. 'This looks interesting. We can make a list of everything we'll need.'

Impatience squirmed round Christine's middle. If she said anything about possibly not keeping the baby… But who was she kidding? The baby kicked against her ribs, as if in protest she'd had the audacity to even think something so outrageous, and Christine massaged her bump. *Of course* she was going to keep her baby. All she had to do here was jolly her mother along. Larissa must have contacted Dad by now. He had to get them out of here, because she sure as hell didn't know how to, short of running off and leaving Sylvie, which would be the absolute last resort. The woman beside her on the sofa needed help. They both did.

'And a sheepskin for the pram, for winter. You know how cold it can be in Aberdeenshire. Oh, darling, I'm so, so happy to have another little one; it's all I've ever wanted. Another little son or daughter now my girl is all grown.'

Christine barely suppressed a shiver. Mum wasn't losing it; she had lost it already. How long would it take Dad to get here? Three, four hours, driving? No, longer. Christine's mouth went dry.

Leaving Sylvie making her list, she went through to the bathroom and splashed her face. She didn't dare suggest calling Ron, so the only way was to do it without Sylvie knowing.

'I'm starving,' she said brightly, going back into the living room and hooking her bag over her shoulder. 'Why don't I go and get us some Chinese, now I've had a good rest? There's a takeaway along the road. Are there any of those fab sugar snaps left from yesterday? You could do them to go with it while I'm out.'

Sylvie leapt to her feet. 'There's no reason for you to go out, Christine. I'll make an omelette for lunch. Sit here and rest, please.' She seized Christine's arm and pulled her towards the sofa.

Startled, Christine wrenched herself free, her bag falling to the floor, but Sylvie lunged forward and grabbed her other wrist and oh no, no, how strong those fingers were, crushing down where there was no flesh to provide padding. Get the shit out of here and call Dad, Chris.

'Let me *go–*'

'I have to take care of the baby, Christine.'

Strong hands were pushing against her shoulders. She was going to lose her balance and fall backwards onto the sofa with Mum and those scary, shiny eyes on top of her. Desperation took over, and Christine kicked against Sylvie's shins.

Sylvie danced back, howling and loosening her grasp, and Christine seized her chance.

'You're being daft, Mum,' she said, grabbing her bag and diving towards the door. 'I'll be back in ten!' She ran from the flat and clattered down the stairs, a high-pitched, animal wail echoing in her ears.

Where to, where to? Not the takeaway, anyway – if Mum decided to run after her that would be the way she'd go. Christine turned right along the street, running away from the centre and away from the shops, but there was nothing she could do about that. She zig-zagged through streets until she was back in the old town centre, and thank Christ, people were here, normal everyday people. If she stayed amongst them, she'd be safe.

Christine turned up a wide street, a pedestrian precinct with small shops either side, and spotted two benches further along. She sank down on one and leaned back thankfully. Now what? There wasn't a phone box in sight. There was a sandwich shop, though. Christine took a few deep breaths, then fetched a hot chocolate, sipping as she returned to the bench. The baby kicked, and she massaged her bump. 'I think it's time for plan B, kiddo.'

The problem was, she didn't have a plan B.

***

Vicky stared at the map on her phone. 'It's just round here.' She crossed the road, and Ron and Ben followed her along a nondescript street with three-storey terraces either side. 'There it is, look. Number twenty-four.'

The tourist information woman had recognised Sylvie on the photo and supplied the address without a murmur. Number twenty-four had a front door leading to a communal stairwell, but like the other house doors here, the door was propped open. Vicky's mouth was dry as they hurried up to the first floor. She could be seconds away from meeting her sister, and she didn't feel prepared. What would she say? What would Erin say? It was going to be odd, seeing someone she resembled so closely. Vicky took a deep breath, then pressed the bell on the first-floor-flat door, hearing it shrill out into the flat.

Ron came to stand beside her, and Vicky took a step back. It would be better if he was the one seen first by whoever opened the door.

No answer. Ron knocked briskly on the door. 'Chris! Sylvie! It's me, let me in!'

Still no answer. Vicky's breath escaped in a loud sigh, and Ben rubbed her shoulders from behind.

'They could have gone out for the afternoon,' he suggested.

Ron turned round. 'We passed a coffee shop a few minutes ago. Let's go there and discuss what we do now.'

Ben put his arm around Vicky as they walked towards the café, and she allowed herself to lean on him. This was nerve-wracking.

Ron was looking up and down the street. 'There's no sign of Sylvie's car.'

Vicky nodded. There was plenty of space to park here, so an outing could be a good bet. And people who were in bad trouble didn't go on afternoon outings, did they? Maybe they'd been too hasty, dashing down to Kendal like this.

A tuna sandwich and a soda water made her feel better, and Ben's suggestion of waiting an hour or two and then trying the flat again seemed the only thing to do. They were sitting in silence when Ron's mobile buzzed. Ron jumped visibly, scrabbling for the phone in his inside pocket.

'Strange number,' he said briefly, then connected. 'Ron Ad– Chris! Slow down, sweetheart. What's happened? Where are you? I'm in Kendal now.'

Vicky heard a high-pitched, emotional voice, but she couldn't make out the words. Ron listened, throwing in the odd *uh-huh*, then, 'Where are you, love? I'm in the café just along from your flat, ah… the one with the green front. No… okay, I'll meet you outside.'

He disconnected, then turned to Vicky and Ben. 'She's coming here. She left Sylvie in the flat just under an hour ago. Sylvie was hysterical, trying to force Chris to stay after destroying her mobile, and Chris was afraid. I'll meet her outside and I think it's best if you stay here in the meantime.'

He strode out of the café and disappeared along the pavement.

Vicky looked at Ben. 'My God.'

He gripped her hand and they waited in silence. Vicky could barely sit still. Was Erin – Chris – all right? What would she say when she heard Vicky was here – would she accept support from a sister she didn't even know? And where was Sylvie?

It felt like an eternity to Vicky, but it was only ten minutes later when Ron appeared in the doorway and beckoned them out. Vicky ran forward, leaving Ben to settle the bill. She pushed the door open and stumbled onto the pavement, tears welling at the sight of the figure beside Ron. Erin was slighter than she was, and paler, but the face looking at her now could almost have been her own; the blonde, wispy hair was the same, and Vicky had a very similar sweatshirt in her wardrobe. She could see why Larissa had mistaken them from behind.

'Christine, this is Vicky, your sister,' said Ron steadily, as Ben joined them on the pavement. 'And this is her partner, Ben.'

'I… I'm so glad to see you safe,' said Vicky. She reached out and rubbed the girl's arm.

Christine nodded, her eyes heavy. 'Wish it was a happier occasion,' she whispered, and Vicky nodded.

'Let's stick to practicalities for now.' Ron started back towards the flat, his arm still around Christine. 'Chris has keys to the flat. We should check Sylvie's not there.'

'The car's gone,' said Christine, staring up the street.

Vicky saw how the girl was clinging to Ron. Good – after all she'd been through, she needed support. Back at the flat, Christine unlocked the door and they all trooped in.

Christine went into one of the bedrooms. 'She's taken her stuff.' She checked the other. 'Mine's still here. Dad, I don't think she's coming back. What can we do?'

Ron looked round them all. 'I'll stay here with Chris tonight,' he said slowly. 'In case Sylvie does come back. If she doesn't, we can think about contacting the police, Chris. They may be able to trace the car. We can drive home tomorrow.'

'What will you do?' Christine glanced at Vicky, but her eyes slid away almost immediately.

Vicky blinked back tears. This was where she had to take a step back; it was only natural that Christine was more worried about Sylvie at the moment. 'I think Ben and I should go home today,' she said. 'This is for you and Ron to sort out. The important thing for me is that you're safe. We can talk later, when you're ready.'

Christine nodded. Vicky wanted to grab the younger girl and hug her, but she could see how distraught Christine was. The girl's hands were plucking at the hem of her sweatshirt, though every so often she would caress her small bump.

'Are you – and the baby – all right?' Vicky was surprised to hear how steady she sounded. Inside, she was shaking like she'd never shaken before. 'If you need a doctor or anything, I can stay and help you.'

Christine's chin shot up. 'Don't worry. It's just been one of those days.'

Vicky gaped at the sudden humour, which seemed hardly

appropriate in the circumstances, but Ron was smiling wryly.

He patted Christine's shoulder. 'That's my girl.'

***

It was three o'clock the following afternoon when Vicky's mobile rang. She was at work, trying to concentrate on the job in hand and finding it almost impossible. Her heart thudded up a gear when she saw Ron's name on her screen.

The voice was Christine's, though. 'Hi. We're driving home now. Would you be able to meet us at my flat around six o'clock? It's 50 Court Avenue.'

Vicky swallowed. 'Of course. Are you okay? Did you find Sylvie?'

'Yes, and no. Dad reported the car missing, but we haven't heard anything yet.'

'I'm glad you're… well. See you later, then.'

She laid the phone down and sipped on her water bottle. How did Christine envisage their relationship developing? There was nothing in her own experience to draw on here; they would have to make it up as they went along, as well as deal with Sylvie and whatever complications that brought.

Ron's face was grim when he opened the door at Court Avenue when Vicky arrived later that afternoon, alone, as Ben was stuck with an emergency at work.

'No more news,' said Ron briefly. 'Come through.'

He led the way into the kitchen, where Christine and Larissa were sitting at the table. Christine smiled but didn't get up, and Vicky realised that she was the one who'd done the agonising and searching; she was the one who'd been alone and desperate to find family. Christine had grown up a well-loved only child with no idea of ever being anything else. They'd need time to build bridges now.

She sat down, and Christine gave her a lopsided grin. 'I guess this is Day One.'

Vicky nodded, quickly touching the thin hand on the table. Day One was a start.

PART THREE

ERIN

Chapter One

Wednesday, 4th July

Vicky exited the flat and hurried across the road to the footbridge over the Clyde, stuffing the umbrella she'd had at the ready back into her bag. It was a grey day, but the showers of early morning had given way to a damp breeze that ruffled through her hair as she crossed the river. She was on her way to meet Anna and Deirdre, the women who'd known her mother back in the day, and this was the first time she would meet them in person. Vicky had called Anna in May, to say they had found Erin, and Anna replied she would get in touch when Deirdre and her husband were in Scotland – they were travelling around for a few months to celebrate her husband's sixtieth. The call came last week, and Vicky hugged herself as she hurried through town. It would be great to hear more about her parents, although the urgency was gone now that Erin was found.

The café they'd agreed on was busy with people having an early lunch, but a woman at the back waved frantically as soon as Vicky went in.

'You must be Vicky. I'm Anna. You're very like your mother, you know,' she said, gazing up at Vicky. 'I was so glad you found your sister – what an odd story that was. This is Deirdre.'

Vicky shook hands with both women and slid into her chair, unsure about how much she wanted to share with her mother's old friends. The story hadn't stopped being odd. Sylvie was still missing, and although Erin was here in Glasgow and part of Vicky's life now, they were still feeling their way around each other. There had been none of the effortless falling into each other's arms you saw on family-finding programmes on TV, and maybe it was only natural. Chris had lived her life loving Sylvie and Ron as her parents. Now she had an almighty betrayal to come to terms with, plus the worry over Sylvie, plus the pregnancy. A new sister who was seething with resentment against poor Chris's vanished mother was unlikely to fit in comfortably. Vicky had mentioned the meeting with Anna and Deirdre, but Christine didn't want to come along, which was probably a good thing, thought Vicky. Who knew what these women would say about Sylvie.

For now, she kept things light. 'I'm glad, too. We see each other a couple of times a week. It's a pity Sylvie has gone away; it means we don't have any kind of explanation for what happened when Erin was a baby.'

Anna and Deirdre both stared, but the waitress arrived and the next few minutes were taken up with ordering food. When they all had heaped plates and full glasses in front of them, Vicky started again with a question.

'When was the last time you saw Sylvie?'

'Your brother's christening,' said Anna. 'We moved to Wales shortly afterwards and when we came back ten years later, Sylvie wasn't part of the crowd any longer. But Deirdre knew her better, didn't you, Dee?'

'Yes. After I left school I was away for a year, tramping round Europe, but when I came home we got back in touch. Sylvie and I went clubbing in a group most Saturday nights as twenty-somethings. She wasn't someone I'd have gone to with a problem, but we were both unattached in those days and she was great fun – very bright and enthusiastic. I could never understand why she didn't have queues of boyfriends. As far as I know, she was working in the north of England at the time of the reunion.'

Vicky nodded. That fitted in with the little they knew. 'When did she move there?'

'Not long before your sister was born,' said Deirdre. 'I remember Sylvie moaning about how she wouldn't see the baby when it was tiny. But as it turned out, she did, of course. I hadn't seen Paula for quite a while, at that point. My mum was ill, and I was busy with her.'

Vicky put down her fork. 'So Mum and Dad and Sylvie went south. And Erin. They were all staying in the hotel, and then–' She covered her face with her hands. Somehow, these women sitting with her at the table brought home what she had lost.

Anna's expression was sombre. 'It was a dreadful shock to us all. I wish we'd kept in touch with you and Jamie.'

Vicky wiped her eyes. 'We were in Edinburgh for a few months afterwards. We didn't come back to Glasgow until we went to the third foster family.' Sipping her water, she thought again about that night in the hotel. Erin would have been with her parents, in their bedroom – how had she and Sylvie escaped the blast? It was something she'd never considered. Had Sylvie taken her out? She must have, and why didn't Paula and Joe go, too? She would have to talk to Ron again, ask directly if Sylvie had told him anything. He was never happy talking about Sylvie's past, but hell, she deserved some answers.

'We're going up to my parents' place soon,' said Deirdre. 'They moved back to Orkney when Dad retired, and the photo albums from my school days went with them. I'll have a look for you and see if there are any of your parents.'

'Good idea, I'll do that too,' said Anna. 'And I know I have some snaps of their wedding. Sylvie was your mother's bridesmaid, did you know that?'

It was Vicky's turn to stare. 'No. They must have been good friends, then. Thanks – that would be great.'

Back at home later that afternoon, Vicky pulled out her parents' wedding album. She had pics of her mother's bridesmaid right here.

A slight, blonde figure in a long, pale yellow dress and carrying a bouquet of white and yellow roses beamed out of the photos. Vicky leafed through the album. Sylvie was smaller than Paula, but that was all Vicky could tell from the official photos. She sighed. Her investigation was still taking baby steps.

Chapter Two

Thursday, 5th July

Kay parked in a side road, smiling at the sight of the American diner on the corner – stars and stripes all over the place for Independence Day yesterday. She locked the car and hurried along Argyle Street towards the charity shop. She was on alone this morning and it was five minutes to opening time already – that second coffee had cost her a few minutes too many.

Open for business, Kay stood at the counter sorting through a box of costume jewellery that had come in the day before. It was always exciting doing things like this; the hope of a real diamond turning up never faded, no matter how many boxes of rhinestones she sieved through. Engrossed in her task, she jumped when the shop bell pinged, then looked up to see a fifty-something woman standing in the doorway, gazing around with wide eyes.

Kay smiled. 'Feel free to browse. Or are you looking for something in particular?'

The woman came over to the counter. 'Baby things, if you have anything.'

Kay took her to the back corner, where children's clothes and toys were set out. 'We don't get much in the way of smallest-size clothes. I suppose most people pass these on to friends and family. We had an unused steriliser last week, but I'm afraid that's gone.'

The steriliser was in her flat, waiting to go to Christine's. There wasn't long to go now – in two weeks or so, that steriliser would be doing its duty.

The woman spun the rack of children's clothes. 'I see. I suppose all the young mothers you know are happy for a heads-up about unused things?' She squinted at Kay, a dimple in each cheek, and Kay laughed.

'That's about it. I only know one at the moment, and she was happy enough to get a still-boxed steriliser at a charity shop price!'

'I'll bet. When's the baby due?'

'Another two weeks. She's quite excited!'

'Lovely. My niece had her first last week – a little girl.'

The woman walked round the rack, then turned to Kay, her eyes uncertain. 'I don't suppose you have any job vacancies? I've been looking for some charity work for a while, and this seems such a nice shop.'

For the first time, Kay noticed the woman's pallor and the lack of rings on her left hand. Was there really a niece, or had that been an excuse to get into conversation and ask for a job?

'We're always looking for volunteers, but I'm afraid we don't have many paid employees,' she said, making her voice as kind as possible, and was drawing breath to suggest one of the bigger chains might be a better bet when the woman leapt in.

'Oh, I meant voluntary work! Would you have anything here? Visiting my niece doesn't take up enough of the week, that's my problem, and I'd love to be a part of something worthwhile.'

'We do need someone for three or four shifts a week, as it happens. You could fill in our online application form.'

'Can I do that here?'

Amused, Kay led the woman, who introduced herself as Susan Allan, to the counter, and brought up the form on the screen. Susan was the keenest applicant she'd come across.

'Okay,' she said, saving the form when Susan had completed it. 'We'll have to check your references, of course – we'll get back to you in a few days.'

Huge eyes met Kay's. Surely those weren't tears?

'Thank you, that's wonderful. I do hope I can come. I only moved back to Glasgow a couple of months ago, and it's hard finding your feet in a new place.'

Kay could imagine it was. 'Well, we're a friendly bunch here. Good luck!'

She waved as Susan left the shop and turned towards the city centre, then scrolled through the application form. Susan had given her landlord as one referee; he wouldn't have known her long. The other was the minister of Susan's church; the same applied to her, but she might be a better judge of character. Kay drafted an email and sent it off to both referees before going back to her box of jewellery, smiling as she sorted through the chains and bracelets. Another volunteer here would make all the difference.

***

Christine stared at the building as Vicky reversed into the parking space on the opposite side of the street. It was an ordinary red-brick block containing six flats, in an ordinary Edinburgh street, and for the life of her Christine didn't know what to say about it.

'So this isn't the flat where you and Jamie lived with Maisie?'

Vicky switched off the engine and leaned back, her gaze fixed hungrily on the building. 'No. She sold that one a year or two after we went into care, and moved here. It's the one on the ground floor there on the left, nice and near the shops and the park. It was here I got to know her properly, as a teenager. I only wish things had been different when I was a kid.'

Christine twisted round in her seat and touched Vicky's shoulder. 'Neither of us could have changed what happened,' she said quietly. 'You shouldn't beat yourself up about it.'

'I'm not,' said Vicky. 'Just wishing. Maisie was such a love.'

Christine closed her eyes, searching for a reply. What she wished now was that Vicky would drive away. They had seen the place, and it was a sickening, unsettling feeling that Sylvie had been mixed up in everything that had happened to Vicky and Jamie, and then hidden it all from Christine and Ron. And by going AWOL so completely now, Sylvie was as good as admitting her guilt, and shit – why didn't she get in touch? She must realise how worried Christine and Ron were. The horror-thought was always in the back of Christine's mind – what if Mum had done something stupid? The police had found Sylvie's car at a garage outside Carlisle where she'd sold it, cash in hand, two days after she'd disappeared. For all they knew, she could have jumped off a cliff months ago, and the police had found out nothing at all.

Miserably, Christine cuddled her bump. Spending the day together in Edinburgh had been Vicky's idea. They'd taken flowers to the garden of remembrance where Maisie's ashes were scattered, and Vicky stood with tears in her eyes while Christine stood wondering if she would ever feel connected to Vicky and Jamie's childhoods. Knowing each other's life histories wasn't enough.

Now, Vicky turned the key in the ignition. 'Sorry. I wanted to see the place when we were passing anyway. Let's go for lunch.'

They left the car in an extortionately expensive city centre car park and found a table at a bistro on Rose Street. Christine gazed round the busy little restaurant and was suddenly glad to be here with Vicky, but oh, if only this had been a family tradition from way back. It was hard to imagine they'd ever have the kind of relationship 'normal' sisters might have – bickering, laughing, making jokes at the other's expense.

The waitress brought their quiche and salad, and Christine nibbled. Hunger wasn't an issue these days; if she ate more than five bites of anything she was full. Roll on having space for a curry in her middle.

'Any more news from the baby's father?' said Vicky, lifting her glass.

'Nope. And there won't be. He's given me money, Vicky, and I've said I'll keep quiet about the parent thing until the baby's old enough to want serious info.'

To her relief Vicky merely nodded, and Christine rushed to change the subject.

'Dad's coming down at the weekend. He's bringing my birth certificate and we're going to have a proper talk about what to do about it. Would you like to be there?'

Christine could see the different emotions going through her sister's head at this. Vicky hated what Sylvie had done, and she was struggling to understand why Christine wasn't yelling and screaming for the police.

'Chris – you know what I think you should do, and to be honest, if there's false information on your birth certificate, I'm sure you won't have a choice about reporting it, eventually. But it's your decision, so I think it's best if you and Ron discuss it alone.'

'Okay. I just thought I'd ask. You can tell me on Friday if you change your mind.'

'Sure.' Vicky smiled across the table, and Christine smiled back.

But wouldn't normal sisters have yelled at each other and flung plates, then hugged and made up? Christine poked at her salad. She had a new family, but in a different way she had no family at all.

***

Whistling, Vicky loaded her coffee mug into the dishwasher. This was the best part about her no-longer-new job – days off during the week, even if she did work at home in the evenings and at weekends to make up the time. And Friday was the best day to have off. She went into the hallway where her bags were waiting.

She had everything, didn't she? Handbag, check, clothes for Jamie, check – he was going to love the tracksuit trousers Chris's neighbour Kay had found at her charity shop last week and snapped up for the boy. Tracksuits were Jamie's favourites, and they were easiest for his carers, too. Vicky rummaged through the contents of her handbag. Car key, make-up bag, wipes – always necessary on a visit to Jamie – purse, yes, that was the lot.

She ran down to her car and started out for Christine's

flat. The sun was sparkling through the windscreen, and Vicky cracked the window open. Today would be the fourth time she and Chris had visited their brother together since she'd found Christine.

Vicky's determinedly cheerful mood evaporated. How she wished her sister hadn't opted to keep the name she'd grown up with. Oh, it was understandable, logical, even, but it still felt like rejection. Vicky pushed the thought away. She was being daft, and there were better things to worry about. Jamie, for instance. It was sad, but she preferred visiting him alone. He didn't understand about Christine, but he was savvy enough to be confused by what appeared to be two Vickys sitting by his chair. It was heart-wrenching to see him look from one of them to the other, a frown on his innocent man-child face. Vicky blinked as she drove up Byres Road. She had no idea if Jamie knew she was his sister. Probably not, but she was a familiar in his life. Or she had been, until she'd produced a double. But Christine wanted to be part of Jamie's life too, which for the moment left Vicky playing chauffeur, as Chris was now too big to drive comfortably.

The girl was waiting opposite the library as they'd arranged, and plumped into the passenger seat as soon as the car drew up.

'I'm sure this baby doubles in size every day,' she said, twisting to get the seatbelt fastened, then pulling the shoulder strap away from her bump. 'I can't wait until it's on the other side of my skin and doesn't wake me up every time it hiccups.'

'Won't be long now. You look great, anyway.'

It was true; Christine was pink-cheeked and blooming in the traditional pregnancy way.

She stroked her bump. 'The all-night gymnastics have

been toned down. Poor baby, it must feel a bit squashed in there now.'

Vicky started the engine again, glancing across at her sister. It was fun, sharing the run-up to the baby with Chris, but oh, it was bittersweet too. The girl must be torn between her old feelings for Sylvie and the sense of betrayal about the past, but she wasn't talking to Vicky about it. Those twenty-two years were a metaphorical wall between her and Chris, and although they had knocked a hole in that wall and were staring through at each other – touching, even, sometimes – neither was finding a way to the other side. And maybe it would always be like that. All the talking in the world wouldn't bring them the years of shared memories they'd missed.

Sirens wailed behind them and Vicky pulled the car to the side to allow an ambulance to speed past. 'I'm glad we had the DNA test done. Even though everyone thought it was unnecessary, given that we could be twins.'

Christine raised her eyebrows. 'Are you saying I look five years older than I am?'

'Obviously, I look five years younger,' said Vicky, her face deadpan.

And there it was. A sisterly dialogue. How lovely.

Vicky drove through Milngavie, green hills in the distance biting into the blue of the sky. Peace descended, in spite of the turmoil inside her. She did love Chris, she did.

Jamie was waiting in the hallway of his unit, and he bounced and laughed in his wheelchair when Vicky walked in. She hugged him tightly. Somehow, since finding Christine, he had become doubly precious. No way did she want Jamie to feel that she now had a 'better' sibling.

'All alone today?' Mark, the carer, appeared from the

224

kitchen, and Vicky handed over the bag with Jamie's new trousers.

'Chris is waiting at the car. No sense her waddling all the way up here only to go back out again.' Vicky hung her handbag over the wheelchair handles in preparation for pushing Jamie. 'We've brought stuff for a picnic – doughnuts, Jamie!'

He whooped, and she ruffled his hair.

Back in the garden, they found a shady spot under an ash tree, and Vicky plonked down on the picnic blanket and opened the basket. Jamie was looking from her to Christine, his brow furrowed, and Vicky took his hand. To her dismay he gave a howl, and jerked his head in the direction of the building.

'It's okay, Jay-Jay. Look – doughnuts!' Vicky kept her voice light, but oh, how it stung. He wanted to go back inside to Mark, who didn't have a double. She fed Jamie some doughnut, and he calmed down enough to allow Christine to offer him his precious Ferrari sippy cup. Vicky watched them hungrily – her brother and sister, doing something together. Visit number four, and they had achieved a few seconds of normality within their new family group. Hallelujah. But would she ever love her sister as much as she loved Jamie?

Chapter Three

Saturday, 7th July

The bell pinged as someone entered the shop, and Kay left Susan sorting the latest batch of donated clothes in the back room – good ones would be steamed, torn or smelly ones went to the recycling. It was her new co-worker's first day. Susan had wanted to start straightaway, and there was no reason not to let her. The church minister had called in response to Kay's email and told her that Susan had been a keen member since she'd moved to Glasgow, was a stalwart in the Women's Guild already and volunteered in the crèche every second Sunday. Susan's landlord had been equally positive, if less gushing. Susan paid her rent on the dot each month, and was a clean and noiseless tenant. The job was offered and accepted.

'Coffee?' suggested Kay, when the customer had left. 'We always try to have it together, though it usually ends up with one of us bopping back and forth as customers come in.'

'I'd love one. Is there a kitty for tea and coffee?'

Kay explained the coffee tin procedure, then opened the packet of chocolate digestives she'd brought to celebrate Susan's first shift. 'How's your niece's baby?'

The other woman beamed, eyes shining. 'Oh, she's lovely!

I could cuddle her all day, but of course there's a queue for that. They're planning the christening soon – I can't wait! What's the news about your young friend who's expecting? I hope she's well?'

Kay dunked her biscuit. 'Blooming! She looks fabulous. She was pretty sick at the start, but that's long gone now.'

Susan turned away abruptly, fishing a tissue from her pocket and dabbing at her nose, then dimpled at Kay. 'Bet you're looking forward to getting some cuddles in, too. Maybe you can babysit for her sometime.'

The bell pinged again. 'I'll go,' said Susan, and Kay sat back in her chair, wondering if Susan had children. When the woman returned, she asked.

'No, but my niece is like a daughter to me. She and the baby are my only relatives now.'

By the end of the coffee break they'd exchanged stories about their respective nieces – Kay's lived in Italy – and she was feeling more and more positive about her new colleague.

Susan was evidently thinking the same. 'Would you like to come to me for lunch on Monday?' she said, blinking at Kay. 'We're both on the afternoon shift.'

Kay laughed. 'Go on, admit it – all you want is a lift to work afterwards!'

A second's hesitation, then Susan laughed too. They put the date in their diaries, and Kay went back to the front of the shop with a smile on her face.

***

Christine emptied the last few items from her shopping bag and stowed them around the kitchen. Ron was coming this afternoon, but Christine had little hope he would bring any new news about her mother. The unanswerable *why?* echoed around in her head. Still, perhaps the birth certificate Ron was bringing would help clarify things. Somehow, Christine had never seen her birth certificate. Sylvie had dealt with the application for her passport, the year she'd gone on a school trip to Italy, and although Christine at fifteen had signed the form, she hadn't seen all the paperwork, and of course the passport was still valid. Was she Erin Cairns on her certificate, or Christine Adams? Or Raynott?

'I'll get off now, shall I? I don't want to get in the way.' Larissa was stuffing running things into her rucksack. She and her boyfriend were taking the afternoon boat across to Arran, where they were having a long weekend running one of the trails.

'He won't be here for ages yet. Wish me luck – he's bringing my birth certificate. I hope it's… correct.'

Larissa zipped up her rucksack and came to hug Christine. 'I hope so too. Don't have the baby until I'm back, huh?'

Shock zipped through Christine when Ron arrived shortly after four. He looked worse every time she saw him now. Dark circles surrounded his eyes, and deep creases had replaced the previously thin lines across his forehead. He gave her a quick hug before sinking into the sofa, leaning his head against the back.

'Was it an awkward drive down?' Christine put a steaming mug on the coffee table for him and sat down opposite with her orange juice.

'No, no. The usual traffic in the central belt, but no obstructions.'

Christine sipped. 'Any more news about Mum?' But he'd have called her, if there had been.

Ron clutched his head in both hands in a helpless gesture

that made Christine jump. 'Where can she be, Chris? I only wish I could do more to find her.'

Christine felt like shaking him. He wasn't doing anything, was he? He'd reported Sylvie missing at Kendal, but as far as Christine knew, he hadn't pushed the police recently about finding her mother. She asked him, and he heaved a long, shaky sigh.

'What could they do? She's a grown woman. She chose to leave like that.'

Christine thought about Sylvie's odd behaviour that weekend. Not much 'grown woman' there, was there? 'She might be ill – she *was* ill, Dad! She might need treatment, or medication.' She might be dead. Was he thinking that too?

'We'd have heard if she'd been admitted to hospital. They'd have got in touch through her driving licence, or her phone. No, she's gone because she's afraid of repercussions after what she did to you.'

His voice was bitter, and Christine didn't reply. He was probably right.

She swirled the juice in her glass. 'Did you bring my birth certificate?'

He reached into the inside pocket of his jacket, lying beside him on the sofa, and pulled out a long envelope, not meeting her eyes.

Christine opened it eagerly. There she was, *Christine Erin Raynott*. So what she and Vicky had surmised was true: Sylvie had registered baby Erin Cairns as her own. The one nod to Erin's origin was the middle name. Out of guilt? Sylvie's name was there too, but no father, and the birth had been registered in Carlisle when she was six weeks old.

'This certificate's a lie, Dad. How could she register me as her daughter?'

He was hunched on the sofa, staring at clasped hands in his lap and clearly hating every minute of the conversation. He shrugged. 'When I first met your mum, I thought you *were* her own child. It was only when we were planning the wedding that she told me you were adopted. I think she thought I'd find out from your blood group or something that you couldn't be hers. She was a bit hysterical about it, and I assured her it made no difference to me. I wanted to adopt you too, but she kept putting it off and after a while I dropped the idea.'

That was Ron. The line of least resistance. Christine replaced the certificate in the envelope, then took it through to her bedroom where she locked it in her wardrobe. She would show it to Vicky next week.

She went back to the living room. 'Dad, I've been wondering. If Mum's in hiding, how can she pay for things?'

'She has her own money, remember. She inherited from her parents, and that's in a separate account. She wouldn't go short, Chris.'

Christine narrowed her eyes. Would he be able to find out if – and where – money had been lifted from that account, if he wanted to? Would the police? But Ron was so wretched now, and what would the police do, if they found out about the forged certificate? Christine's stomach sank to the floor. This was all going to come out, at the latest when she needed a certificate for her own baby. Did she really want the woman who'd brought her up to be prosecuted? Sylvie had loved her. Christine leaned back in her armchair, tapping her fingers on her thighs. What she needed was answers, but the only person who could supply them was Sylvie.

***

230

Susan's flat was off Hawthorne Street, north of the city centre. It was the first time Kay had been in this part of Glasgow, and she looked around curiously. The accommodation here was a real mixture: new red-brick houses in a little scheme to one side, older tenement blocks like her own home further along, and the high-rise flats Susan lived in. Kay parked in the visitors' area, then lifted the flowers she'd bought. This was a lovely change to her normal Monday morning-off routine.

She was approaching the door to the building when she saw the notice in the entrance: *Furnished flats to rent. 1 and 2 bed. Call…*

Surprised, she went on through the entrance hall. Did Susan live in a furnished flat? It seemed a little unusual for a woman her age. But then, she was recently separated, wasn't she? This would be a stopgap until she found something permanent. Kay went up the tiled staircase, and rang Susan's bell on the second-floor landing.

'Come in! Did you find it all right?'

Kay presented her flowers and assured Susan her satnav would find anywhere, within reason. Susan led her into the living room, and Kay's suspicion was confirmed. The room had a definite 'furnished flat' feel. Unless Susan was a whole lot poorer than she appeared to be, she wouldn't have chosen the sagging dark brown sofa and elderly black armchair, or the pine bookcase that clashed with the shabby oak coffee table. The general effect was cheerful enough, though – several plants were dotted around the room, and a trio of Charles Rennie Mackintosh prints above the fireplace added a splash of colour to faded magnolia paintwork.

Susan fussed around arranging the flowers. 'I'm living for the day when we sell the house and I can get a better place,' she said. 'Dave's still dragging his feet, unfortunately.'

'It must be hard,' said Kay, sympathetically. 'But the main thing is you're happy with your new situation.'

'Exactly. Let's have a coffee, and you can talk to me while I'm getting the pie into the oven.'

Kay leaned on the work surface in the tiny kitchen, sipping coffee and watching while Susan chopped chicken and mushrooms and assembled the pie, and they chatted about the shop and the new and expected babies in their lives. Susan had visited her niece on Saturday evening, and was full of baby Laura's gurgles and coos.

'No smiles yet, of course, but I can't wait until she gets to that stage. She's such a love. Did you see Christine at the weekend?'

'No. Her dad was down from Aberdeenshire.' Kay hesitated. She hadn't told Susan about Christine's situation; it wasn't anything she wanted to gossip about. She compromised. 'Her mum's gone off somewhere, but they're hoping she'll be back soon.'

Susan's eyes were round. 'Oh my. And the baby coming, too. I'm sure she'll come back then – she'll have to see her grandchild.'

Kay felt uncomfortable. Time to change the subject. 'You must let me see some photos of little Laura.'

Susan's arm jerked, and she nearly dropped the pie she was about to slide into the oven. 'Whoops! That was close. I have loads in an album, but I'm afraid I left it at a friend's place yesterday.'

'Don't you have any on your phone?'

'I take them with my camera – you get a better quality. I left it too, though. Let's go through while this is cooking. You can show me some of your photos from your phone, maybe?'

Later that afternoon, and pleasantly full of chicken pie, Kay was sorting through a new batch of kitchenware in the shop when her phone rang. Oh, it was Chris – was everything all right?

'Kay, I feel really odd. I've got this weird pain in my gut and my heart's going like the clappers and Larissa's still on Arran and Vicky's not answering her phone.'

She was panicking. Kay hurried in with some reassurance. 'Take nice even breaths. Are you at home?'

'Yes. It's been like this since lunchtime and oh, Kay, I feel like I'm going to pass out.'

'Hang on, lovey. I have the car here. I'll be with you in ten.'

Leaving Susan to call one of the other volunteers in, Kay drove towards the West End as speedily as traffic would allow. This could be the start of Christine's labour. Or was it a false alarm?

Christine was pale, and her hands were fluttering about the place as she described what had happened. Her face shone with sweat. Kay came to a decision.

'Let's get you checked,' she said firmly. 'Then we'll know what's what.'

Christine had a bag packed and waiting, and they set off for the hospital, where Kay supported the girl into Maternity.

The midwife checked Christine over, then patted her shoulder. 'We'll monitor you for an hour and see if anything's happening, but I don't think you're in labour. Practice contractions can be pretty intense, and you panicked, that's all.' She attached leads to Christine's bump, and switched the machine on.

They all watched as an almost straight line appeared

across the screen, and Kay squeezed Christine's hand. 'I reckon the run in the car calmed the baby down again!'

The midwife pulled a sheet over Christine. 'Something to remember for when it's here!'

Shortly after five, they were given the all-clear to go, Christine reassured that the baby was fine.

'I feel a bit daft,' she said, pulling on her trousers.

'If in doubt, get checked,' said the midwife. 'It won't be much longer now.'

Kay wandered over to the window while Christine was in the loo fixing her make-up. It was busy out there, visitors arriving after work, and some of the hospital employees would be going home, too, glad to get Monday over with. She caught a glimpse of a familiar figure disappearing into the building. Goodness – wasn't that Susan? No, she'd have said if she'd been planning a visit. They did say everyone had a double…

Kay drove back to Court Avenue, then went in with Christine and made her a cup of tea.

'Thanks, Kay – you've been brilliant,' said Christine, and Kay felt herself blush with pleasure.

Larissa was due home any time, so Kay left Christine with her feet up, reading a magazine. Home again, she sat down to call Susan – after being left alone in the shop so unceremoniously, she deserved to hear the outcome.

'False alarm, all's well,' she said cheerfully.

Susan gasped. 'Oh, thank goodness. About the all's well bit, anyway. Is she home again?'

'Yes. They said it wouldn't be too long before the real thing. Susan – were you at the hospital this afternoon? If you weren't, you have a twin – a woman I saw going into Maternity.'

A heartbeat's pause, then Susan laughed. 'It was our day for going there, wasn't it? I popped in after work with my cousin, to visit her friend. She's on bed rest.'

Kay chatted for a few minutes then rang off and poured a chilly glass of Fendant. Something was niggling her. Sipping, she thought back over the day, then frowned. How odd. Susan had said her niece and the baby were her only relatives, but now she'd spoken about a cousin.

Chapter Four

Vicky stood on the pavement, waving Ben into the tight parking space on Pollokshaws Road. It was a dismal evening; dark grey clouds spitting fat raindrops onto pavements slimy with city dirt, and a stiff breeze that was anything but summery.

'Inside, quick,' said Ben, taking Vicky's arm as they hurried the few yards to the Italian restaurant. 'I wonder what she has to say to you?'

They were meeting Deirdre, Paula's old school friend, and her husband, who were back from visiting Deirdre's parents in Orkney. Vicky thought back to the older woman's phone call. 'She said she's found some photos, so that'll be interesting, and there's something she didn't mention last time, but she thinks I should know about it.' Which would be even more interesting.

Vicky pushed the restaurant door open, and they went in, shaking the rain from their jackets.

Ben slid his umbrella into the stand behind the door. 'We're early. They won't be here yet.'

The waiter showed them to a table for four by the window, and Vicky sat down, pulling Ben into the chair beside her.

She wanted to be able to see Deirdre properly while they were talking.

The other couple arrived a few minutes later, and Deirdre introduced her husband, Paul. An odd thought went through Vicky's head. If her parents had lived, she might have known these people well. They might have been 'Auntie Deirdre and Uncle Paul' all the time she was growing up. A wave of grief and anger rose in her throat, and she swallowed it down. This part at least wasn't Sylvie's fault.

'Let's leave the complicated stuff for after food, shall we? I've printed off a load of photos for you.' Deirdre indicated the plastic bag hooked on the back of her chair.

'Definitely after food, then – I'd hate to get oil all over them.' Vicky sat back as the waiter brought wine plus bread and oil and balsamic, and took their food order.

They chatted about Deirdre's school days over tortellini, and Vicky listened avidly to funny stories about what her parents and their friends had got up to. It was… healing, she realised, soaking up the details and picturing it all in her mind.

When the waiter had removed the plates, Deirdre pulled out a large envelope. Vicky brushed away tears as she pored over the prints – ordinary kids having fun. Her parents were younger then than she was now. Come to think of it, they'd died around the age she was. Heck.

'Have they found Sylvie yet?' Deirdre leaned over the table.

'No. She's done a total runner. Christine's really upset, but I just feel angry,' said Vicky, dabbing her eyes with a tissue. Would she ever be able to look at those photos and not cry? 'What was it you thought I should know?'

Deirdre pulled an envelope from her bag and produced

more photos. 'I didn't print these off, but I will if you want them,' she said. 'I took them at your parents' wedding reception.'

Vicky accepted the handful of snaps. Wedding guests dancing, drinking, laughing – it had been a big reception. There was Sylvie, chatting to the best man. And there she was dancing with a little boy, both beaming at the camera. And there she was again, with Dad.

Vicky stared at the photo. Her father was standing with a wine glass in one hand, the other on Sylvie's shoulder, and she was laughing up at him. It was a strangely intimate picture of the two; they'd obviously known each other well. Vicky shivered. Why hadn't Sylvie kept in touch with her and Jamie? She could understand the woman not adopting all three of them, especially Jamie, but to vanish like that with Erin was… odd.

'Sylvie was in love with your dad,' said Deirdre slowly. 'It was before he got together with Paula, and to be fair I don't think he felt the same way about Sylvie. She was gutted when he split up with her, and terribly jealous of Paula. I told Sylvie several times she should move on, but she didn't seem to care. Paula never noticed, and I'm not sure Joe did either. Or if they did, they didn't care.'

Vicky sat back. 'But she stayed friends with Mum. Heck, she was her bridesmaid.'

Deirdre shrugged. 'Sylvie has no children of her own. Maybe she can't have them, and maybe she knew it, back then. Your dad was always pretty nice to her, you know. That might have given her false hope.'

Vicky's head swam, and she clenched her fists on the table top. 'No… you don't think… she kept Erin to compensate for losing Joe? And then disappeared with her?' How totally unsettling that thought was. And short of Sylvie telling them, there was no way to find out if it was true. Vicky sat struggling not to cry as Ben rubbed her back. Deirdre reached for Vicky's packet of tissues on the table top and handed one over.

Maisie's face swam into Vicky's head. Had she *agreed* to let Sylvie take Erin away so completely? It didn't sound like Maisie.

Vicky took a deep breath. 'I'll talk to Chris. One thing – Sylvie couldn't have known the hotel was going to explode, so taking Erin wasn't planned.' But vanishing with her afterwards must have been…

Vicky and Ben started back home shortly afterwards, having waved goodbye to Deirdre and Paul.

'Nice couple,' said Ben, turning up a side street to make a U-turn. 'What are you going to do about Christine?'

Vicky glanced at the clock on the dashboard. 'Nothing, tonight. I'll call her in the morning.'

***

Christine folded the last baby outfit and laid it in the drawer of small garments. Someone had brought a box of baby clothes into the shop that week, all unworn, and Kay had picked out a few for Christine to look at. She'd bought them, of course, but was there anything more sad than unused second-hand baby clothes? They were even worse than those ads you saw: *Wedding dress, size 12, never worn.*

Wistful thoughts of her birth mother followed Christine through to the kitchen. Paula would have had clothes waiting for her, little outfits she'd never worn. Christine massaged her bump, tears springing into her eyes, because right behind the sorrow about poor Paula, came the uncertainty and disbelief about Sylvie. Life could be a real bummer. It was time to put the kettle on.

Her phone buzzed while she was drinking her tea. Vicky. Good. Christine lurched through to her bedroom and lay down in careful slow-mo to chat. All this being alone was doing her head in, and she couldn't even flop onto the bed now. Roll on not being pregnant.

As soon as Vicky spoke, Christine knew this wasn't going to be a jolly ten minutes.

'Chris, honey, there's something you should know, so I'll tell you about it now, and you can have a think before we talk again, okay?'

Christine closed her eyes as she lay listening to the story of Vicky's evening out yesterday. Sylvie and Joe? What a mess this was.

'I wish you'd asked me to go too.' Christine swallowed the left-out feeling. 'I wonder if I should have a look through Mum's stuff at home? She might have something that'd give us a clue about all this, or even about where she might be. I could go up this week and see.'

'Wouldn't Ron have given anything to the police?'

'Doubt it. He had a lot of contact with the police in Kendal, but as far as I know, no one's visited him at home. The police seem convinced she's just gone off somewhere.'

Vicky sounded doubtful. 'Is it a good idea, going all that way when the baby's due so soon? What if you go into labour?'

'I'm seeing the midwife tomorrow. I could ask what she thinks. Would you come too, if I went – to Aberdeen, I mean? We could go on Saturday and come back on Sunday.'

'I'm not sure Ron would like that.' Vicky sounded more

than doubtful now, and Christine couldn't blame her.

'He can lump it. I'm sure he'll be fine, though, Vicky. He always tries to make the awkward stuff all rosy and harmless, so as far as this mess with Mum's concerned, he comes over as uncooperative, but he's not really. I'll handle him.'

'I don't understand how he's able to ignore what she's done.'

'That'll be one reason she got together with him in the first place. He wouldn't ask too many leading questions about Sylvie 'adopting' me.'

Vicky's sigh blew down the phone. 'If the midwife okays it, I'll come. I'll drive. Call me after your appointment tomorrow.'

Christine ended the call and allowed her thoughts to drift. Tomorrow was another day.

***

Vicky slowed down as they swept past Dundee and continued north. 'This is new land for me. Pity we're not on the coast road.'

Christine glanced at the satnav. 'We should hit Stonehaven in an hour or so – that's by the sea, and it's a good place for lunch.'

Vicky concentrated on the road. They'd left Glasgow at ten, and were planning to arrive at Christine's old home by mid-afternoon. This allowed for a couple of generous stops. Vicky still wasn't happy about taking her heavily pregnant sister so far away from the maternity unit she was booked into, but the midwife had said there was no sign of labour starting any time soon, so here they were.

'Have you had any more thoughts about your birth

certificate?' asked Vicky, when they were sitting in a seafront café in Stonehaven, pancakes and maple syrup in front of them.

Christine sloshed a piece of pancake around in her syrup, then leaned forward to transfer it to her mouth. She waved her fork, chewing. 'I did some research online, and as far as I could see it's a full certificate. And apparently if I'd been adopted, Sylvie would have needed to provide an adoption certificate to get a birth certificate. So I ordered a copy of all my birth documentation, and the certificate that came is identical. That seems to be proof I was never adopted.'

Vicky swallowed her impatience. 'You have to get that sorted, Chris. Now you know it's false, you can't use that certificate.'

'I know. I'll do it. But it would be nice to talk to Mum before they yank her off to prison for stealing me. Anyway, I can't report it without at least telling Dad first.'

Vicky was silent. It jarred horribly every time Christine said 'Mum' or 'Dad', but she didn't like to say anything in case she sounded too critical. The new sibling relationship was so much more painful than she'd anticipated the day she started the search for Erin.

At Stonehaven, they had a walk along the beach in companionable almost-silence, then continued the journey and arrived at Christine's home at three o'clock. Vicky took a moment to appreciate the beauty – what a lovely place to grow up. Money obviously wasn't an issue here, and there was fresh air and fields to play in everywhere you turned. Lucky Chris. Poor Erin.

Ron had left a note to say he'd been called into work but would be back at five, so Vicky went for a walk round the garden, leaving Christine to search through Sylvie's things.

The younger girl joined her after just twenty minutes.

'Apart from baby snaps of me, I can't find any photos that predate Dad, and nothing that would help find her. It's as if she deliberately got rid of everything with a connection to her old life.'

Vicky sighed. Another dead end.

Ron arrived at five with a bag full of groceries. 'Pizza from the Italian place you like, so all we need to do is heat it up,' he said cheerfully, adding, 'We can talk over food,' when Vicky caught his eye.

She leaned against the work surface. 'We have a couple of things we'd like your opinion on before Christine takes them further.'

Ron's lips were a thin slash, but Vicky wasn't sorry she'd spoken. Best to make it clear right at the start things would be going further. She wasn't going to let Ron sweet-talk Chris into letting everything slide.

The pizza was good, and talk about Aberdeen kept them going until coffee. Ron listened, his face expressionless while Christine told him about Deirdre's photos, and Sylvie being infatuated with Joe.

When she had finished there was silence round the table. Ron sat with his glass clutched in front of him, breathing quickly and staring at the table top.

'Dad?' Christine leaned forwards.

'It was a long time ago, Chris – your mum was a youngster. I wouldn't think it had any bearing on her adopting you. Having a crush on someone doesn't make her mentally ill.'

Vicky felt like a pressure cooker in imminent danger of exploding. This man was deluding himself as much as his wife was. Fortunately, Christine was already halfway down his throat.

'For God's sake, Dad – that's the whole point. She *didn't* adopt me. And she *is* ill. She might need urgent help now, and she might not be getting it.'

Vicky almost applauded, but Ron's reply was nothing but peeved.

'Christine, there's no indication that your mother's in trouble. I'm convinced she'll come home–'

'Why?' Vicky banged the table in her frustration. 'I don't understand why you're so blasé about it. She's been gone for months, Ron. Why should she come back now?'

His eyes slid away. 'She deserves a chance to come home and put things right.'

Vicky lost it completely. 'Nothing will ever be right. Sylvie abducted – yes, she did – she *abducted* my sister. Heaven knows how much grief that caused my great-aunt, and it deprived Jamie, Erin and me of the chance to grow up together and personally, Ron, I can't forgive that. You want things to be fine and good again. Well, they won't be.'

'That's why we have to make the bes–'

Vicky stood up. 'The *best* of it? There is nothing here that will ever be remotely 'best'. Don't you see how hard this is for Chris?'

'Vicky.' Christine gripped her arm and shook it. 'Let me talk.'

Vicky fell silent but remained on her feet while Christine spoke quietly, her eyes fixed on Ron's.

'Dad. *Ron*. This is what we're going to do. In a week or so I'll be having this baby, and after I do I'll go personally to register it. I'll take my birth certificate along and explain there's a problem, and ask their advice. I'm pretty sure they'll take it further. So you have until then to find Sylvie and get things 'sorted'. And now my sister and I are going back to

Aberdeen to find a hotel for the night.'

She rose, and Vicky followed her out to the car.

'Are you sure about leaving him? You can stay if you like, though I'll go to a hotel. You were great in there, by the way. I'm sorry I lost my temper.'

'I'm sure,' said Christine. 'It's tough, but it might make him understand. I'll call him in the morning before we start for home.'

She got into the car and sat cuddling her bump. Vicky hesitated before turning the key in the ignition. 'You okay?'

Christine gave her a wry grin. 'Please don't keep asking. I'll tell you as soon as I'm not okay – okay?'

Vicky nodded sheepishly. She reversed into the road and turned the car towards Aberdeen. If the journey had done little else, it had cranked her relationship with Chris to a new level of intimacy. It was worth it for that alone.

Chapter Five

Tuesday, 17th July

The shop door swung open and Kay rushed to hold it for the woman struggling in with three boxes piled on top of each other.

'There's more in the car. It's all right just to bring stuff, isn't it?'

'Yes, of course. Let me help you.' Kay took the boxes and laid them on the counter, then propped the door open and followed the woman to a Ford Escort parked ten yards away. The inside space was jam-packed with stuff. Kay grimaced. They had scenes like this several times a week, and it was usually a grieving son or daughter bringing a carful of a parent's earthly goods.

'You're breaking up a household?' she said sympathetically, allowing the woman to pile bags and boxes into her arms.

'My mum's. She passed away two weeks ago. I can't take all this stuff. I hope you can make use of some of it, at least.'

'Oh, we can use most things,' said Kay, leading the way back inside, where Susan was busy with a customer. 'Anything that can't be sold is recycled in another way. And it's for a good cause, so thank you very much.'

The woman sniffed, and Kay thought back to the time

she'd had to do the same thing for her father's home. It wasn't easy.

'Stay and have a cuppa,' she said, when the last bag was in the shop. She settled the woman, whose name was Connie, in the back room, and put the kettle on. Charity shops dealt out charity in more ways than one.

She was listening to Connie's account of her mother's funeral when Susan put her head round the door.

'We're out of tenners. Shall I run across to the newsagent's? There's no one here.'

'Please. I'll listen for the bell.'

Susan disappeared, and the shop door banged behind her.

'Your assistant looks familiar,' said Connie, frowning into her cup. 'I'm sure I've met her somewhere recently.'

'She hasn't long been in Glasgow,' said Kay, realising she had no idea where Susan had moved from. Funny, the things you don't discuss…

'She could have been in our shop,' said Connie, putting her mug on the table. 'We have a jeweller's at the other end of Argyle Street.'

'The posh, city end?' said Kay, smiling, glad when Connie smiled back.

'Posh pure, that's us. Thanks for the tea – I feel better now. I'll leave you to it.'

On the way back to the door, Connie stopped to spin a stand of costume jewellery.

'I have this dream we might find something valuable one day,' said Kay, as Connie lifted a chain with a silver cross, then replaced it.

'Hm. I don't think it's here today, unfortunately. But I've remembered where I met your assistant. She bought a pendant a few months ago and wanted it engraved, but we

247

couldn't do it immediately. She was quite cross about it. I'll pop off before she gets back.' She grinned at Kay and ran back to her car.

The rest of the morning was uneventful, and Kay handed over to the two afternoon volunteers at one o'clock then went through to the back for her jacket. She would go home via the good baker's shop and get some apple cake – Chris was coming for afternoon tea. Perhaps Susan would like to come, too.

'Fancy coming back to mine for apple cake this afternoon? You'd meet Chris.'

Susan's head shot up, and she dropped her handbag. 'Oh! Yes – no – what a pity, I have an appointment at the bank at half past two, and it might be a long one. I'm so sorry. Another time, perhaps?'

Her laugh was half hysterical, and Kay gaped at the other woman. It wasn't such a big deal. Or did Susan feel bad because it was the first time Kay had invited her home?

'Hey, no problem,' she said, leading the way to the door. 'Tell you what, why don't we pop across the road and have a ploughman's in The Fox and Badger instead? A half of cider and some cheddar sounds about right to me.'

Susan agreed gushingly, and they stood on the pavement, waiting for a break in the traffic. Kay took her new friend's arm on the way across the street. Susan was a complicated creature, but she meant well.

***

Christine gathered up the last few crumbs of cake, then put her fork down. She hadn't expected to manage such a huge chunk, but Kay was right. It was the best apple cake ever.

'How was your trip to Aberdeen?' Kay poured them both more coffee.

Christine slumped in her chair. 'I've given Dad an ultimatum.' She told Kay about the birth certificate, and the other woman sighed.

'I think you're right to get that sorted, but it might be better to do it before the baby comes and you have broken nights and babysitters to worry about.'

'You could be right, but I don't have much time left – my due date's this week. In a way, I'm really sorry for Ron, but he makes me so mad, too. Whatever Mu– Sylvie did before he met her wasn't his fault, and neither is whatever she's doing now. I just hope nothing awful's happened to her. Vicky thinks I should go to the police.'

'That's a big decision. I think your idea of reporting your certificate when you register the baby is a good one. They'll know what has to be done.'

Christine sat straighter. She would call Ron when she was home again, and then she'd decide. Whatever Ron thought, someone should be actively looking for Sylvie.

Half an hour later, she was sitting on the sofa at home with her mobile. Ron answered on the first ring.

'Chris – I had the phone in my hand to call you. Everything okay?'

'Fine. Any news?'

'Nothing specific yet. I'm sorry about the weekend. I've done some thinking, and I've hired a private investigator to look into your mum's disappearance. He's starting around Carlisle, as that's where she registered you. I can't think of anywhere else she might have gone. Apart from Glasgow when she was a kid, the only other place I know Sylvie lived is Aberdeen, where we met. I don't think she'll be in either of these places; there'd be too many people who might recognise her.'

'Can't you trace her via her bank account?'

'I wouldn't know how to begin, but it's a good point. I'll tell the PI.'

Christine said goodbye and rang off to call Vicky, who was pleased to hear about the PI but dubious about Carlisle.

'I don't see her going anywhere so obvious, do you?'

'Hard to say. She wasn't thinking straight, last time I saw her.'

Christine chatted for a few minutes, then rang off and went to run a bath, and wow, this might be the last bath before the baby came. She should make the most of the solitude.

***

The first pain came on Thursday morning when Christine was walking up Byres Road, and she hunched her back, gripping her handbag and breathing slowly. The 'practice contractions' hadn't been coming so often for the past few days, but this was a hefty one.

'Are you all right, hen?' A woman was staring at her, a poodle clutched under one arm and a concerned expression on her face. She stepped closer and the dog growled.

The contraction eased off, and Christine straightened up. 'I'm fine, thanks. They're just practice contractions.'

'Looks like the real event isn't far off. Good luck!'

The woman moved away, and Christine continued on her way home. Every day was exciting now – waking up with the feeling that this could be the day she'd meet her baby. To think she'd contemplated adoption…

She massaged her bump and was rewarded by a faint kick.

'It's just you and me, baby,' she whispered as she continued up Court Avenue. 'But don't worry. I've got your back.'

Maybe the very reason she wasn't giving her baby away was because she'd been taken herself. Christine mulled this over as she climbed the stairs to her flat. She should stop being so introspective. It would– oh hell, another pain. She stumbled into the hallway.

An hour and three further contractions later, and Christine knew it was for real this time. Her baby was coming today. Or tomorrow, if she was unlucky. Larissa was at work in the hospital, but it wasn't quite time to go there. Christine lifted her phone and called Vicky.

'Ooh! I'll be right over. Got your bag ready?'

'Uh-huh.' Christine went to get it from her wardrobe, and laid it by the front door.

She felt better when Vicky arrived, and spent the next few hours alternately walking around the flat, and lolling on the sofa. By three in the afternoon she was ready to go to the hospital for some kind of pain relief.

Larissa met them in Maternity, her eyes shining. 'You can do this, Chris. We're all cheering you on.'

It was true. Most of the staff from the rehab unit came by and waved from the door of Christine's room over the next hour. Eventually, the midwife hung up a 'no visitors' sign. 'Let's have this baby.'

Christine paced up and down the labour room, Larissa by her side. Up and down and up and down, and it seemed as if the pains would never stop.

Vicky was perched on the edge of her chair. 'Don't you want to lie down?'

Christine shook her head and wiped a hand over a face slick with sweat. 'Another one.' She leaned her forearms on the bed, sucking greedily at the gas and air machine.

Vicky gripped her free hand from the other side of the bed, and Christine held on tightly. Oh God, this wasn't like the other pains, this was–

'It's coming!' she screamed, and the midwife made a grab for the baby sliding out.

'Whoa – here we are! One speedy baby! I've got… her – it's a little girl!'

Christine clutched the baby the midwife was passing up to her. Shivering and laughing, she allowed the others to help her onto the bed, and here she was, cuddling the next generation.

Vicky was leaning over the bed, her face pink. 'Congratulations, Chris, she's gorgeous! You did so well!'

Christine kissed the baby, dripping a tear onto blonde fuzz on its head. This baby would always know who its mother was.

'Oh, Vicky – a girl! And I'm calling her Erin Joy.'

***

Anticipation fizzing inside her, Vicky lifted the bag with the present and ran down to her car. This was the best way ever to spend Friday morning – with her sister and her day-old niece. She drove across the river and turned towards the hospital. The first part of the trip was the same route she took going to Jamie. One day soon they would take little Erin Joy to see her uncle; oh, what would Jamie think? He didn't often see a baby, unless someone's visitors brought one in.

The maternity unit was busy, with four-bedded bays around a nursing station in the middle. Christine was sitting beside her bed, and Vicky ran to hug her.

'You look great – did you sleep okay? How's the baby? Hello, Erin Joy! Chris, I'm so glad you chose Erin. Mum would be, too, I'm sure.' She bent over the see-though crib. Little Erin had sparse blonde hair and the usual baby smudge of a nose, and she was asleep, small hands tucked under her chin.

Christine joined her, and touched the baby's cheek with one finger. 'She's great. I wanted her to have a family name. At first I thought of Erin Paula, or Erin Maisie, but then–' She looked at Vicky, her face vulnerable. 'You remember our mother and Maisie, and I don't, and you might want to call your daughter Paula one day. And I wanted her to know how much she means to me, in spite of how I got pregnant. So it's Erin Joy.'

A lump rose in Vicky's throat. 'Oh, sweetheart, you're every bit as much Mum's daughter and Maisie's great-niece as I am. But Erin Joy is the perfect name.'

Christine kissed the baby. 'We'll need to have lots more daughters for the other names, that's all.' Gripping the armrests, she lowered herself into the cushioned chair by her bed.

Vicky winced in sympathy. 'When are you going home?'

'Tomorrow morning. Kay called; she says she'll pop over regularly until I'm fully fit again.'

'She's a star. And of course the same goes for me, even though I'm not just around the corner. We'll all rally round. And talking of families, I brought you this.' Vicky handed over the parcel she'd gift-wrapped. 'It was Maisie's. I thought you and Erin might like it.'

Christine pulled the paper away and held up Maisie's paisley shawl. 'It's lovely,' she whispered. 'My first family heirloom.'

She draped the shawl over her shoulders, and tears came into Vicky's eyes. Christine's face was turned towards her sleeping child, the decades-old blue shawl round her neck and a new peace in her eyes. Vicky leaned back in her chair, feeling the same peace in her soul. Erin was here. Chris had been through so much, and it was still ongoing, as far as Sylvie was concerned, but keeping the baby was definitely the right way forward.

***

It was wonderful to be away from the noisy maternity ward. Christine had the headache from hell because she'd barely slept since giving birth, she was leaking from places she really didn't want to leak from, and her boobs felt like hot air balloons gone wrong – but oh, the quiet in the flat.

'Lunch coming up,' said Larissa, beating eggs for an omelette. 'Then you can skedaddle off to bed and sleep while Erin and I entertain each other. When are you expecting Ron?'

'The usual. Four-ish. Vicky's coming too,' said Christine, holding the baby upright for a post-feed burp.

She waddled into her bedroom half an hour later. The silence was divine, and it was still there when she awoke. Christine stretched luxuriously. Ten past three. Fifty minutes until Ron appeared to see the baby who was no relation to him, and presumably to try and talk her out of reporting her false birth certificate next week.

Erin was fast asleep, and Christine grinned at Larissa. 'You've been brilliant, but I don't want to take up your entire Saturday. Doing anything nice tonight?'

'Jason and I are going for an Indian. I'll be breathing

pakora over you later.' She blew a kiss at the baby and left Christine alone with her daughter.

Ron arrived first, and bent over the baby in her carrycot on the sofa, his face expressionless. Abruptly, he turned and handed Christine an envelope, then sat staring at her while she slid out a card and four crisp fifty-pound notes.

'I didn't know what you'd need,' he said, twisting his hands together. 'Your mum'll be better at this. I'm sure she'll have lots of ideas when she's home.'

Christine put the notes back into the envelope. What planet was the man on? But everything would soon be out in the open; she didn't need to rant at him.

'Thank you. I'll put it towards a good pushchair for when she's older.'

The doorbell rang and Christine limped – she was so looking forward to not being sore – into the hallway to admit Vicky and Ben with a huge bunch of flowers already in a vase.

'I didn't want you to have to fuss with vases.' Vicky put the bouquet on the shelf in the living room. 'Hi, Ron. Down for the weekend?'

He nodded, but Christine noticed he wasn't meeting Vicky's eyes.

'No news of Sylvie?' Ben was bending over the baby. He straightened up and went to perch on the arm of the sofa.

'Not yet.'

'Let's hope the authorities find her quickly, once Chris registers the baby next week,' said Vicky, and Christine was surprised at the gentleness in her sister's voice. But then, you only had to look at Ron to see he was suffering – the bags under his eyes were as big as her own, and didn't his cheeks use to be fuller?

He shot Christine a hunted look. 'I was going to suggest you wait up with registering the baby. It would give Sylvie more time to come home.'

Christine dropped her eyes. Thank heavens Vicky and Ben were here too – they'd back her up.

'I'm doing it next week,' she said flatly. 'It needs to be done, Ron, private investigator or no private investigator. Sylvie isn't coming home. I don't understand how you can still think that.'

To her horror, he began to weep, face buried in his hands. Christine and Vicky met each other's eyes, and Christine saw the same pity she was feeling, but mingled with Vicky's frustration.

'Ron. This isn't what Chris needs now,' said Ben, getting up to stand in front of the other man. 'Come on. I'll buy you a beer at your hotel.'

It was all Christine could do not to burst into tears in sympathy. The door closed behind the two men, and Vicky came to hug Christine.

'Ben'll look after him, Chris. He'll come to see that he's not thinking straight about Sylvie.'

Christine clutched her head. 'He was my father all those years. I can't believe what's happened to my life.'

'I know. Me too, and it must be worse for you. Hang on in there.'

A mew came from the cot, and Christine lifted the baby and sat cuddling her. She had her baby. And her brother and sister. She would manage, with or without answers from Sylvie.

Chapter Six

Tuesday, 24th July

Kay hurried along Argyle Street. She was late for work; she'd gone by to see if Chris wanted anything from the big supermarket she was going to after work that afternoon, and stayed for a cuddle with the baby.

Susan was already in the shop, hanging jackets on the circular rack, and Kay could smell the mixture of humidity and damp material that lingered around the shop when the steamer had been in use. She glanced at her watch. Twenty-six minutes to nine. It could have been worse. Thank goodness Susan had a key now.

'You've got the steamer going early today,' she remarked, going into the back room to leave her bag and jacket.

'I've been up since six, so I thought I might as well come in and get started,' said Susan.

She sounded snappy, and Kay went out to join her. 'Everything okay? You sound a bit down.'

Susan clunked the last hanger on the rack. 'I'm tired, that's all. I was babysitting for Mona last night, so it was a late one, though of course it was lovely to be with baby Laura. And you'll never guess what Mona told me.' She stared at Kay, her eyes round, indignation positively streaming from her.

'What? Is the baby all right?'

'Oh yes. But a woman Mona knows, such a lovely person – she's a bit older, and incredibly kind and caring – she was looking after a little girl she wanted to adopt. She'd had her for months, *years*, and then the birth mother decided she wasn't going to give the child up and the adoption fell through. She was *gutted*. Things like that shouldn't be allowed. *Years* of her life she gave that child, and now…'

Kay listened, initial sympathy turning into concern. There was spit in the corners of Susan's mouth, and she could barely articulate. She wasn't looking at Kay, either, and it felt as if the tirade was as much for herself as for anyone else. Eventually she paused for breath and Kay jumped in.

'Can the authorities do anything? Social workers, or fostering people?'

Susan almost spat the answer. 'Useless, the lot of them. Birth mothers have all the rights. My blood boils when I think of it.'

Kay moved round the clothes rack and put a hand on Susan's shoulder. 'Poor soul – come round the back and we'll have a quick cuppa.'

She went to put the kettle on, glad when Susan followed her into the back room. The other woman's hands shook as she grasped the mug Kay gave her, but she was quiet now, sipping slowly. The lines around her mouth were more pronounced today, and her face was bleak.

'Do you know the woman?' asked Kay. If it was a friend, she could understand the anguish, but Susan had said 'a woman Mona knows'.

Susan's eyes were swimming. She shrugged, blinking. 'No. But all she's ever wanted was a little girl to love and bring up, and now that's being taken away from her. It's heart-breaking.'

'It may still work out for the best. The birth mother could change her mind,' said Kay, regretting the words the moment they were out. She didn't want to set Susan off again.

Susan's lips were still trembling. 'She won't, I'm afraid. It's quite hopeless.'

Her head sank while she heaved an enormous sigh, then she braced her shoulders and gave Kay a shaky smile. 'Sorry. I shouldn't let it get to me. Do you have any photos of Christine's baby yet?'

Kay reached into the drawer where her handbag was and pulled out her mobile. Thank heavens for a change of subject; that had been intense. She opened the gallery on her phone and Susan cooed over the collection, her eyes soft.

Kay remembered about the niece's baby photos. 'Have you collected your pics of little Laura yet?'

Susan leaned back in her chair. 'I'll get them this week, I hope. Meanwhile, I'll enjoy yours – what a little love baby Erin is!' She went back to a miniature photo on Kay's phone, one finger stroking the baby's face.

The shop bell went and Kay hurried out to the main room. She helped an elderly woman try on 'a nice blouse for Mandy's wedding', then found her a string of pearl beads to complement the blouse. Kay waved as her satisfied customer set off up Argyle Street.

In the back shop, Susan was wielding the steamer again, shaking the folds from a grey linen jacket.

Kay lifted a bag of books waiting to go out. 'I keep forgetting to ask – how's the woman you know, the one on bedrest in Maternity?'

Susan shrugged, her eyes blank. 'Oh – um, fine, I think. I haven't seen her again. At least she'll get to keep her baby…'

She went back to the jacket, her head turned away.

Kay took the books through to the bookshelf. There must be something in Susan's past that was making her so uptight about this adoption story today. It wasn't logical for her to be this upset about someone she'd never met.

The steamer hissed unremittingly in the back shop as Kay filled her bookshelf. Poor Susan.

***

A thin baby wail came from the Moses basket at the other end of the sofa, and Christine dragged her eyes open. She'd been half asleep for the past hour. She inched over until she was beside the baby. Erin's face was red, and small fists waved in the air as the wails increased in volume.

'There, my lovely. I'm right here.' The howls continued. Christine put a hand on the baby's face and stroked gently. Eventually she lifted Erin and rocked her, but it was a clean nappy and some grub her daughter was after, wasn't it? Would she manage that without dying of exhaustion? Her head heavy with fatigue, Christine changed the wet nappy for a dry one, then sat with closed eyes, the baby suckling valiantly on her left boob. At least the wails had stopped.

She sat for a while after the feed, but Erin was still fussy, and eventually Christine got up and walked around the flat, feeling the warm baby solidness against her shoulder and trying to convince herself she could do this. That she wanted to do this. But yes, that was now a definite, even though she hated how she was feeling today and if Larissa didn't come home soon she didn't know what she would do. Eventually, Erin fell asleep against Christine's shoulder. Good... Please, baby, please don't wake up. Back in the basket with you.

Christine laid the baby down and stepped back, then froze as the doorbell shrilled into the flat. She held her breath, but Erin didn't waken. Christine dragged her feet to the door.

'Kay – come in. I'll make a cuppa, shall I?'

'I'm so glad you're here. I need some advice from someone who knows what they're talking about.'

'What's up?' Startled, Christine led the way to the kitchen, and put the kettle on while her friend perched on the edge of a chair.

Kay was nervous. Her hands were moving around in front of her, and her eyes were twice as large as usual. And she hadn't even asked about the baby.

'I've lost my phone. I don't know if it dropped out of my bag somewhere, or if it's been stolen, or what. And you hear so much about people's email and bank accounts getting hacked…'

At least it was something fresh to think about. Christine reached for mugs, then leaned against the work surface while the kettle boiled. 'It's definitely lost?'

'Yes. I was at the shop until lunchtime, then I went to the supermarket and had a wander round the shops at Braehead. I didn't notice it was gone until I arrived home an hour or so ago. I went back to the shop and searched for it, but it was nowhere to be found, so I called Susan with the shop phone, but she hadn't seen it. It could have been stolen from my bag somewhere, or maybe it fell out when I was paying for something, and I suppose it's not impossible someone went into the back shop and lifted it this morning. We were busy, we were often both in the main room. What should I do?'

'You should change your email password,' said Christine, racking her brains. She didn't know much about this kind of thing either, but she knew who did. 'I'll send Vicky's Ben a quick message, shall I? He's one of those clever IT people. He really helped me when I couldn't open a file last week.'

She left Kay to make the tea while she tapped out her message, then pressed send.

The reply pinged in two minutes later. *Call you in 5.*

Kay relaxed visibly. 'Thank goodness. I feel so helpless with technological stuff. Anyway, how was your day? How did you get on registering Erin's birth?'

Christine propped an elbow on the table and rested her head on her hand. It was hard to judge how she'd got on. The registrar had been incredulous about the Sylvie story, and had taken all the details, as well as Christine's birth certificate 'to check', and a copy of the DNA test result that proved she and Vicky were full siblings.

Christine related all this to Kay. 'He said it might well be a police thing, but they'll get back to me in a day or two. Meanwhile, Erin's registered, though I don't have a full certificate yet.'

Her mobile buzzed as Ben's call came in. Christine handed the phone to Kay and went to make sure the baby was still asleep. When she returned, her phone was on the table and Kay was looking happier.

'He's coming round to help me on my laptop. We'll get my passwords changed and anything else done, too. He said he'll drop Vicky off here to visit you. What a nice young man he is. Thank you so much, Chris.'

Christine went to the door with Kay, then flopped down on the sofa, smiling in spite of the tiredness. Kay had helped her so much with stuff from the shop and everything, and now she'd been able to help Kay. It was a good feeling.

***

Friday morning sunshine was streaming down as Vicky drove across town to the West End. Today was an important day in their new family life; she and Chris were taking baby Erin to visit Jamie, and hopefully, Chris would be in better shape than yesterday.

She pulled up outside Christine's flat. The girl was waiting on the pavement, the baby in her carrier over one arm and the folded buggy on the ground beside them.

'What a love she is,' said Vicky, accepting the carrier and belting it carefully into the back seat.

'She was less lovely at four this morning,' said Christine, sinking into the passenger seat and leaning back, her eyes closed.

Vicky got in too and turned the key in the ignition. 'Well, she's sleeping like a baby now. I can't wait to see how Jamie reacts to her.'

Christine nodded, and Vicky drove without speaking. Half an hour's nap would do Chris good. They were having a picnic lunch with Jamie, so hopefully he and Erin wouldn't take one look at each other and start howling.

They were approaching the home when Christine gave a little snore. Vicky grinned and pulled into a lane fifty yards from the car park. A moment's pause while her sister rearranged her hair and un-smudged her lipstick might be an idea.

'Wha– are we there?'

'Another minute. I thought you might prefer to arrive looking less, um, natural.'

Christine stuck her tongue out, then rummaged for her make-up bag and peered into her mirror. Vicky looked on indulgently. It did feel more like sisters with Chris now. They were going to make it past the sordidness and the tragedy of their separate pasts.

The car park was empty of people, and Vicky left Chris and the baby in the car while she ran up to the unit for Jamie. It was a lovely day – perfect for a walk in the grounds.

'Actually, Vicky, it might be better if you didn't take Jamie outside today.' Steve, the head of the unit, came out of his office while Vicky was in the coat cupboard looking for Jamie's jacket. 'He didn't sleep well – he's been a bit off-colour all week. Nothing specific, but it's breezy out and we don't want to take any risks.'

Vicky could only agree. She phoned down to Chris while Steve settled Jamie into the interview room where they could be undisturbed.

Jamie's reaction to the baby was sweet: he stared for a moment, then opened his mouth in a big, goofy, dribbly grin, his eyes shining. Erin was in Christine's arms, and Vicky guided Jamie's hand to touch the baby's head. Another smile flickered over Jamie's face as Erin blinked up at him, then he twisted his head round to look at Vicky. She hugged him. Jamie and Erin. What a bittersweet moment.

Back in Glasgow, Vicky dropped Christine and the baby off, and was turning the car to return to the main road when her phone rang. She pulled in to the side. Kay didn't often call her; hopefully nothing was wrong.

'Vicky, you said once you were looking for a travel cot for your flat – an almost-new one came in today. Do you want to see it?'

'Yes! Are you there now? I could swing past on the way home.'

Vicky parked ten yards away from the charity shop, inwardly blessing Kay, who had provided Christine with most of her baby equipment. It was good to know her sister had such a supportive friend.

Kay was draping a red handbag over the shoulder of a mannequin in the shop window, and Vicky waved from the pavement.

'Looking good,' she said, as Kay stepped back into the front room. As usual, it was jam-packed with goods, but apart from a teenager investigating the jewellery stand, the place was empty of customers. The steamer was hissing away in the back room.

'I change the window once a week at least – makes us more eye-catching,' said Kay. 'Time for a cuppa?'

Vicky shook her head. 'Ben and I are going to a posh work dinner tonight – his work. I need to get home to make myself suitably elegant.'

'I'm sure you'll look lovely. He was so nice about my mobile and laptop, Vicky. And the stupid thing is, the phone was here all the time. It had fallen down the back of the handbag drawer in the back room.'

A smile curved round Vicky's mouth. 'Ben's a lamb, and he loves tinkering like that, so don't worry. I'm really happy you've found me a cot for little Erin's visits. I want to help Chris as much as I can.'

The teenager left the shop without buying anything, and Kay pushed the door more firmly shut after her.

'I'll get the cot, and you can meet my friend Susan,' she said, hurrying into the back.

Vicky wandered over to the bookshelf. She was leafing through the photos in a book about glaciers when Kay came back out, a large, slim box in her arms and her brow furrowed.

'Susan can't come out; she's having a kind of migraine attack. Cluster headaches, she said. She's in agony.'

'Oh, they're horrible,' said Vicky, opening the box. 'One

of my colleagues in Manchester had them – he couldn't even sit still. They only lasted twenty minutes or so, but it was grim to see. I'll meet Susan another time.'

Uncomfortably conscious of Susan pacing up and down in the back shop, Vicky examined the cot and paid for it. Kay opened the door for her and they stood outside.

'I hope your friend's better soon,' said Vicky, balancing the box on her foot.

'She's the nervous type.' Kay glanced over her shoulder. 'Very nice, though. Hasn't long been in Glasgow. I'd better go and see if she needs anything.'

Vicky said goodbye, and slid the cot into the back seat of her Clio. Auntie Vicky was ready to babysit.

Chapter Seven

Saturday, 28th July

K ay drove along Argyle Street, hoping Susan wouldn't have another headache today. It had been terrible to watch yesterday; the poor woman had stumbled up and down the back shop, her head clutched in both hands, throaty moans coming from her throat for a full half-hour before the pain eased. Kay had gone home that evening and googled cluster headaches. Apparently they were even more painful than migraines, and often came every day for a while.

Susan arrived at the shop a few minutes after Kay, looking her usual self.

'Don't worry. They never last longer than half an hour,' she said, when Kay asked how she was. 'I get them nearly every day for a week or so, then that's it for months on end. Not a big deal. I'm sorry I didn't get to meet Christine's sister, though. Christine must be glad to have her close by. Family's so important, isn't it? And friends, of course.'

Kay frowned. According to the internet, cluster headaches could be a pretty big deal. But maybe Susan's weren't as bad as some. She put it to the back of her mind. 'I was round at Chris's last night,' she said. 'Erin's such a love.'

'You must let me know if you're ever babysitting,' said

Susan, switching the steamer on. 'I can come and keep you company. I was at Mona's again last night. I'd have called it off, but they had theatre tickets and Mona's been looking forward to it for ages. I couldn't let her down, but I'm half-dead this morning.'

'You should have called me,' said Kay. 'I'd have gone with you. Imagine if you'd had a headache while you were alone with the baby.'

'Oh, I never have more than one a day,' said Susan, confirming Kay's thought that she didn't have the worst kind of cluster headaches.

Two women came into the shop, and Susan went forward to help them, chatting brightly about the new blouses they had in. Kay watched her. No sign of tiredness now, anyway, but Susan was the type to exaggerate, bless her. Kay began to sort through a new bag of clothes, thinking about Susan's babysitting offer. Maybe she could help babysit for Mona's Laura, too. That would be fun.

***

Christine lay in bed, gazing at her daughter in the crib attached to her bed. It was another of Kay's finds, and it made all the difference. Erin was lying in what was basically an extension of Christine's bed, so all she needed to do in the night was reach out and touch the baby when she cried. And she'd just had the best sleep since giving birth.

Christine slid out of bed, scooped up her clothes and went for a quick shower. Hallelujah, she could blob all day. Larissa was home so it wouldn't be lonely, and Kay or Vicky might come by. She would phone Ron, too, and hopefully catch him before he hit the golf course. Had the PI found out anything new?

She made tea and sat in the kitchen thinking about the articles she'd read online last night. According to those who knew, parents could expect to pay around a quarter of a million pounds to raise their children to adulthood. It had given her what you might call a nasty jolt. Two hundred and fifty grand was a lot of money, and it made the twenty grand Drew had given her look like a bad excuse. When was he planning on paying the other hundred and five thousand of his share?

And now it was Saturday morning. Christine picked up her phone – there was every chance Drew was still in bed with his wife this minute. Schadenfreude filled her as she pictured the scene: Drew half-asleep, grabbing his mobile, seeing who it was and stumbling from the room. But that might put him into the mood to refuse a request for money. On the other hand, the law was on her side, and a DNA test would prove whose child Erin was. Christine pressed connect.

Oh. It was one of those 'the number you want to call is no longer available' messages. Had he changed his number? Well, that wouldn't work. She could still get Drew through Ron.

She was swallowing her last bite of toast when Erin wailed from the bedroom. Breakfast and a change of clothes had the baby content again, by which time Larissa was up and dying for a cuddle. Christine left them to it. Time to call sunny Aberdeenshire.

Ron sounded pretty down, and Christine's heart sank. He asked after her and Erin, though, and Christine was drawing breath to mention Drew casually when he hurried on.

'I was going to call you today – the PI phoned last night.

He has some information about your mother's past, he said, and he wants to meet me tomorrow afternoon. He said it was 'potentially a little upsetting'. I can't imagine what that means.'

Christine's brain was whirring. The logistics of getting to Aberdeen by the following afternoon were tricky, but she wanted to hear what the PI said with her own ears. Ron was capable of making the most upsetting event in the world sound like a day at the seaside. Still, at least he'd told her about it.

'Could I be there on Skype while you talk to him?'

'You can be there in person; we're meeting in Glasgow. I'm driving down in the morning.'

Christine made a note of the time and place, then chatted about various Aberdeen friends before eventually working round to Drew and Jess.

'It'll be a while before I see them again, if ever,' said Ron. 'They've gone to Australia to join Drew's brother, and the idea is they'll stay there. He said the permits and so on were all applied for, and they're hoping to have it settled within the next few months.'

Christine slumped. Had he done this to get away from her and the baby – his baby? 'That sounds very sudden. Or had they been planning it for ages?'

'No idea. They've never mentioned it to me.'

Christine ended the call, struggling not to cry. Getting more financial support out of Drew was now a million times more unlikely. She would have to fend for herself.

Chapter Eight

Sunday, 29th July

Vicky rose to take the brunch plates to the dishwasher. They'd had a fabulous evening at an Enchanted Forest event in Pollok Estate last night, and for the *nth* time Vicky rejoiced they had returned to Glasgow. Now she and Ben had eaten the most enormous brunch, and it was just a pity she had to spend the afternoon listening to Ron's PI telling them whatever details he'd dug up about Sylvie.

'I'm beginning to feel we'd be better off simply ignoring the fact that the woman ever existed.' Vicky wiped the table and slid the fruit bowl back to the centre.

'You need to get things into the open, and settled,' said Ben. 'Or you – and especially Chris – won't be able to move on. Sylvie did you both a huge wrong. She should account for herself at the very least.'

'I suppose so. Chris wanted me there, anyway, so I'll go.'

The meeting was at two o'clock in the Gairhead Hotel, not far from Christine's flat. It was a posh venue for a meeting with a private detective, thought Vicky. She collected Chris on the way and they arrived at the hotel five minutes early to find Ron already waiting in the old-fashioned, elegant foyer.

His eyebrows nearly hit the ceiling when he saw her, and

Vicky treated him to her best sweet smile. He'd probably thought he'd be able to sweep anything the PI said under the table. Well, she wasn't going to allow that.

'Hello, love.' Ron kissed Christine, then clapped Vicky's shoulder. 'And Vicky too. Where's little Erin today?'

'Ben's babysitting, so she's being thoroughly spoiled,' said Christine.

A tall man strode through the entrance door and marched up to where they were standing, and Ron made the introductions. Peter Spencer was a retired detective from Edinburgh, now based in Glasgow, and he was nothing like the shady PI Vicky had pictured. She shook the hand that was extended towards her, feeling more optimistic. This man was must be well into his sixties, older than she'd expected, but the smart suit and resolute expression gave him an air of authority that did come over as very policeman-like.

'Let's go through and have coffee,' he said, leading the way into a leafy conservatory.

The waitress knew him, Vicky noticed; he was evidently a regular here. Coffee arrived with a selection of cakes and biscuits. She and Chris had arranged that Christine would do the talking, which suited Vicky perfectly. She didn't want to lose her temper with Ron again.

Peter Spencer placed a folder on the table, then clasped his hands over it and locked eyes briefly with each of them in turn.

'I've come to the end of the investigation Ron commissioned me to do, and it'll be up to him to extend it if he feels it's necessary. My conclusion is, without police help it will be difficult to find more information about Sylvie. She appears to have vanished off the face of the earth. The only suggestion I have here is that you consider any other names she might be using, and I could look for them. But the chances of that succeeding seem... remote. I'm sorry.'

Ron cleared his throat but said nothing, gazing at the folder.

Christine leaned forward. 'So what *did* you find out?'

Peter opened the folder, and Vicky, who was sitting beside him, saw several sheets of closely typed paper.

'There's no record of Sylvie in Carlisle after she left there when you were a few weeks old,' said Ron, addressing Christine. 'She hadn't been there long, either. Details such as addresses are in the report; I have a copy for you here. After Carlisle, the next time she is traceable anywhere is almost a year later when she was treated in the Western Isles Hospital in Stornoway, after falling off a ladder and breaking a bone in her foot.'

'Stornoway?' Ron's voice came out in a squeak. 'Was she on holiday? She never mentioned Stornoway, as far as I remember.'

Peter shook his head. 'The address she gave was a large house, which at the time was owned by a group, or business, providing "alternative therapy". There isn't much online about them, but they moved away from the island around a year later and went to America. They're still active there, but are judged to be more sect than regular business. What we don't know is Sylvie's involvement with them. There's no trace of her with them now.'

Vicky leaned forward, forgetting she was supposed to leave the questions to Chris. 'So Sylvie might have been in the clutches of some sect? My God, Erin was there too and she was just a baby...'

Ron glared at her. 'There was nothing remotely sect-like about Sylvie when I met her in Aberdeen. *Chris–*' He stressed the name, '–was eighteen months then and Sylvie was working as a receptionist in a gym.'

'And where did she tell you she was before then?' Chris was glaring too, but at Ron.

'She said she'd been in Aberdeen for several months, and before that at her parents' in Devon, and travelling around a bit. I had no reason to disbelieve her.'

Peter gathered his papers. 'She may simply have done a course, or had some treatment with the sect. We don't know, and it would be very hard now to access any records they might hold about that time.'

'Her parents are dead, aren't they?' Vicky saw the tears in Christine's eyes at this, and wished she was close enough to squeeze her hand.

'Yes.'

For a moment there was silence round the table. Christine and Ron were sunk in their own thoughts, and Vicky struggled to find something to say. 'What... what else would you advise us to do, Peter?'

He sighed. 'I would think about – and discuss, of course – *why* you want to find her. What would you gain by it? And if it's something you feel you have to do, then go to the police. If not...' He allowed his voice to tail away, then handed a copy of his report to Ron and waved another at Vicky and Christine. 'I'm sorry, I didn't know you ladies would both be here.

Vicky reached for the print-out. 'I can scan it over to Chris.'

'I'll leave you to talk. You know where to find me, Ron.' Peter stood up.

Ron leapt to his feet. 'I'll see you to the door.'

Vicky slid round into Ron's chair and leafed through the

report, Christine peering over her shoulder. Five pages were filled with details of who, what, when and where.

Ron reappeared behind them. 'I'm going back to Aberdeen,' he said abruptly. 'I have work tomorrow. This was a waste of time and money. Think things over, Chris, before you do anything hasty – like report that birth certificate.'

'I've done that already,' said Christine, flinching.

Ron was silent, his face expressionless, then he bent and kissed Christine, gave Vicky a vague nod, and left.

Vicky saw the tears in Christine's eyes, and gave the girl a quick hug. 'Let's go back to yours and read this more thoroughly. Something here could give us an idea, you never know.'

Christine stood up. 'All I want is to cuddle my baby and never let her go. I hate not knowing what Mum's motives were.'

***

Reading the report helped them no further, though, and the following day saw Christine rolling her shoulders in the passenger seat – she had slept poorly and wakened with a stiff back – as Vicky drove out of the city. Monday evening sunshine had chased away the afternoon's clouds, and the rosy glow in the sky stretched across the windscreen.

'*Red sky at night*,' said Vicky. 'Maisie always used to say that.'

Christine sighed inwardly. Another family memory Sylvie had stolen from her. She glanced at Vicky, who was driving with a set face. They were on the way to visit Jamie, who was apparently still feeling a bit off.

'Did you let them know we were coming?' she asked,

more for something to say than anything else.

'Yes. He's still the same. It doesn't seem to be anything specific… I wish he was back to normal.'

'Me too.' This was what you might call a family worry, but Vicky was more worried than she was. Christine sighed. Thanks, Mum.

The staff in Jamie's unit were bustling around getting the youngsters ready for bed. Squawks and laughter as well as flying pillows and pyjamas filled the air, and Christine and Vicky grinned at each other. The positive moment passed, though, when they went into Jamie's room. His roommate was nowhere to be seen, but Jamie was in bed already, dozing with half-closed eyes.

Mark was tidying away some clothes, but he came over to the bed and gave them a half-smile. 'He's still not his usual bouncy self,' he said in a low voice. 'We're wondering if he's brewing an infection of some kind, so we sent off blood and urine tests today. We'll know more when they come back.'

'No temperature?' Vicky touched Jamie's forehead.

'Nothing to speak of. I wouldn't worry too much – it's probably nothing a course of antibiotics wouldn't zap out of his system.'

Vicky went to sit beside Jamie's head, and Christine pulled out her phone as it pinged. Kay was babysitting… The text was from a friend in Aberdeen, though, and Christine switched her phone to silent and went to fetch another chair.

'Has the doctor seen Jamie, Mark?'

'He took the bloods and he'll be back tomorrow. Shout if you need anything.' He touched her arm and left them.

Christine sat watching as Vicky leaned over the cot sides, stroking Jamie's face. He didn't waken properly, but his face twitched sometimes, so he might be aware of them. 'He'll be tired, Vicky,' she said, trying to sound reassuring. 'He must have been more awake during the day or Mark would have said. Maybe he's just starting a cold, or something.' That wasn't much comfort, though, was it? A cold could be life-threatening for someone in Jamie's condition. Watching her sister with her brother, Christine realised that Vicky felt the same about Jamie as she did about Erin. God, this was complicated, and once again, she was the outsider in the family.

They sat with Jamie for half an hour, then Vicky suggested a quick drink on the way home. All Christine wanted was to get back to her baby, but Vicky looked so wretched, and Kay would cope for another half-hour, wouldn't she?

'You should have a talk with Amanda, see what she thinks,' she suggested when they were sitting with glasses of cider in front of them.

'I called her this morning. She said that Jamie's defied the odds all those years, and that probably won't change any time soon. I hate seeing him like this, though. Anyway, have you had any more thoughts about Peter's report?'

Christine shrugged. 'What I'd like to know is how Sylvie got me out of the room at the hotel, but she's the only one who knows that. As far as keeping me is concerned, I'd have been okay with that if she hadn't lied about it. She kept us apart, that's what's so incomprehensible. She was a good mum, you know. Until I grew up and ripped her perfect family apart.'

Vicky stared into her glass. 'So she was happy until you left home?'

'I'd have said so. But I couldn't stay at home forever because Sylvie wanted to be a mother, could I? What she did wasn't rational then, and her behaviour's definitely not rational now. And that's scary.'

Christine's phone vibrated, and she fumbled for it, her breath catching. A text from Kay. Seconds later she was smiling and holding the phone out for Vicky to see. 'Look. Nothing like a photo of a sleeping baby to cheer up its mum and auntie, is there?'

Chapter Nine

Thursday, 2nd August

Thursday was a 'home office' day, and Vicky settled down at the dining table with her laptop and files long before eight o'clock. She would work for an hour or so, then call Jamie's home to see how he was. It was hard to judge how much to worry. He'd been off-colour for almost a week now. If it had been going to develop into anything nasty, surely it would have happened by now. Vicky forced herself to concentrate on her job, a mug of coffee to provide the caffeine boost by her side. She was still working through the morning's quota of letters when her mobile rang.

'Hi, Vicky, Steve here. Just to let you know the doc'll be in to see Jamie again this afternoon. Is there anything you want us to ask him?'

Vicky abandoned her letter, tapping her index finger on the desk as she considered. 'Just why they don't know what's going on with him. Is he any better today?'

'About the same. It's probably just a virus. Speak soon.'

Vicky put the phone down. Did it have a sinister undertone, when the head of the unit called you? But she should stop being so neurotic. These people knew Jamie better than she did. And how depressing that was. She would wait to hear what the doctor thought, then call Amanda again. Her old foster mother had visited Jamie yesterday and thought it was 'just a virus' too – nobody else was worrying unduly about Jamie. But nobody else loved him like she did, either. The thought did nothing to motivate Vicky to work.

She lifted her phone to let Chris know about the doctor.

Her sister sounded ragged, and Erin was wailing in the background. 'Poor old Jamie. Let me know as soon as you hear anything.'

'I will. Tough night?'

'The second in a row. And oh, Vicky, the registrar just called. Mu– Sylvie's going to be investigated about the certificate. It'll all come out, and I don't know if I want it to!'

Vicky's stomach lurched. 'It's the right thing, Chris, and the police are much more likely to find Sylvie than we are.'

'It might be better if she was never found.' Christine was crying now.

Vicky made a decision. 'Listen, I need to work for a couple of hours now, but I'll come to yours later and bring some lunch. Then I'll look after Erin and you can have a sleep. Okay?'

'A sleep sounds divine.'

Vicky rattled off a couple of letters, but her mind kept returning to Sylvie. That woman would persecute them all their lives if she wasn't found.

Persecute… Vicky's thoughts jerked back to the note that had come through the door. *Stop persecuting us.* No… or… could it have been…? Sylvie and Ron had been in Glasgow around that time; Chris had told her. But how would Sylvie have known where she lived?

Vicky stared blankly into the room, jumbled thoughts whirring in her head. Sylvie had always known her name and who she was. It wasn't impossible she had tried to stop Vicky finding Erin, and she wouldn't have had to look further than the online phone book to find the address. Vicky glared at the house phone. The Capodimonte rose was sitting beside it on the shelf, and a new thought struck. That photo Maisie'd had, the one of an older baby – Sylvie must have sent it. Vicky tapped a finger on the table. It might be better if she kept this new suspicion to herself for the moment. Poor Chris had enough to deal with.

***

Kay lifted another jacket from the pile in the back room, hung it up and attacked it with the steamer. This would be a good find for someone: a classic navy jacket, the kind you could dress up or down depending on the occasion. There was a rough patch on one lapel where the owner must have attached and reattached brooches, but it would be easily hidden if the new owner did likewise.

She was working down the second sleeve when her mobile vibrated on the desk behind her, and she twisted to see who it was. Oh – Chris, and she almost never called while Kay was at work. Was something wrong?

'Kay – I need someone to take Erin for an hour or two. We've just heard Jamie's being rushed to hospital; he's had some bug all week, and now he's deteriorated.'

Kay put the steamer down on its stand. 'Oh no – of course I'll help. I'm at the shop, but I'm sure Susan won't mind coping until closing time. I'll be with you in twenty minutes.'

'I'll have her ready. Thanks, Kay.'

Susan put her head round the door. 'I heard you – what's happening?'

Kay explained, pulling her jacket on.

Shock spread over Susan's thin face. 'Oh dear, those poor souls. Will you take the baby to yours?'

'Yes. Oh God, I hope poor Jamie isn't–' Kay swallowed hard. Imagine if Chris lost her brother so soon after finding him… It didn't bear thinking about.

'On you go. I'll finish here, and then come to yours, shall I? I can help with the baby, and I'll bring something nice from the deli for dinner, how's that?'

'You're an angel.' Kay sped off down Argyle Street to her car.

As promised, twenty minutes later she was in Christine's living room. Erin was asleep in the carrycot, her cheeks rosy, but Christine was pale and Vicky looked as if she was staring into hell.

Kay hugged Christine and patted Vicky's arm. 'Don't worry about Erin, Chris. She'll be fine with me and if she's not, I'll call you straightaway.'

'There's a bottle in the bag, but she should be okay until after eight. I've packed her bouncy seat and a few toys and stuff too.'

Christine's voice was… not exactly shaking, but her apprehension about what lay ahead was plain. Kay lifted the bag of baby things. Better just stick to practicalities. 'Any special instructions?'

'Don't worry if she's grumpy; she often is in the evening. It helps when you walk around with her.'

Kay tried to sound like an efficient babysitter. 'Good tip, I'll do that. I'll take her round to mine now. Susan from work's coming to keep me company, so Erin will have two pairs of eyes to watch out for her.'

Christine kissed the baby, and Kay manoeuvred the

carrycot and the bag through the hallway and round the corner to her own flat. This wasn't how she'd anticipated her next babysitting job.

Erin was still sleeping when Susan called an hour later. 'I'm on my way. Is everything all right?'

Kay almost laughed. 'There hasn't been time for anything to go wrong. I'll leave the door unlocked so you can come straight in. The baby's asleep, bless her.'

Susan was flushed when she arrived, and her eyes were brighter than usual. She thrust a deli bag into Kay's hands. 'Has Christine gone? I'm dying to see little Erin!'

'Yes. She and Vicky are distraught. Poor Jamie seems to be pretty bad.'

Kay led the way through, and Susan made a beeline for the carrycot. To Kay's astonishment, her friend clasped both hands under her chin and gasped.

'Oh! What a little love.'

Were those tears in Susan's eyes? It seemed rather an OTT reaction to someone else's baby.

Kay opened the sandwich bag. 'She takes after her mum. Let's eat while she's quiet, shall we?'

The baby woke up while they were still chewing Parma ham and olive baguettes, and Kay went to lift her, Susan hovering at her elbow.

'Be careful to support her head. She sounds hungry.'

'She's not long been fed. She's often grumpy in the evening.' Kay patted the baby's back and strolled up and down with Erin snuffling damply into her neck, aware of Susan's eyes following her every move. The baby settled down and Kay felt proud. She was coping. 'How about a coffee now?'

She jumped as Susan spoke sharply. 'You can't drink

coffee with a baby in your arms.'

'Of course not. I have her bouncy seat. She loves it, don't you, sweetheart?' Miffed now, Kay went through to the kitchen and laid Erin in the bouncy seat on the table, glad when the tiny girl was obliging enough to remain quiet. She searched for something to break the awkward silence.

'Here – why don't you butter a couple of pancakes while I get the coffee? And tell me, what's happening with your niece's friend, the one who was adopting a little girl but the mother wanted her back?'

Susan's lips were thin as she swiped butter over the pancakes. 'She's still gutted, but I think she's hopeful of a good outcome now. It's heart-breaking for her that it's come to this.'

Kay sat down and tipped the baby's seat to set it rocking. 'It's so sad. Someone will be hurt no matter what happens.'

Susan turned her head away. 'The birth mother is wrong. And people who do wrong things always get what's coming to them in the end, don't they? One way or another.'

***

Christine sat by Jamie's hospital bed, touching shoulders with Vicky, who was nearer the head end and leaning over the still form under the blanket. This was horrible. Half of her was here with Jamie, but the other half was with her daughter. Leaving Erin with Kay for an unknown amount of time was a physical ache, but that was her gut talking rubbish. Erin wouldn't want a clingy, nervous mother. A mean little whisper in her head: That's what you had. Like mother, like daughter. Christine pushed the thought away. Jamie gave a little moan, and Christine dabbed her eyes. Thank God for waterproof mascara, and how could she even *think* that, with her brother fighting for his life here. The turmoil inside her was choking.

Jamie was in a single room, which probably wasn't a good sign, but at least they had privacy. Christine squeezed the spastic hand on the sheet, her breasts aching at the thought of her baby, that precious cross face nestling into another woman's neck. Was Kay coping? She eased her phone from her bag, but no message had come, no missed call. Oh God, no, she was going to cry. Christine pushed her chair back and rushed to the door.

In the toilet she let cold water run over her hands, then dried them and held them to burning cheeks.

'Chris? You okay?'

It was Vicky. Christine opened the door, and Vicky's face creased.

'Sweetheart, I know it's hard, but Jamie needs us. As soon as the doctor appears we'll grab him and ask exactly what's going on. Oh God, Chris – I can't lose him.'

The last sentence had Christine in floods again, and for a moment they clung together. Christine was first to break away. Her baby was safe, and she and Vicky and Erin would have years and years – decades – to be together. Jamie wouldn't have that long, and she should go back to him now.

Drawing on strength she hadn't known she had, Christine led Vicky back into Jamie's room.

***

It was harder than she'd expected. Kay paced up and down the living room, Erin grizzling quietly in her arms. It wasn't that Susan meant to make things difficult, but she was, wasn't she? Anxious eyes were following Kay everywhere she went, and it was making her nervous. She shifted Erin to an upright position, glancing at the clock on the mantelpiece; help, it was only ten past seven. It was stupid to allow Susan to get on her nerves like this. The poor soul was only trying to help.

Kay smiled at her friend over the baby's head. 'I wish I'd had one of my own, don't you?'

Susan's eyes rounded, and she shifted on the sofa. 'Well, yes. Sort of. Families are important. But I've got one, you know, in spite of... everything.'

Old family memories were floating through Kay's head, distant as a black and white film. Mum and Dad... her granny... 'You're lucky to have a niece. It must have been difficult for you, losing your sister.'

Susan slumped into the sofa, wiping her eyes with a tissue. Erin started to cry in earnest, and cold despair washed through Kay. This evening was churning up the emotions, no mistake, and few of them felt good. Susan's face was white against the blue of the sofa – did she have another headache coming on?

'It was a long time ago. Mona and Laura are my life now.' Susan sprang to her feet. 'For heaven's sake, Kay, let me hold the baby while you heat a bottle for her.'

Needy hands were grasping Erin, and short of starting a tug of war with the baby in the middle, there was nothing Kay could do. Some milk was worth a try, anyway. She hurried through to the kitchen and fumbled in the changing bag. The bottle was small; she'd soon have it ready. Was it wrong to be glad Erin was howling even harder in Susan's arms?

Swirling the bottle in a jug of hot water gave Kay a much-needed break for thought. Susan was nervous tonight, but whatever was going on there had nothing to do with her or Erin. She shouldn't allow the other woman to undermine her confidence like this.

Back in the living room, Kay set the bottle on the coffee table and claimed Erin back. Susan dropped into the corner of the sofa, then twisted round to face Kay in the other corner. Bright eyes watched as Kay held the bottle to the baby's mouth.

'Be care–'

'Susan, we're fine. Relax.' Wishing she felt as calm as she sounded, Kay concentrated on the baby, who was sucking in a half-hearted manner. Hunger hadn't been the problem. Kay wriggled into a more comfortable position.

'When I was small, my mum used to babysit for the neighbours. I loved that,' she said, forcing a smile for Susan. 'Funny, though – I never did any babysitting when I was a teenager.'

Susan didn't lift her eyes from the baby. 'Neither did I, at that age. Young girls are too immature to babysit. It makes me sick how they can have unplanned babies just like that and think they're doing the right thing by keeping them.'

They were back at the niece's friend's adoption problems. Kay sighed inwardly. Susan had never been this uptight before; there must be something else wrong that she wasn't up for talking about tonight. The feeling in Kay's middle now wasn't a comforting one. The truth was, she didn't really know Susan.

'Have your headaches been troubling you again?'

Susan's eyes froze for a second, then slid across to Kay, and back to the baby. 'No, no. Look, she's drinking so nicely now. I'll change her when she's had enough, shall I?'

'Let's wait and see if she falls asleep.' Please, baby, fall asleep.

'She's a lucky girl, having you in her extended family.'

Susan was inching along the sofa, and Kay felt like screaming, go away, leave us alone.

The voice was almost in her ear now. 'You'll do the right thing by her. Some so-called families don't. But it's ten to midnight for some families. And the clock's ticking.'

***

The room was silent, apart from Jamie's laboured breathing and the hiss of his oxygen mask. Leaning over the bed, with Vicky leaning over the opposite side, Christine felt the walls close in on her. The doctor had been in and assured them Jamie was being kept 'comfortable', and they would 'have a chat' when they saw how his condition developed. It didn't sound very positive.

Christine shifted in her chair. 'I wish we could do more. And I wish I'd brought Erin with me.'

Vicky's eyes were haunted. 'You're not worried about Kay looking after her, are you?'

'No, Kay's lovely. It's… I don't know.' Christine wiped her face with the hand that wasn't holding Jamie's, not looking at Vicky. The real problem was she'd never forgiven herself for planning to have the baby adopted. And for some reason, tonight just felt wrong.

Vicky's attention was fixed on the thin form in the bed. 'Ben should be here soon. We can stay with Jamie. Why don't you give Kay a call and say you'll be back in an hour or so? It would put your mind at rest.'

Sixty minutes. Three thousand, six hundred seconds of pain in her gut. But it wouldn't hurt as much if she had a quick word with Kay. Christine took her phone into the corridor and stared at the screen, where a dark, ghostly image of worry was reflected – a mother, aching for her child. Had Paula ached too? Had she realised her baby had been saved but she was going to die? It was terrible to think that the last moments of Paula's life might have been filled with the pain of separation, like this, but a hundred, a million trillion times worse. What would be three thousand, six hundred seconds – fewer, now – for Christine, had been empty forever for Paula.

Christine connected to Kay's number. 'Kay, hi – a quick update. Jamie's the same, but Ben's on his way now and I'll be back in an hour. Everything all right?' She should get an Oscar for that.

'No problem. Erin's had some milk, and she's quite happy sitting with Susan now.'

That voice in the background. Christine's world sharpened as adrenaline kicked in. *No. Oh Christ, no.* That jingly-jangly nursery rhyme, how many hundred times had she heard it sung in that voice? High pitched and quavering, a good enough soprano, but untrained…

The nightmare reared up and engulfed Christine. 'Tell me that's not Susan singing?'

'Yes, she's–'

'The *shit* it is, Kay – that's *Sylvie*. Get my baby away from her, get–' The phone slid from damp, shaking fingers and clattered to the floor at Christine's feet, the back cracking open and the battery flying out. Outrage shrieking from her soul, Christine dropped to her knees, scrabbling to put it all together and get Kay back. But the phone was dead.

***

The hallway swirled around Kay and she lurched against the living room doorway. She must *not* pass out. *Sylvie*? Her fingers slid on the screen of her phone as she fought to get Chris back. Silence in the phone, no, no. Deep breath, Kay, you have to stay calm. Ignore the crashing in your ears, your heart will take it, but if anything happens to this baby tonight, it's all your fault. The police, she had to call the police. The bathroom–

Too late.

'Who was on the phone?' Susan was standing in front of her, the baby in her arms.

Kay forced a smile. She needed a nice convincing lie now. 'Vicky. They're going to be a bit longer than they thought.' And yes, that was a flash of relief on Susan's face. Kay moved into the living room and plumped onto the sofa, silently thanking God when the other woman followed and sat down beside her.

Kay forced a laugh through dry lips. 'I think Erin liked your song – look how she's watching you!'

This at least was true. The baby was staring up at Susan, apparently mesmerised by the woman's eyes.

Susan beamed. 'I've always had a way with babies. Mona's often said she wished she'd inherited it.'

Did Mona even exist? Kay touched the baby's cheek with one finger, her mind whirling ever slower as sick certainty descended. Susan. It had all been a lie, an elaborate hoax, right from the start. And all those weeks spent cosying up to Kay, even to the people at the bloody church – it had all been part of Susan's plan. The plan to get Christine's baby.

But Chris would call the police. They'd be on their way already, blue lights flashing. All she had to do was get the baby away from Susan.

'Why don't you see if Erin'll sleep in her carrycot? I'm not very good at getting her down, but you might be. And I'll fetch us some of that elderflower cordial I bought yesterday.'

The eyes staring into hers had never been brighter, but somehow the person behind them was invisible. Kay released her breath slowly as Susan laid the baby in the carrycot, still on one of the armchairs.

No howl of protest came, and Kay leapt into action. 'Oh, well done! Let's leave her to sleep.' She hurried through to the kitchen. Now to keep Susan away from the baby until the pol–

The door behind her slammed shut, and Kay whirled round. She was alone in the kitchen. Heart thundering, Kay dived for the door and yanked it open, only to fall head first over the hall chair, planted on its side across the doorway. The flat door was open...

'Susan!' Kay pulled herself up and limped across the hallway, pain searing up her leg. The living room was empty and the carrycot was gone. And so was the baby.

***

Vicky rubbed Jamie's hand, terror chilling her soul and love for her sweet man-baby brother warm in her heart. *Please, Jamie, please don't die.* Thank God Chris was here. Why, oh why hadn't Maisie talked about Erin sooner? If they'd found Chris even ten years ago, how different their lives would have been.

And little Erin wouldn't be here at all. The thought thudded into Vicky's head. This was why 'if only' never worked.

A nurse put her head round the door. 'Vicky, your sister–'

Vicky twisted round. Chris was on her knees in the corridor. Heck, had she turned faint? Vicky wrenched herself away from Jamie's bed and hurried out as the nurse went into the room.

'Chris?' Was it Erin? Wild visions of the baby ill, or in an ambulance – in hospital – charged through Vicky's head, and she knelt to grip Christine's arm. Whatever this was it must be massive; her sister was shaking all over.

'Sylvie.'

Whimpers mixed with hiccups were shuddering through Christine's body, and the terror in her eyes…

Vicky's heart began to pound. 'What about her?'

But the fear had taken possession of Christine; the only sounds she was making were moans. Vicky seized the girl's shoulders and shook, then bent until their eyes were level. 'Chris – you have to talk to me. Tell me what's wrong.'

Christine was gulping and shivering, but she was speaking now, staring into Vicky's face, her eyes wild.

'Kay's friend Susan – she's there at Kay's and she's… Sylvie. She's holding my baby!' Christine collapsed against Vicky.

'No. *Shit!* Police – we have to–' One arm clutching her sister, Vicky fumbled for her phone, her ears buzzing as horror blurred everything around her. She'd never done this before. 999. 'We need police. There's a baby at number ten Court Place and she's in danger. A woman known to the family, who's…'

Somehow, she managed to summarise the events of the past in a few sentences. Help was promised, and Vicky ended the call and pulled Christine to her feet.

'Come into Jamie's room, Chris, I'll–'

Horror and vulnerability were chasing across the girl's

face. 'No, no, I have to go to my baby, I have to go now. Vicky... Will you come–' She stopped, her eyes agonised.

Vicky's head swam. Christine's eyes before her; Jamie's laboured breathing in the room at her back.

Her brother... or her sister...

Christine jerked away and ran along the corridor, and emptiness welled in Vicky's gut. She had lost her sister once... *I'm sorry, Jamie.*

'Wait! I'm coming with you.'

Vicky grabbed Christine's hand as they raced across the car park. The girl's panic was infectious. What was happening at 10 Court Place?

She fumbled to open the car doors. 'Sylvie must be mad.' Vicky dropped into the driving seat, jabbing the key into the ignition. Jamie...

And oh, there was a God, in the form of Ben's car, crawling along another row and parking near the doorway. For a split second, Vicky closed her eyes. Thank you, thank you. Not waiting to speak to him, she drove towards the hospital exit.

Christine shivered uncontrollably all the way along Great Western Road. Traffic was light, but a bus had broken down halfway along, and they had to join a queue to manoeuvre round it. At last, the traffic lights at Byres Road came into sight. Red, of course. Impatience singing through her, Vicky slowed down again. *Come on...*

Then Christine jerked upright in her seat, her voice a thin shriek. 'That's her! That's Sylvie! Vicky, follow that taxi – Sylvie just got in with my baby!'

***

The taxi turned into Great Western Road, followed by

several other cars before the lights changed and they could follow. Christine yanked Vicky's mobile from her bag as the car weaved forwards, trying to get closer. She connected to Kay's number, then held the phone to her ear as her eyes concentrated on the taxi, four cars in front.

'Vicky – Susan's got–'

'It's me – I know. We're following her taxi. What's her address, Kay?'

'Oh God, I can't remember. North of the centre, around Possilpark way.'

This meant nothing to Christine. She clicked on speaker. 'We're on Great Wester– wait, he's turning into…' The car lurched after the taxi, three cars in front now. 'Belmont Street.'

'I'll try to find the address– oh, the police are here, I'll–'

The connection broke. Cursing, Christine called again, but Kay didn't answer. The taxi crossed the river, then turned right, then left, then right again, driving through streets lined with sandstone tenements. Christine moaned as a group of boys ran out of a little park and jostled along the road in front of them. Vicky slammed her foot on the brake.

'Shit.' Cold despair in her heart, Christine stared ahead as they continued on across another junction. The taxi was nowhere in sight now, and this road was– hell, it was a cul de sac.

Vicky pulled up. 'We've lost him. He was heading for Maryhill Road, but God knows where he went after that. Try Kay again.'

Christine's fingers slid on the screen. This was the biggest nightmare possible. Her baby.

'The police are on their way to Sylvie's, Chris. I found the address, it's…'

Christine leaned back and ended the call, a wave of dizziness hitting her as Vicky keyed the address into the satnav and started the engine.

'The police'll find her now, Chris. Hang on, that's all.'

Bitterness engulfed Christine. 'How do we know she's going home? Last time that woman disappeared with a baby called Erin, it was twenty-two years before anyone found her.'

***

The police cordon stretched across the road, stopping them entering Susan's street. Two officers were standing to one side. Christine shifted in the passenger seat, but her legs had turned to so much jelly.

'I'll go.' Vicky ran across and spoke to them, and one man followed her back to the car, opening the passenger seat door and bending towards Christine.

'Your baby's in there, and so are our officers. Wait here – we're doing everything we can.'

Christine couldn't stop shaking. She wanted to scream but she couldn't because she could hardly breathe, and if she lost her baby tonight she would shake inside for the rest of her life. She managed to nod at the policeman, then closed her eyes.

Terror.

This would be what Paula had felt, those last few seconds. If she'd felt anything. Please God she hadn't, poor Paula, her baby gone forever. All those people whose children disappeared, how did they live on, searching, not knowing, aching inside – no baby, no child, their future gone? She couldn't do this.

And waiting, and waiting. What the shit were they doing in there?

She seized Vicky's hand. 'If I lose her–'

Vicky's voice was shaking too. 'They must get her out. Hang on, Chris.'

Christine hung on to Vicky's hand, and Vicky was hanging on to her. Sisters. Erin had no one to hang on to, just like little Chris hadn't, all those years ago. The cycle was repeating...

Then a shout further up the street, and a tall police officer was hurrying towards them, a white bundle clutched to his chest. Her *baby*. Christine forced her legs out of the car, stumbling towards him, grasping the bundle, and oh, her Erin, she was awake and gazing around, flexing small fingers.

It was sunrise after a decade of ebony. Christine raised a wet face to the sky. *Paula, Paula, Erin's safe*. Vicky was sobbing beside her now, but Christine was laughing through tears. It was the fifteenth day of her baby's life and the first day of the rest of hers.

Epilogue

Six months later

V icky stepped out onto the balcony and gazed across the river. The Clyde was flowing rapidly, blue-green in February sunshine, and Chris and Erin were on their way across the footbridge, heading here for a celebration lunch with one of Ben's majestic homemade pizzas. A wistful thought struck Vicky. In a different life, Paula and Joe would have been coming too. Now it was just her and Chris. And Erin. And Ben, of course. Vicky twisted the new diamond and emerald engagement ring on her finger. They'd come a long way since that awful day last summer, but they still had no answers.

Vicky waved to her sister and niece, and Christine bent down, pointing her out to Erin in the buggy. And maybe they didn't need answers after all. Sylvie was in a psychiatric hospital, but Christine had been advised not to visit her yet.

The tears that welled every time she thought about Jamie were back in Vicky's eyes as she stood watching the waters of the Clyde glide past. They had scattered his ashes into that water. He'd survived the bug in August, but succumbed to another in November, slipping out of his life with Vicky and Christine by his bed. They'd taken the ashes to a quiet spot on the north side of the river and released their brother there, hugging each other close as Jamie flowed swiftly downstream, moving easily and painlessly towards the ocean and eternity.

Christine was at this end of the footbridge now. She lifted a blue bottle from the bag on the back of the buggy and waved it up at Vicky.

'Don't just stand there, woman – get the glasses out!'

Vicky laughed and turned back inside, glancing across at the Capodimonte rose on the shelf. Maisie would have been happy today.

Acknowledgements and Author's Note

As always, love and thanks to my sons, Matthias and Pascal, for help and support in all kinds of ways, especially for technical and IT help. Thanks also to my editor, Debi Alper, and to Bloodhound Books for publishing the earlier edition of this book.

More thanks to Evelyn Tingle for taking such great photos of the Glasgow locations of this book after I lost my own, and for tramping around Glasgow with me while I looked for a good place for 'Vicky's flat'.

A special mention for The Cover Collection, who have covered nearly all my books and worked with me to create the perfect image for each, and to Yvonne Betancourt for formatting the paperback.

And to all those writers, book bloggers, friends and others who are so supportive on social media – a huge and heartfelt 'THANK YOU. So often it's the online friends, people I may never have met in real life, who are first port of call when advice and encouragement are needed. I hope I can give back as much help as I get from you.

Biggest thanks of all, though, go to the readers – knowing that people are reading my books is a dream come true. If you've enjoyed *Stolen Sister*, please do consider leaving a rating or short review on Amazon or Goodreads. One sentence is enough, and every rating and review counts towards making a book more visible in today's crowded marketplace. Thank you!

For more information about my books, and also about the writing life and life in general here in lovely Switzerland, visit my website: www.lindahuber.net or follow my blog there.

Daria's Daughter: a taster

If you enjoyed *Stolen Sister*, why not try another of Linda Huber's suspense novels? Here's the first chapter of *Daria's Daughter*:

Day One
Friday, 17th April

Chapter One

They would miss their flight if the taxi didn't come in the next five minutes. Daria stood at her first-floor living room window, peering up the street. And, oh, glory, as if there wasn't enough to worry about – look at those clouds! Her shoulders slumped as the sun vanished abruptly and fat raindrops spattered across the window, transforming the dusty Glasgow street below into a slick dark stripe, punctuated by scattered hailstones that melted to join the torrents scudding along in the gutters. Daria rested her head on the windowpane. A rainstorm when she had to get her daughter, along with everything the two of them would need over the next two weeks, into a taxi, out again at the airport, into the terminal building and through departures – it was exactly what she didn't need.

'Where's Daddy?' Four-year-old Evie pushed in front of

Daria's legs to see outside, her pink 'ready for the taxi' jacket matching the hot little face under her beloved bobble hat.

Daria held out her hand. 'Come on, we'll wait downstairs. Daddy's at a conference in Stirling – remember he said 'bye-bye yesterday? Got your rucksack?'

Evie ran to fetch the pink elephant rucksack she'd left on the sofa. 'Daddy's in Stirling?'

They'd been through it a million times, but what did Stirling mean to a child who'd never been there? Daria dredged up a calm-Mummy smile.

'That's right. And today we're going to visit Grandma and Grandpa in Spain, and Daddy's coming to join us next week.'

And how good it would be to escape the coldest spring on record for a little while. Daria pulled out her compact and checked her make-up. She would do. Okay – case, daughter, handbag, travel bag. Come on, Daria, you can do this.

Downstairs, they stood in the shelter of the doorway, Evie leaning out to catch stray raindrops on her tongue while Daria fumbled for her phone. She was still scrolling down her contacts for the minicab company when a blue and white taxi screeched around the corner and pulled up by the gate. At last. Thank heavens the airport was a mere fifteen minutes away; they would make it. Daria grasped Evie's hand and wheeled the case down the path to meet the taxi driver, who was standing beside his vehicle glowering at them. He heaved the luggage into the boot, and Daria opened the back door.

'In we get, Evie, love.' She fastened the child's seat belt, then her own. Evie was a slight little thing and it was never a good feeling being in a cab with no child seat. Another reason to be thankful the airport was so near. Daria sat tapping her fingertips together as the driver organised his meter and turned on the engine. Come on, come *on*, we have to go.

The rain intensified as they crawled along to the main road and joined a column of blurry red lights as every commuter in the city headed homewards for the weekend. A band of tension tightened around Daria's head. They had less than twenty minutes now and they were inching along at a speed she could have matched on foot.

'We'll take the back road.' The driver pulled into a side street, and Daria breathed out. Traffic was flowing here, albeit slowly, but they were on their way at last. She put an arm around Evie and the little girl beamed up at her, then reached across to take Daria's hand and, oh, it was so lovely to be travelling with her daughter. They were picking up speed all the time; it was going to be all right. They cut round the back of the cemetery and came to a wider road. This was better.

Daria leaned over to kiss Evie's damp little forehead, then jerked back in horror as a long, deep horn blared and headlights from an approaching lorry swept through the cab. A single, sickening scream left Daria's soul as Evie's rucksack scratched across her face. The taxi skewed sideways, only to be hit from behind and flipped skywards. Daria's arms opened in search of her girl, but she was pitched across the car, twisting in the air as metal screeched and tore around her and—

She was flying. Daria clutched at empty air then crashed down, rolling over and over on something hard, more screams coming from a distance. Hers? Her leg, her arm... Oh, please, Evie.

Silence. Stillness. Pain. Daria sank into darkness, but far, far away, something was buzzing. Find Evie, you have to find

Evie. Swirling grey shapes replaced the darkness. Breathing was agony and she couldn't move her leg. Darkness was hovering; God, no, she mustn't die here. Stinging rain was soaking through her hair, running down her cheeks, her neck. Far off voices screamed behind her, Evie's high-pitched wail the nearest.

Evie, oh, baby, Mummy's here.

Daria fought to call to her child, but black pain was all around now. No, no, she was going to pass out. Her fingers splayed and met wet plastic: Evie's rucksack. Wailing sirens swooped closer as Daria fought to stay awake. Please, somebody, come…

The voices shouting in the background were still too far away to help when the choking smell of petrol reached her nose. And everything went black.

Printed in Great Britain
by Amazon

19763044R00174